Hen Night

Hen Night

Cocktails and Confessions

L.E Zentner

authorHOUSE°

AuthorHouse™
1663 Liberty Drive
Bloomington, IN 47403
www.authorhouse.com
Phone: 1 (800) 839-8640

Published by AuthorHouse 03/14/2016

ISBN: 978-1-5049-8448-5 (sc)
ISBN: 978-1-5049-8446-1 (hc)
ISBN: 978-1-5049-8447-8 (e)

Library of Congress Control Number: 2016903853

Print information available on the last page.

To my best friend, who is so much fun she is worthy of writing a book about.

To all of the Hens, you know who you are, who have let me publish this crazy shit!

To my husband, who literally supported me in every way through this project. I love you.

To my favourite pedantic cousin, Marie, for all the hours you invested editing and all your honesty.

To Kathie and Karlie, my first fans … for your encouragement, support and editing contributions.

Cover design and illustration by, Dana Lynn Pouteau, who did a remarkable job bringing my vision to perfection. Thank you so very much.

Cast of Characters

Laura

Ter-ri: noun

Opinionated, energetic, loyal, logical, happy. Speaks with confidence and passion.

Linda

Les-lie: noun

Expressive, hysterically funny, sexy, hyper, insecure, happy. Speaks with exuberance and prefers to talk rather than listen.

Sha-ron: noun

Serious, humorous to the dark side, lethargic, opinionated, cynical. Speaks very monotone unless she is very excited about something.

Iz-zy: noun

Tough, witty, aggressive, gossipy. Speaks either with a smile in her voice or disdain, depending on how she feels and what the story is about.

Col-leen: noun

Survivor, introspective, nurturing, kind. Speaks with caring and encouragement or rants, depending on the subject.

Table of Contents

"You're running with me; don't touch the ground
We are the restless hearted, not the chained and bound"
Bryan Ferry

Week 335 - About Leslie

"Who's out tonight?" I ask as I walk through the door.

"We have a full house tonight baby! Look out, things could get crazy…"

"Leslie, when I'm with you there's no other option … you do know you're certifiably crazy, in the most adorable way of course. Well, guess what girlfriend … I did something crazy myself, something completely out of character, something I have never done before in my life and always wanted to. Something …"

"Enough already, get to the point … spill."

"I, Terri Vetnor, seduced a man. No was not an option I was going to accept, and I fucked him and he didn't know what hit him!!!"

"Jesus girl, get those hideous boots off, this needs all hands on deck."

"Girls!" Leslie shouts from the doorway, "Terri cheated on John!"

"My boots are not hideous."

I hear all the ooohhhhhs and aaahhhhhs coming from the kitchen and Sharon hollers out, "Get in here! We need details and leave nothing to our imaginations."

Leslie and I walk in and all the usual faces are all glowing and can't wait to hear my gossip. I am at the Hen House, which was affectionately named because three of the hens live here ... Leslie, Sharon and Izzy. Colleen and I are regulars most every Thursday along with whoever may be in the neighbourhood, because everyone knows we meet here around 7:00 pm. No phone calls are required; the sistas will be here to greet all.

"Leslie you don't have to make it sound so horrible ... I feel bad enough, but at the same time ... so liberated! I've known in my heart for a while that I can't marry John, and it took his car accident for me to finally wake up and get some balls and end it. Now, a month later I still haven't ended it! Girls ... I have no balls! How can I break his heart?"

"John's a douchebag and if you don't do it, I'll do it for you," Leslie says and means it. "If I have to hear one more time how you had to take the bus to return from shopping in the freezing cold, WHEN HE HAS A CAR ... don't get me going! Our dear Lord did a great job bringing you redemption when John's little car got totaled ... no one more deserving. I'm so grateful he didn't get seriously hurt cos you probably would've had to take care of him for the rest of your life ... prison sentence x10! And, if you'd gone out with John that night, you'd be dead, I've seen the pictures. My life would've changed overnight." Leslie puts her palms together, raises her eyes upward and says, "THANK YOU!"

"John has his good points and he was my first love, but I couldn't agree with you more. For two years things haven't been great. I have to break up with him."

"Shit Terri, you lived in Toronto for one of them. Obviously things aren't great."

The impatience of the group is growing and Sharon redirects the conversation, "Terri, you made quite the announcement ... the affair ... that's all we want to hear about. We already know aaallll the other shit."

"DO NOT call it an affair. That makes it sound like it'll be something long term. I much prefer ... seduction ... I'm about to be single soon and I really don't want another boyfriend right away! It was sooooo fun luring him to my place after the class Christmas party and asking him to come in for a drink. Just like in the movies! I knew I was going to try to get him to sleep with me and I was doing it just to see if I could. You girls and your one-night-stand stories ... well dammit I wanted one of my own!!!"

"Are we going to be here all night or can you just get on with it?" Sharon says completely irritated.

"Well I'm sure you ladies ... and I use the term loosely..."

"Funny..."

"...all know who it is since you've been drilling me on every guy in my class since I started back to school."

"Yeah, we all figure it's Alex P. Keaton. What's his real name again?"

"Michael J. Fox."

Sharon is losing it by now. "Not the fucking actor bonehead, your classmate," she says exasperated.

"Gotcha!" Now we all high five each other because if you can get one of the girls riled up in a totally innocent way, we all celebrate like children.

"It's Andrew, and the reason I decided I had to sleep with him was because he taught me how to drive a standard ... oh, and I find him dead sexy. Every time I see his cute little arse I want to bite it! A few of us went out for lunch before the Christmas party and he drove. On the way back he asked me if I would drive so he could roll up a joint."

"So he has his own car and he buys his own dope, so far so good," Colleen states with approval.

"I tell him I can't drive a standard. He just says, 'well let's fix that now,' and in the parking lot right then and there he makes me get in the driver's seat and teaches me to drive a stick. Do you have any idea how many times I tried to get John to teach me? He always had the same excuse, 'you're a brand new driver you'll wreck my transmission.'"

Izzy smirks, "Well his transmission is in the fuck'n scrap yard now baby!"

"The only thing left of that car was the driver's seat! I couldn't believe he walked away from that."

"Are we ever going to stay on track here?"

"Yes, so I was shocked that a guy I just met a few months ago would be so generous of heart when my own fiancé won't allow me to drive his car. Leslie you're so right, John is a douche bag! I really have to end it. OK, back to the seduction before someone has an aneurism! He agrees to come in for a drink, phase one complete. We get a beer and sit in the living room. I'm distracted because I'm thinking what if John, for some crazy reason, left his parents' place and decided to come home … I don't want it to end bitterly like that, but it would bring the relationship to a quick finale. So I decide I'm OK with it and I relax. Andrew asks why he's there since I'm engaged and I tell him that it's over in my heart, but I have no balls and I'm having a hard time ending it. I'm such a fucking idiot … I just moved back in with John in September … could none of you have stopped me?!"

"We have made plenty of comments on his unworthiness. You had to go through this final stage in order for you to be able to end it. Everything happens for a reason and you've encountered so much change lately. It's given you the clarity you need to move on," Colleen chimes in with her older wiser self.

"You're right, but shit … I have to move out and leave all my stuff behind. I can't leave him and then empty out the apartment!"

"Can we get back to the fuck'n affair please!!!"

"Sharon, it was a seduction … let's get it right. I'll be single so it was a one-night-stand! OK, once again, getting back on track. So, I just come out with it and tell him I want to kiss him and that I have wanted to kiss him since I first met him. I don't give him a moment for a reply and I just do it. We neck on the couch for a bit and we get touchy feely and I'm so freaked out that I've had no resistance. I'm feeling like we can move on to phase two. I invite him into the bedroom. Well, we're all naked and I am thinking yes, yes, yes and doesn't the poor bugger's conscience get a hold of him and he decides he can't fuck me. Not that he doesn't want to … so he said, but he can't. Of course a million different scenarios go jamming my brain with disappointment, always reading more into it than I have to. BUT, he doesn't leave. He asked if he could stay the night and I agree, because he is naked and pretty drunk. But the bitch side of me wants to say, NO … GET OUT you have not completed phase three and right now I'm completely and utterly embarrassed, which I also mean literally cos I'm bare assed and horny and he just pulls the plug!!!"

"That sounds uncomfortable."

"Thennn in the morning he wakes me up and says, 'I've slept on it and I'm not one to miss an opportunity like this.' He leads me butt naked into the shower and washes me down from head to toe and I love every second of it. He hands me the soap and I wash him down. We dry each other off and then I have the hottest sex of my life."

"I hate to break it to you chick, but that was no one-night-stand. They don't go down like that girl. Trust me I've had a few and they're drunk and sloppy," Sharon informs me.

"I have to agree with her," Leslie concurs. "This guy is going to be your new boyfriend!"

"Don't you dare take this away from me!!! I Terri Vetnor seduced a man. I made the first moves and I got him to sleep with me! Although I do know him … I guess technically that would negate the one-night-standness! Shit guys, I want be single after John. I want to be promiscuous and screw men like it's no big deal! I want to add some notches to my bedpost! You have to be wrong cos what if we start dating and then another five years goes by, and I've wasted them away too?"

"Terri, stop analyzing. You're just getting way ahead of yourself, and don't ever think that any moment of your life is wasted. Every experience has value and meaning."

"Yes, Mast'r Splinter." I say this to Colleen cos that's what we have nicknamed her when she gets all philosophical on us.

"Not to mention the fact that you haven't even dumped John and it'll be a miracle if you actually do it."

"Izzy is that a challenge?"

"I'm just saying that it's been over a month since you decided to end it."

"Enough about all of this you bone heads are freaking me out. So where are we heading tonight?"

"I checked the paper and there aren't any good bands around so we're going to the usual watering hole."

As we get ready to head to the bar there is much chitchat and lots of laughter as always. A full Hen House consists of Leslie, Sharon, Izzy, Colleen and me of course. We have some other friends who show up here and there, but the five of us have made Thursday girls night a ritual. We all met in high school except for Colleen; she is the mom of one of Leslie's ex-boyfriends and joined our outings when they were dating. I have returned to Ottawa where I was born and raised because this is where I was accepted into college. I had lived in Toronto with my sister Laura for the past year because John refused to move there, while I desperately wanted to. I have been in love with Toronto since I was 11 when mom finally let me go spend March break with my older sister. I have five older sisters. John and I moved back in together in September. He is attending university and I am going to be a photographer after five years of retail and office jobs. Typing was probably the single most useful class I ever took in high school.

Paul's Pub is a ten-minute drive from the Hen House, chosen as our favourite based on location alone. Although they do have a sweet bartender, and the French fries are awesome. We arrive at the bar with the usual staff and patron excitement. I often feel like I am in an episode of *Cheers*. I have no doubt that once word got around that we frequent this pub on Thursday's, business picked up. Five rather outgoing personalities, all of which are attractive in their own ways, can spike liquor sales and drive customers. We often joke that we could make a viable business where a bar would hire us to live'n things up and make their customers' day. We would work for free booze and food, yet we are unsuccessful in convincing any of the managers that it is a brilliant idea.

It is our usual bartender tonight and he is familiar with the order and starts to get it ready … beer for Leslie, Sharon and Colleen, rye and ginger for Izzy and me. We always sit at the bar because we are there to experience people, to share stories and listen to stories and of course to meet men! Well the single ones anyway. Which I will soon be! I think the bartender is smitten with Leslie, but she is oblivious to it. If she were interested she would have given off the scent already and he would have happily followed it.

"So Leslie, has any lucky guy stolen your heart yet?" he asks.

"No, but I was just about to tell Terri and Colleen about a crazy drunk thing I did the other night. You see there's this cute guy that lives with his parents in our townhouse complex and we say hi and have shared small talk. We've been doing this for months now! I'd go on a date with him, but he never asks and I get the feeling he's super shy. I arrived home and I was pretty drunk. I got out of the car and I saw his Porsche in the garage. So I said screw-it, I'll make the first move."

"Only because you were drunk!" says Sharon.

"Who cares why, I felt brave and I did it."

"Did what exactly?" the impatient bartender adds.

"Right, so I find a piece of paper and I write on it: Want a date, Unit 48 and my phone number. I want to put the paper under his windshield, but before I can I have to take the stupid car cover off. That was no easy task let me tell you. So I have the cover in a heap on the floor and the note is on the windshield. Then I have an epiphany … I put some lipstick on and take the note back and give it a smack. There, perfect. I put my note back and start to put the cover back on. Then I'm thinking to myself do I really want to date a guy who covers his precious car? I'm thinking guys like that tend to like their cars better than their girlfriends and while I'm thinking all this shit I cannot figure out how to put the fucking cover back on. I really tried and I was so frustrated, and let's not forget slightly drunk."

"So you left it like that and took the note?"

"No fuck, I took the note back and just added … sorry about the cover I really tried! And then I put it back under the wiper, I grabbed the cover and put it on top of the hood as neatly as I possibly could."

"So has he called?" We almost say in unison with extreme anticipation.

"No he didn't, but he did show up on my doorstep at around 7:00 pm the next day and he was mad as a fish on a hook. He's on a rant and I'm thinking, yes I was right he's the kind of guy who loves his car better. Then I tune back in and I register he's not upset about the cover one iota. The poor bugger was so pissed cos he couldn't understand why in hell I would go through all that trouble to put that note on his car and give him the wrong fuck'n phone number!!!"

We all break out in laughter and each one of us is imagining this poor schmuck all excited about receiving a note from the hottie in unit 48, and how he can't wait to get home from work to call and arrange a date, only to find out that it is some tasteless prank.

"Seriously Leslie, you didn't?"

"Yeah, I did! I gave him Stan's number … must have been more drunk than I thought!"

"That's too hilarious. So what happened then?"

"It did take a bit of convincing that I totally didn't mean to do that and we have a date on Saturday."

"Ok this guy's a good sport and that's the best … 'So, how did you meet your husband' story ever."

"Fuck Izzy, relax we haven't even gone on a date."

I can tell the bartender is disappointed with the outcome, but he keeps a brave face and continues his duties.

"Even with my own crazy story of the night, which I don't have often, you have managed to trump me again."

"I wasn't around for your crazy story Terri, do tell," I hear as my second drink arrives unordered.

"Mine is for Hen ears only young man. Thanks for the drink."

The night carries on as most Thursdays do. Some of us in conversation with one another; some of us conversing with the regulars, or Leslie off making the lone person at the bar feel welcome and important. Whether they are male or female, young or old they will feel better after talking with her and they will go home having had a great life experience. Provided they can appreciate life and understand that all experiences are great, simply because you are alive to experience them. Just reaffirming those wise words from Mast'r Splinter!

As per our customary routine we head back to the Hen House for a nightcap and recount the conversations and highlights of the evening. One of us will roll up a joint and Leslie will put on a pot of tea. If I had actually broken up with John I could sleep over. He is not the kind of guy who would make that easy. He had a hard enough time with me going out each week. But we made a pact and we made it before I ever met John. Every week, nobody does that, and we were going to be the ones. The boy that couldn't handle our pact was the boy who didn't last and the boy who wasn't the right one, so it was almost like a collective dump. If the Hens did a thumbs down it wouldn't be long before he would be adios amigo. Colleen is married and I have been with John and we met Izzy because she was dating one of our friends and they are still together, so it has been the other two who have gone through the boys. Although at the moment Sharon is in a pretty steady relationship. She met Stan at work. Sharon is fucking her boss ... so cliché but it seems to be working out well so far. He is an older divorcee ... quite scandalous!

Leslie arrived in my grade 10 homeroom. She had moved from Nova Scotia and her dad was in the RCMP so she was never able to settle any place for very long. Leslie was awkward and had this Farah Facette hairdo gone wrong. I remember sitting in class thinking she actually got up in the morning and turned on a curling iron and did that to herself. She curled it in a flip all around her face so that it almost looked like she had a big round head. If Leslie's face were an animal she would be a Lassie dog collie. If you asked her what animal she looked most like, she would want to be something from the sea, so she would pick a dolphin. Apparently they love sex too. Her figure you could only describe as tits on a stick. That was enough for me to decide I didn't want anything to do with her. I had a hard enough time attracting boys … I didn't need or want competition like that. Nobody in high school wanted to add a beautiful booby girl into their crowd so Leslie remained on the outs, with the girls anyway.

But the boys were another story. She piqued the interest of many young penises. Looking back, that is what most high school boys were. They were just a bunch of dicks waiting and hoping to get used. I was not the type of girl who was of interest to these walking erections. I guess it was because I am completely flat chested, although I am cute in a wholesome Spanish way, but I looked 12 years old. I was called every name in the book, but the one that stuck was 44D. I don't know how I survived that time in my life. And no, this will not be a man hater book. I love men it is just that in high school they didn't love me. Not one guy ever tried to hit a home run! Ironically enough, John was the boy at his high school that was the totally hot jock that every girl wanted. The prom king so to speak, and once high school was over I won the prize. Well, at the time he was a prize and I was madly in love.

Over the next few months Leslie would try so hard to be my friend, but I was a bitch. There is no other word for my behaviour other than the "C" word and I will refrain from using it … I have my limits on self-deprecation. Besides, Leslie had found herself a wonderful boyfriend (the type I could never dream of dating) and she was doing just fine … until that fateful day in the bathroom where I found her sobbing. I may have bitchy tendencies, but I am not heartless. I asked her what was wrong and she informed me that Paul had dumped her. It was the middle of grade 11 and I was going to a party on the weekend so I invited her. We talked for a while and she pulled herself together. Just the thought of a party perked her right up. We headed off to gym class together. It was the track and field portion of the year and I suck at running. Gymnastics was my thing. But I had to run and I got through it. I saw Leslie was up in the next group and the girl I hated most in school (or was most jealous of) was running with her. In my heart of hearts I wished Leslie would kick her ass. She was the Prom Queen of our school (but she wasn't on the gymnastics team!) and super snobby. Way worse than me.

I was on the sidelines watching Leslie, and I had never in my life seen a girl run like that. Those stick legs of hers kicked everyone's ass by a long shot. I was overcome with joy and ran over and hugged her. Awkward, seeing as we had just had our first conversation since she arrived over a year ago. Leslie was a little flustered, but took my affection in stride. She joined me at the party that weekend, and I have loved her from that night on. She was kind and generous and easy to talk to with a wicked sense of humour. She was quite simply the sweetest, most fun-loving person I had ever met.

"I don't need a friend who changes when I change and who nods when I nod; my shadow does that much better."

Plutarch

Week 336 – About Sharon

I walk through the kitchen doorway; the girls only want to know one thing.

"Well, did you do it yet?"

"No, I've let it go too long and it's way too close to Christmas to dump a fiancé. This can't happen till after the New Year. He feels my distance, he knows something is up. I never say I love you anymore."

"Likely because you don't! How has it been with Alex P since the big affair?" Izzy asks.

"Seduction dammit … will you queers get that right! Actually, weirdish because he confided in me the other day at lunch that he has been having a fling with another girl in our class! I was relieved in a way, cos now we're on the same playing field. I didn't feel as dreadful. I thought … you're a cheater too!!! Once I reflected back on this news I should have guessed. She looks at him with total puppy eyes."

"Do you like her?"

"She has a perfect body and she's attractive, but she has this sadness about her. I suppose it's because her Spanish boyfriend is coming to Canada for the Christmas break and she won't be able to fuck Andrew anymore. He says she's crazy about him, with the emphasis on crazy. She asked him to marry her and they have been undercover dating for two months. I mean he's cute and sexy but that's crazy! At least he recognizes it. He's been totally spooked by the whole thing. He told me he broke it off with her, but she didn't take it well."

"1988's going to be some year for us. Terri leaving John and me potentially getting a steady date!"

"Jesus Leslie, I'm so sorry. I'm self-absorbed these days. The date with Porsche boy must have gone well."

"He showed up with flowers. And his name is Jean-Francois."

"He covers his car and he has a hyphenated name … and she still went on the date! Does he know he doesn't have to keep both of them when he introduces himself … c'mon buddy pick one, Jean or Francois or better yet JF, now that's sort of cool."

"Sharon, that's his name and he didn't choose it."

"But he could use one of my suggestions which would be much better. You may want to mention that next time you see him."

"Or, I may NOT, cos I'm pretty sure I'd like a second date, but thanks for the input. Can I go on now?"

Sharon gives one of her smirks that only Sharon can give. She means what she says, but she also understands she is being ridiculous.

"So I put the flowers in a vase and we have a drink in the kitchen. He made a reservation at some restaurant I had never heard of. Then he has to break the news to me. He looks me up and down and says, 'I don't think this place will let you in with that outfit. They don't allow jeans.' So, I go to change and he grabs our drinks and follows me upstairs. Mr. Shyboy … maybe not so shy! I ask him what on earth he's doing and he promises he won't look, but he doesn't want to sit downstairs alone because he knows how long it could take for me to change and he doesn't want to miss a moment of our date. I quickly reply that I'm not like most girls. He smiles this adorable smile and says,

'I've noticed.' Then we laugh and I start looking through my closet, and I hate everything. So I ask him to pick out something. It was more like a test, but doesn't he rise to the occasion and start flipping through my clothes. He does it quite willingly to my surprise. He picks out dress pants and a top that I've never put together, and I like it.

I then dismiss him from the room because now all I have to do is change."

"Has anybody had a first date pick out their clothes?" Colleen asks.

"My ratio of first dates is so small I don't count." I say with a tone of longing for more.

It is only Leslie with her wide open heart that seems to bring on the oddest situations. I remember in high school we were at a dance and this gauche boy asked her to waltz. Of course she said yes, but didn't really want to, but wouldn't hurt his feelings. She made it through the song and at the end of it he grabbed her hand and walked her back toward us. In high school it doesn't take much for a rumour to spread and someone told someone who told someone else that Leslie and Dwayne where dating. They saw them dancing and holding hands! She didn't freak out she talked to Dwayne and explained that under no circumstance where they seeing each other, but did he want to play it up and have some fun with all the gossip? So Dwayne had the best week of his life, because for the first time in his life he wasn't invisible.

"So did he leave the room?"

"Yes he did and I met him back in the kitchen, we finished our drinks and left. The restaurant was a swishy Italian one in the Glebe. The food was amazing and no one had jeans on."

"We don't really need to hear about the food."

"Terri let's just say Izzy and I had breakfast with him in the morning!" Sharon states while rolling her eyes. "I nearly choked on my coffee when she introduced us … what a fuck'n name."

"Leslie how many times do I have to tell you not to give it up on the first date? That practice hasn't served you well so far."

"Well he was so sweet and he spent a fortune on dinner and then he came over after and the girls were all out and then he kissed me and he was a really good kisser and then I thought of the Porsche and it was actually unbelievable that he wanted to kiss me and then one thing led to another and he was not as shy as I had thought … at all."

"Breath girl … judging by the huge smile on your face I'm guessing you weren't disappointed."

"Not one iota and let me tell you neither was he. We're going to a movie on Tuesday."

"That's cheap movie night."

"I know, he suggested it and of course I'll offer to pay so I jumped all over it. I'm not the one who owns the Porsche!"

Leslie works in a law office doing real estate files and Sharon will start working there in two weeks. Leslie referred her because Sharon did not want to continue her employment as 'the one fucking the boss'. We met Sharon in grade 12. It was her first year at our high school and she came from our rival school not far away. Leslie's maritime manner welcomed all, and she soon became a good friend. She was a bit more challenging to warm up to. Leslie and I were on overdrive most of the time and if Sharon moved any slower I don't think the friendship would have worked out. We would just have left her behind all the time. If Sharon's face where an animal she would be a cat, a Siamese cat with piercing blue eyes. When she irritates us and she does often, I look into her eyes and find it impossible to be mad. I am not sure if it is because

I'm afraid she will pounce, or because I know her, and she has had some hard times.

"So girls this is our last Hen Night before Christmas and I have a little something for us." I pull out two grams of some amazing hash I bought from Andrew's contact. I am the poor student so I am always smoking everybody else's dope. Doing this makes me feel good!

"What are you waiting for girl, roll one up."

"I'll roll it all up and you guys put yours away for the night. If there's anything left over … well I'm taking that home. And I say that loosely cos I don't have a home. I hate being at that apartment. Do you have any idea how big it sucks to still be living there, but so totally gone. And it's Christmas, and I feel like such a bitch. I lie in bed and think of Alex P, then I have a shower and think of Alex P … then I have a drink and think of Alex P. My only salvation is John is going to his parents on Christmas Eve and I won't see him till Boxing Day."

"Ok Miss … NO … it was a one-night-stand! Right … enough of that shit. I told you it was an AFFAIR," Sharon says in her customary compassionate way and trying to sound seductive as she says 'affair'.

"Well it doesn't mean my ONE-NIGHTER couldn't turn into a casual affair! And by the way are we staying in tonight?"

"Yeah we're all broke from holiday shopping."

"I was hoping you'd say that."

Izzy looks at us all as if in a quandary and says, "Maybe we should be phoning the bar and calling in sick or something?"

"Funny … they'll miss us no doubt! Who needs a cocktail? You have to wonder how that word came about. It's used for alcoholic beverages, and let's face it, most of our accumulated "cock tails" are a result of excessive cocktails! Is that how the word started? I'd love to know."

"Leslie I promise to research that for you next time I'm in the school library."

Izzy adds, "While you're there why don't you find out why we drive on a parkway and park on a driveway? English is a fucked up language."

Leslie remembers something, and has to blurt it out before she forgets, because her brain is on fast-forward at all times, and her next thought might wipe out this one altogether.

"By Jesus, I was on the phone with mum and dad the other day. Mum's telling me about her pap smear. The doctor couldn't find her cervix, and told her she needed to check by hand. Mum said fine, I must still have one, check away. So the doctor finds it, and tells her that it has 'atrophied' some. Well dad doesn't miss a beat and hollers into the phone, 'No Odette … I think what the doctor meant to say was 'A TROPHY.' Fuck we laughed."

"You're parents are so great. Wouldn't it be wonderful for you if they moved back one day."

"Yes, they're mostly awesome, but let's not forget they left me to move to Newfoundland on my graduation day and never sent me a penny to help out. Could they not have waited a day? It was my fucking graduation!!! I mean they drove away waving out the back window. Once they were out of sight, I turned around … and balling my head off I walked to Terri's with my suitcase, comforter and pillow. They didn't even drop me off! That still upsets me. It's a hard one to let go of. So hard I obviously haven't been able to!"

"That's pretty crazy. Eighteen and launched on your own. We wouldn't have let you move to Newfoundland. I'm sure it's gorgeous, but it's fuck'n no man's land. I don't care how nice the people are. Nobody moves to Newfoundland unless it's for a dam good job. And the price of airfare is stupid … you could never fly back, and we could never visit you. You can practically fly half way across the world for the same price. That's so fucked up about Canada. I get supply and demand, but do you not think that if it was affordable there may be some more demand!"

"Sharon you're right … you need to write a letter to Air Canada and get that all fixed up will you."

"Wack-off."

"Keep the claws in girl its Christmas and I brought the dope and I won't share with you!"

"You will too, cos you know you love me no matter what!"

It is midnight and I am heading back to John's and my apartment. I don't drink very much, but I am pretty high and listening to music to keep my mind off the fact that I am still engaged to a man I no longer love. I am driving cautious and the roads are clear and the song playing is *Roxanne* by *The Police.* I'm cruising along and groov'n and singing like a rock star. The song changes to one from the Bread album that we used to play at parties in grade school, and you could waltz to the entire side. In grade school you were not expected to have breasts yet, so I was desirable then! It brings back memories, so I don't change the channel. I sing, 'I want to make it with you' and that just fuels my despair.

What happened next is why I feel much more confident getting in a car with a stoner over a drunk any day and twice on Sunday! I am feeling sorry for myself, and I do my usual quick check of the back mirror and speedometer. I am driving 30 KM in a 50 KM zone and have changed my speed to match the rhythm of the song. All I need is a cop around and I could play out that scene from the *Cheech and Chong* movie *Up In Smoke.* Typically we stoners are very laid back and pot doesn't have the aggressive affects that alcohol will have on men. I say men because I really haven't witnessed a girl brawl in a bar … yet.

I know they happen I just haven't seen one first hand. And let's face it statistically the jails are full of men. They are just different.

I know a man's rage when he is drunk. I have been the recipient of it time and time again. John's turning point is the 13th beer. I did count once because then I would try to pace him, or somehow control his intake. I would suggest just buying a 12 for a party instead of a 24, but that never flew. He was never physically abusive because he was very close one time, and I made it very clear if he hit me it was over. It was the first time I ever yelled back at him. He hit the kitchen cupboard instead. My sister Laura introduced us. He was three years older than I, and way out of my league. Never had I had a boyfriend of that caliber in my life. He completely swept me off my feet. I was 18.

"A friend is someone that knows everything about you and loves you anyway."

Kushandwizdom

Week 337 - About Izzy

"I hope you enjoyed yet another Vetnor Christmas."

"You know I love hanging with your family Terri, I've been doing it long enough now."

"And you know you're part of our family! If only you could stop calling mom Mrs. Vetnor. Call her Winni or Witcho. We've been calling her that forever. Even the boy's friends call her Witcho!"

"I could never do that. I don't know why, but for as long as I'll known you and your family it will be Mrs. and Mr. Vetnor."

"Fine, but sometimes I feel like mom takes offense to it. It's so formal, and she does love you like one of her own. She loved it when you lived with us after graduation. You just have a way of spicing things up! Lord knows I was ecstatic. Being alone in the house with just mom and dad was eerie. I suppose it must have been even stranger for them."

"Are you kidd'n … if you raised nine children I'm sure you'd be in your glory when your house finally emptied out. Besides it didn't take long for the house to fill up again."

"It was a good thing you were paying rent, or you'd have been sharing a room with me if any more of them came back!"

"Who was back first Ed or Michael?

"I don't remember. All I remember is that within eight months we had eight adults in the house."

"It was Ed, then Michael, then Laura dumped her boyfriend and she moved back. Michael came back from out west and had to move into Ed's bedroom although at that time I may have preferred he move into mine!"

"Shut up! Leslie your little crush on my brother completely took me by surprise. I'm happy nothing came of it. That would have changed everything."

"I know it was a crazy moment where I lost my sensible side."

"Do you have a sensible side … I haven't seen it!"

"Funny … then Ann moved in when she got kicked out because she was dating the older widower … bloody Born Again's, aren't they so righteous and pious that they need to kick their kid out cos she wasn't following the rules … who makes those stupid rules anyway!"

"Laura was happy to share her room, and hear all the gossip and give her two cents. Speaking of gossip where are Izzy and Sharon? I need the scoop on their Holidays."

"They went to get some beer. They'll be back in a bit. Izzy didn't have the best of holidays, but I'll let her tell you about that."

Just as Leslie says that, the girls walk in full of snow and shivering.

"Did it start snowing?" I ask.

"No, Izzy the queer decided it would be funny to push me in the snow and I'm not in a particularly playful mood."

"Tell me when have you ever been in a playful mood? I would love to hear about it!"

"Funny … so, I brushed myself off some, and we keep walking through the courtyard, and I see the tree is snow laden and I can reach the branch. So I take one quick step faster and before she can figure out what's happening, I grab the branch, jump out of the way and sweet justice. Izzy is full of snow. Another proven case of what goes around comes around."

"Genius, I'm impressed."

"I know right, I retaliated and didn't get another drop of snow on me!"

"I was talking about the beer still being intact. Now that's impressive wouldn't you say Leslie?"

"Do you really think I would push her in the snow if she was carrying the beer?!"

"They're lucky it's still intact, or they would be heading right back out again to get some more. I paid for that beer."

"Now that I'm back in school I really have to start drinking pints again. It isn't that I don't like beer it's just that it doesn't like me. And no one wants to hear me belch all night. I get tired of listening to myself!"

"We're used to it, and everyone knows a good belch isn't as satisfying when you're trying to be ladylike. Besides, everything makes you burp."

"Yeah, but beer's in a class of its own on the belch scale. I can actually talk in a burp, and beer is the only thing that'll do that."

"Yes … we all know all about your gas, let's move on."

I take a big swig of beer, and as loud and I can in a big glorious roaring belch, I say, "ffffiiiiiinnnee!"

The girls don't even flinch. I have to introduce people slowly, and carefully to my little issue. It can gross them out. I can do it quietly when I stop and think about it, but it has been part of my character for as long as I can remember. If I don't let it out then cramps and bloating will follow, and who wants that. But, I will secretly admit that sometimes I enjoy freaking people out. I have been at parties and a guy will look at me in complete awe that such an accomplished gaseous explosion could release from such a little wee girl.

"How was Christmas everyone?"

"We heard all about yours from Leslie. I just can't even imagine all those people in that little house. How many were there?"

"We had 26 this year and it's so fun having little ones around. Miles is the cutest baby ever. I'm one of those people who is absolutely sure she wants to have children one day. Babies are so amazing. My nieces and nephews were the best part of the day. So Izzy, I heard there is trouble in paradise."

"Did Leslie tell you?"

"No, just that you didn't have the best holiday."

"Sam and I spent Christmas Eve together and it was really nice. Christmas Day we spent with our respective families. I had a great day because all four of us girls were there for a change. I wish I was as fond of all my sisters as you are of yours, but it was still great, and mom was in her glory. She's an amazing lady. At least thinking about her makes me happy. Telling the Sam story just makes me feel like I could punch a fucking wall with his picture on it."

"Or better yet, put that old picture of his hard-on up on the wall. Punching the 'springboard' may feel more satisfying! You don't have to repeat it if you don't want. I can wait."

"Naw, I just love gossip even if it's my own! So we had plans to go shopping Boxing Day and he cancels, says he isn't feeling well. Sharon and I decided to go anyway, but Sharon wants to go downtown for a change. So we do. Well don't we walk right into Sam fucking shopping with Brenda Skanks … I mean Spanks. Of all the girls he could run around with … why her, my nemesis?! The one it took him so long to get over and finally realize that I was the one. I would have dropped her right there if it weren't for Sharon. Then I would have beaten the shit out of Sam."

"Wholly crap, Sam you idiot. So what was his excuse?"

"He claimed he ran into her there, and didn't want to shop with me cos he was looking for something special for my birthday."

"Your birthday isn't till May, but it would be just like Sam to want to buy it during Boxing Day sales. He doesn't part quickly with his hard earned dollars!"

"He was quick with the story, and that's the only reason I'm giving him any benefit of the doubt."

"So what happened after you wanted to kill them?"

"I told him to have a good day with the 'Skank' and not to fucking call me ever again! Sharon hustled me out of the mall pretty fast. It just happened to be 11:00 am so we headed straight to a bar and I drowned my sorrows. She could barely get me in the car, but I felt so much better."

"Do you think he has been with her again?"

"We spend a lot of time together, I don't see where he would fit it in … except for Thursdays of course!"

"What'll you do if he really doesn't call you again? But, I'm sure he will!" I say with great enthusiasm.

"I'll slash his fucking tires on his precious car. Then I may track down the 'Skank' and do the same with hers!!!"

Leslie and I met Izzy at the very end of Grade 12. She was dating Sam at the time. From the moment I saw her there was something very familiar. If Izzy were an animal she would be a wombat with her thick hair, round face and small pencil thin mouth. It didn't take me too long to piece together that she was the leader of the girls' gang who terrified me and my friends all through grade school. She had put on a few pounds, and back then she wore her make-up like a whore, so the association wasn't instant. Her gang would call us names and try to start fights. We would avoid them at all costs. They were bullies who wanted to beat us up, so we always ran away. It was the classic case of the public school girls hating the Catholic school girls. There was also some history between one of my friends dating some guy Izzy liked, so she became an instant enemy. Oddly enough it turned out that Sharon and Izzy were best friends since kindergarten, but I don't ever recall Sharon with that group of butches. Happily, we have all matured, and I really like Izzy now, but she means every word about slashing Sam's tires. I never want to be in her bad graces.

"You know Sam is going to call, and I really think you'll have a grand old time making the little shit sweat some."

"Leslie he'll be drenched and panting once I'm through with him … oh and we haven't had a chance to talk since the second date. How did it go?"

"It was fun. He made me laugh…."

"Which you love!"

"Yes, and we had much debate over which movie to see, and he finally caved when I reminded him I was paying. We saw Moonstruck and it was excellent. He just gave me a quick peck and left quickly so I'm not sure what to make of that. He said he had some stuff to do at home and he would call soon."

"You know he'll call, don't fret."

"Maybe you were right and I shouldn't have slept with him right away. I hope I didn't fuck it up … excuse the pun!"

"Well it appears sleeping with Alex P even before any first date didn't scare him away."

"You didn't sleep with him again?!"

"No, but he knew I was spending Christmas Eve at moms with my family and doesn't he show up with his best friend Al, whom I've never met. I didn't even know if I should invite them in, but it would have been weird not to. So here he is at my parents' house meeting my whole family, as my classmate who lives nearby."

"OK, yes that's strange, and a smidgeon on the arrogant side I'll add."

"He is a little on the arrogant side I think. Or, it could just be total confidence, because he doesn't seem arrogant. Sharon, from my take so far I would say he's just very confident. He must have been stoned because he was so chatty with everyone and then he and Teresa start talking. She is one person who's in love with the Christmas season, and she's going on about all the presents under the tree and how important it is to give, and doesn't he pipe in, half interrupting her and says … 'that's so great, we're going to get along wonderfully because I'm Jewish, and we love to receive.' Well at first Teresa didn't know what hit her and when Al and I broke out laughing she joined in. I'm not entirely sure if she did find that humorous, or if she was just faking it."

"It appears the man likes to make an entrance … but, that's pretty fucking funny! I don't know how I'm feeling about this guy?"

"It's not like I have had many to compare to. But I'm planning on changing that."

"Does that mean you broke up with John?" Izzy asks already knowing the answer, but now that question is a weekly ritual.

"Operative word there was 'planning'. Are we going anywhere tonight?" I ask trying to change the subject.

"No, we're all going to Robbie's New Year's party so we need our beauty sleep. Are you going?"

"I expect we'll go. It's on the agenda, and I'm going to buy the beer and only get a 12. John and I are so off these days I'm afraid of what verbal diarrhea may spew if the consumption threshold is crossed. So Sharon I hear you met some of Stan's family … ooohhh getting all serious!"

"I went to his house for Christmas Eve dinner. What I didn't know is I was going to have to do most of the fucking cooking! Stan has been a pampered boy. His aunt and uncle were amazing, and they were super helpful. I just loved them. His dad is getting on and has some difficulties, but a nice, nice man. I can't believe I'm dating a guy who has a fucking ex-wife. Everyone made a point of telling me I was so much better than his ex. It was a tad peculiar."

"Thankfully there aren't any children to keep them attached."

"If there were any of those, we would never have made it this far. I'm not a rug rat lover like you guys."

"Some people just know they absolutely do not want to ever have children. Charlotte, Laura's best friend is one of those people. She had her tubes tied when she was 21. Could you imagine being that sure? She asked her doctor to do it when she was 18, but he refused. She finally wore him down."

Leslie is standing over the music as she always does, ready to skip over the songs she doesn't want to hear. The girls have a big ghetto blaster that plays tapes and CD's or you can listen to the radio. There is a beautiful stereo in the living room with a bunch of albums that her ex has not removed yet. He made her promise not to use it. They never lived together, but when he bought it he had nowhere to put it and she had the space.

"Leslie that thing is a piece of shit. Let me play DJ with the stereo. Gary will never know."

"Fine let's do it. You're right, fuck Gary! What does he think I don't know how to use his precious stereo?!"

"Leslie you're miss music critic, so you pick out a few albums. I'll know which songs you want to hear."

"OK then, we're having a dance par-tay tonight babies!"

We all grab our cocktails and move to the living room. I have my music selections ready and we start to sing and dance the night away. At one point Leslie runs up to the kitchen and brings back a broom, a long pepper grinder, a finished roll of paper towel and a fat marker. These become our microphones as we strut around to Genesis, Steely Dan, The Police and Madonna, to name a few. I put on George Michael's … *I Want Your Sex* and Leslie clearly approves. She loves that song. She is hopping around the sunken living room and her performance is sinking to new lows of obscene. Her prop is the pepper grinder and as she dances she takes it and treats it like she would a big cock and is pelvic thrusting toward it. Then it starts disappearing between her legs. After a time she then moves it up to her mouth and animates giving it a blowjob. Then all hell breaks loose and Izzy takes her broom stick and puts it behind Leslie's arse and we are all still dancing and singing and laughing at how ridiculous we are, but we are all just blowing off inanimate objects … I mean steam. Everyone tries to outdo the other with sexual acts to their respective props. If only I could bottle that contagious energy that Leslie has, I would make a fortune. Even on your most exhausting day you will show up on Hen Night and get your second, third, and fourth winds just by being in her presence.

I finally get myself out of there at 1:00 am and I am driving home and thinking about music, and how I love it. Every album I bought I would pray they had the words on the sleeve and I would play it over and over again till I knew them all. Do I love the music, or do I just love the lyrics? It has always been important to me to understand the songs and make sense of the lyrics. Some lyrics have clearly had very little thought put into them but I typically don't like those artists. I love the poetry and stories of the song as much as the music. Dad bought the house headphones so he didn't have to listen to my music anymore. Laura and her boyfriend had a big influence on my choices. I used to visit them all the time and he introduced me to a variety of artists and drugs! My absolute favourite was Roxy Music. Bryan Ferry had the sexiest voice I had ever heard; winding it around the most stirring lyrics. It was through the bond of Roxy Music that I had my first civil conversation with my brother, Ed. I was 17 when we both showed up at home with the same album.

"Female friendships that work are relationships in which women help each other belong to themselves."
Louise Bernikow

Week 338 - About Colleen

"Holy Mary Mother of GOD it is 1988. Yet another year of the par-tay!"

"Don't mean to burst your bubble chick, but it's technically the Year of the Dragon. The next time it will be a dragon again it will be 2000. We'll be 36 at the change of the millennium. It seems like a lifetime away."

"I wonder what it will be like. Shit we could be married and have kids."

"Yeah, we may have decided to grow up."

"We are so grown up already. We just haven't turned into bores! I know one thing that will always remain the same … a par-tay on Thursday!!!"

Colleen walks into the bar because we have all gathered here first and she has an expression that I can't quite read. Colleen is 15 years older than us. If Colleen were an animal, orangutan comes to mind but only because she is big boned and strong and a strawberry blond with freckles. What is special about her is her aura. To me, an aura is that sixth sense you feel when you first meet someone. Anyone who first meets her can't help but feel her warmth. I may as well be Sherlock fucking Holmes because I am so good at nailing down my like or dislike on the first few seconds of an introduction. Just shake my hand and that old sixth sense will kick in like a barometer. In my short quarter of a century life I have learned to always go with my first instinct! But do I? Absolutely not and I always regret it. The day I stop second guessing myself will the day when life falls into place. We have decided to go to Moe's Place because there is a band playing tonight. We are all sitting around the bar and Sharon starts the query we are all dying to know.

"What the fuck happened with you and Hank after the New Year's Party?"

"We've seen you two bicker plenty, but nothing like that. We were all relieved once you managed to get him out."

"I just let him go on shitting all over me cos I know once he's that drunk and stoned there's no point in arguing."

I rudely interrupt, "Don't I know all about that!"

"So, I finally snapped … that night my whole life flashed before me as if I was watching it on TV! My fucking husband is a few bricks short of a wall. I put him on the couch, threw a blanket on him and I smiled because I knew I wasn't ever going to do that again. I went up to bed and slept like a bear in winter."

The bartender brings us our drinks and then asks Colleen what she would like. In a playful singing voice, and a dance in her step she replies, "One bourbon, one scotch and one beer … naw, just kidd'n … but I do want a round of tequila shots and a Blue please."

"What's up?"

"I have kicked Hank out, and he actually left. I can't even believe it was that easy. He packed a bag, and moved in with his uncle temporarily.

He doesn't even remember the party, but some of the boys have been telling him bits and pieces and he knows he was a dick."

"Don't you mean he knows he IS a dick? The party was just another night of Hank being Hank. This is celebrated news Colleen! You'll be so much happier without him!"

"Ah … here we are. Everyone get your shots ready and I would like to make a toast … to new beginnings … may all our lives be full of them because that's what will keep life interesting."

We all finish and make our 'why do we drink this shit' faces and slam our shot glasses on the bar. Because that is what you do when you drink shots … you slam them down because drinking shots means you're tough! But tequila does feel good at times, and we are all excited for Colleen. She has been out of love for a long time, but when there are children involved it is another matter entirely. Hank had two boys from a previous marriage (one of whom is Leslie's ex) and he and Colleen had two more children. Hank and Colleen raised all the kids. When Leslie was dating Gary we used to party at their house all the time. Colleen is a totally different type of mother than what I am used to, but then again she is nearly 30 years younger than my mom. I suppose she ought to be hipper.

"I feel like Jed Clampett when his shot-gun found the oil. I may as well be living in Beverly Hills when I walk around my house and don't have to deal with him anymore."

"How are the kids?"

"They're fine. They can come and go as they please and visit their father whenever they want. I don't think they will very often, but we'll see. And I don't give a rat's ass. I've made him look like a much better father than he is. Now they'll see all his true colours."

"Jesus you split with your husband of 20 years and I can't dump my fiancé of two and a half years! I figured I would answer the question before one of you queers asked me."

"We'll keep harassing you till you'll be too embarrassed to come out on Thursday if you don't tell him. What if he gets in another car accident and this time you aren't so lucky? Put that in your pipe and smoke it!"

"Yeah, yeah, yeah … that was a fun party." I say changing the subject. "I had a ball despite my inner turmoil. I was watching John interacting with our friends and thought he may never see these people again. I'm dreadful. So I had another drink. I may have outdrank him that night. I had the biggest hangover ever! I was in a coma all day."

"I hope this night can be of some inspiration … if I can do it anyone can. It's never easy, but infinitely worthwhile."

"All I need is one night were John behaves like Hank did and I will be golden."

We see the band members head to the stage. I had been checking one of them out at the bar, practicing the new techniques I will have to master for the dating scene. There is something about a musician. I think girls feel like they must be sensitive and romantic and will write songs about them. When Leslie and I had our band nights out with Laura and Charlotte I had a new crush every time. It was always Leslie they went for, but it never bothered me. I had long since resigned myself to the fact that I was not an object of desire. The first set of music was pretty good, but didn't get us all up dancing.

"Great, now we can hear again. I hope they get a little peppier next set. I'm itch'n to dance, but I hate it when I'm the only one."

"You know I'll come and rescue you because I love you."

"And you know when we start … the sheep will follow. That dancefloor will fill up like a hooker's mouth on a busy night."

"You have such a way with words! What is that poem you are always reciting … that Johnny Tucker one?"

"Mary, Mary cunt so hairy, how does your garden grow? Ask Johnny Tucker that little fucker he got her three times in a row!" Leslie recites with a mixture of pride and reflection.

"Is that what you did in Antigonish to pass time? You must have been extremely bored."

"I was just happy to memorize something!"

"That was the missing link for your education Leslie. If they could have somehow made your school work with sexual undertones and a catchy little rhyme … you would've been an A student! History class could have been something like, Christopher Columbus sailed his seamen across the sea in 1492, so he could finally get screwed."

"That would've been way better!"

The other girls have gone to do a bathroom run. Leslie and I are sitting at the bar when two drinks show up unexpectedly. The bartender points and they're from the very cute band member. He's sitting with a friend. When this happens, and it does quite often because Leslie simply oozes sex appeal, we'll always take our drinks over and say thank you and have a little chat.

"Are you ladies enjoying your evening?"

"Yes, we always enjoy Hen Night!"

"What night?"

"Never mind, we're having a good time, but I have to say I'd love it if the tempo was a bit faster. Do you take requests?"

"Leslie shut up. You'll give the poor guy a complex."

"We have a set list we have to stick to because we haven't been playing together for that long. But, I can assure you we have some good dance tracks coming up."

"Good to hear. We just wanted to come over and say thank you for the beer."

"Hope to see you on the dance floor."

"Hope you play something I want to dance to."

"Leslie, for a super nice person you can sound like a right bitch!"

We walk back around the bar and the girls are giving us the look. It's the 'What is Leslie up to now?' look.

"He bought us a drink so we just went to say thank you."

"Was he the one playing guitar?"

"Yes he was," I reply quickly as I'm looking over at him. "I was already checking him out before he went up to play. He's totally gorgeous. But, he bought Leslie the drink and I just got to ride on the coattails of her free alcohol! Sharon if you didn't go to the bathroom you would have a free drink too!"

"You sound ridiculous. You don't mean that. You may have been the one he wanted to buy the drink for, and I'm just riding your coattails."

"I'm just speaking from experience that's all!"

"Colleen, I would like to buy you a drink. I'm so happy for you."

"Sure, since you will likely get free ones why not! The band typically drinks for free so take advantage of this one girl. If he wants to get you liquored up we'll take care of you!"

"Funny."

"I heard a good joke today."

"Ok let's hear it."

I put on my best Deep South accent and proceed: "There are three southern bells meeting for tea in the afternoon trying to make some interesting conversation. One suggests they play a little game. They each have to pick a soda pop that would best describe their husband in bed.

'Oh, I got one the first girl announces. I would call mine Mountain Dew'. 'And why?' The other two ask. 'Well because when he mounts, he do!'

OK, that's good they agree. Then the second one says, 'I got it. Mine would be 7-UP because when he's up he's 7 inches.' The other two agree that that was well played.

The third one is stumped so she is thinking for a bit. Then finally she says … 'I got it! My husband would be Jack Daniels.' The other two say, 'Honey that ain't no soda pop … that there is a hard liquor.'

'Yeah girls … that's my man … he's a hard licker.'"

The girls enjoy that as best as they can because they are a tough crowd. We are all getting a glow on and feeling like all that exists at the moment is this moment. I mean that is all that ever exists, but who really lives in the now? You are supposed to, but I sure don't. I'm thinking about the past and the future all the time. I am in a perpetual state of regret or hope. There are always moments during Hen Night where we are all just in the moment and no one gives their real life a thought and that is why we do it every week. It is therapy for the soul. The band heads back to the stage.

"OK, I can't sit to this one. C'mon let's dance."

Leslie will plead with all of us, but she knows I will be the only guaranteed dance partner. I started joining her because if you don't she will just dance alone and start pointing at random strangers to join her. At times that practice has gotten us into some trouble. There are men who think that a dance invitation is also an invitation to get laid. That somehow they go hand in hand! They are playing *Start Me Up* by

The Rolling Stones, which isn't one of Leslie's favourite bands, but it is danceable and she has been waiting a while. I, on the other hand, am a huge *Stones* fan so I am right behind her. The boys in the band look pleased. Like clockwork about half way through the song the dance floor starts to fill up. Sometimes I wonder if we didn't start would all these repressed people just sit in their seats, tapping their feet wishing the dance floor wasn't empty.

"Check out the guitar player … he can't take his eyes off of you." I try to holler over the music.

"As if! Just shut up and dance."

We have an awesome time and our band buddy tried to get Leslie's number, but she told him she had a boyfriend. He did insist on giving us the next four gigs they had in case they split up. I guess Porsche boy has intrigued her enough to wait and see what happens because if that hunk of flesh wanted my number I'd write it real large with lipstick on a napkin and stick it down is pants. We are all back at the Hen House and there is a note on the door and Leslie reads it: "Hey Unit 48, would you be my date on Saturday night at eight?"

"That's so cute, but I didn't get his number yet … I guess cos he lives four doors away I didn't think about it."

"Let's all just get in the house. I'm freezing. I'll grab a pen and you can just write, 'yes' and put it in his mailbox … or does he still have Stan's number? Maybe you should add your real one too … just in case!"

While Leslie does that I get the lowdown on the Izzy and Sam saga. Sharon puts the tea on and rolls one up.

"So how long did it take before he phoned?"

"He didn't phone. He showed up here with my so called birthday present and decided that may be enough restoration. He knew I would love it. Whether he had already bought it or bought it after I left, I have no idea."

"That doesn't matter. He obviously loves you and you love him. It isn't like you caught him in bed with her."

"I know and we're back on track, but I'm still pissed off. It takes me a while to forgive and forget."

"Yes, I remember this from our grade school days!"

"I was a bitch then. My tough chick days are over."

"Are you sure about that? You can still give it out girl!"

"Funny."

"So what was the gift that released the knife from your clenched fist?"

"It's a gold necklace of two hearts entwined and where the hearts meet there are tiny emeralds."

"Your birthstone, how sweet, but why aren't you wearing it?"

"I'm just not ready yet. That would show him it is over and I need a few more days of groveling!"

"I can't wait to see if Sam buys her another present for her real birthday or if that's supposed to be it!"

Leslie puts the radio on. Sharon lights up a joint.

"Did you guys hear that they are building a tunnel under the English Channel, so you can drive from England to France? Isn't that amazing?" Izzy says as she goes upstairs to put on her jammies.

"I would hate to be the one digging it. You have a whole freaking ocean above you. No thanks."

"Good old England has been in the news lots this year. Can you imagine Ottawa with no power? Well London is way bigger and they had a huge storm blow out their power!"

"We're fragile and so vulnerable to mother nature. We think we're so smart, but let's face it, if she rears her ugly side … we're fucked. If we lost our power in the winter what would we do?" Colleen asks.

"We would all have to move out of our homes and go to some community building run by generators. Just like on TV when you see the disaster relief efforts. We would have a little section of the floor in the gymnasium with some creepy stranger sleeping beside us."

"The only person sleeping beside me will be Izzy or Sharon."

"I wonder what Thatcher was doing through all of it?"

"Trying to get it fixed I would imagine. She's quite a force there. She's in her third term. That doesn't happen every day!"

"She's a huge cue for women. A female Prime Minister of England and guess what …"

"She's actually a man!"

"Funny … she's doing a great job! Although I'm sure not everyone would agree, but that's politics. There's nothing perfect about it."

"Oh, hurray … a good song is on. You queers are putting me to sleep. Come dance."

"Leslie finally likes *Bruce Springsteen*! She admitted that *Tunnel of Love* is a good song! It's a moment in history!"

"I just had to see him in concert … that's all it took! I never knew how hot he was either! I wouldn't kick him out of bed for eat'n crackers."

Leslie and I have quite different taste in music, but I have her warmed up to Bruce finally, and Roxy … well she likes what she likes. I am learning to respect Madonna, more for her business acumen than her music, but I do love to dance and she has very danceable music, but so does Steely Dan and Earth Wind and Fire, and … well you get my drift! In high school we usually went to my place for lunch because I lived five minutes away. We would eat and then do hot knives if mom wasn't home. Mom worked shift work at the hospital as an RNA. She went back to school when she was 42. Every once in a while dad would surprise us and arrive for lunch. He worked for a mobile pressure washing company. One day, after our hot knives he walked in with a brand new haircut. I have no idea what was so funny about this haircut, but we started to giggle when we saw him walk by the kitchen window. Dad walked up the stairs and sat in his chair to say hello. Dad always said hello when I had friends there. By now we were using full restraint, trying not to look at him or each other, trying desperately to keep composed. Then Leslie took a sip of her tea and we looked at each other and lost it. The tea came flying out of her nose and I had to run to the bathroom for fear I may pee myself. I left Leslie out there, alone with my father for way too long while I was hysterically laughing, locked away, and safe from my father's accusing stare. I was not a good friend that day.

I'm heading home and thinking how much I will miss having use of a car. When John had his replaced it wasn't a standard. I was so hoping it would be, and I would shock the shit out of him when I drove it perfectly. I would have loved to have been able to do that. My stomach is in knots and I know when I go home, if John is up I will tell him I do not want to marry him. If he is not up, I will tell him in the morning. I have to untie the knot that will never be tied.

"Regret for wasted time is more wasted time."

Anonymous

Week 339 – About Time

"Terri, get in here. I have a big reefer ready with your name on it. Leslie has kept us posted on the whole miserable break up."

"It would be so much better if it was more miserable. That's why I'm so miserable. John is taking it much better than I ever imagined. He's hurt, and mad and trying to figure out what the hell to do with the apartment. I figured he could maybe find some student to move in with him, but he'll have nothing to do with that. I called and gave my notice, but they won't be able to find anyone before March 1. Fuck I hate myself right now. Where's that reefer?"

"That man has had a chip on his shoulder for as long as you have been with him. I call him the coulda, woulda, shoulda man. You know he wouldn't be in university if it weren't for you pushing him there. Mister I had three football scholarships, but I couldn't go, because my parents moved to the country and I had to work cos I had to buy a car and on and on, and cry me a fucking river! He'll find his way."

"Sharon you have a nickname for him! The things you learn about after you break up! When I brought my clothes bag back to mom and dad's place and told them I was moving back in, dad surprised me when he said … my dad of very few words says, 'Glad to hear it. I never liked him anyway.' And I ask him why cos I'm sincerely shocked by this. I thought everyone liked John. Then dad continues … 'Because every time he would come over he would head straight to the beer fridge and he would grab a beer and then offer me one. And I would always think the gall of this guy offering me a beer, that I paid for! If I wanted a beer I would get myself a beer. Why don't you bring some for once in your life, then you could offer me a beer?' Dad was so right. That's exactly what he would do and I never realized how dreadful his behaviour was … doesn't say much for me either."

Colleen is quick to shut me up, "Don't you go cutting yourself down. It's taken us years to build up your self-esteem and you'll need that confidence during the next journey."

"I have acquired a significant improvement in that department, and let's not forget that John did have a lot to do with that. He's very cute, and he only had eyes for me. Now why don't our efforts ever work on Leslie?"

"Her lack of confidence is so deep rooted it may never change."

"In high school she always struggled with English. For Leslie, reading in front of the class was equally as painful as the thought of getting a needle. When we were lined-up for our TB shots she nearly passed out! One thing I learned in Toronto while reading all the self-help and spiritual books is you have to love yourself. It is the common thread in all of them, but really hard to do! I soon realized that my purpose in leaving and spending that time there was to try to find myself … to establish what I wanted to do with my life, and how best to live it. I changed so much that year. Speaking of Leslie is she with Izzy?

"Yeah, I can't believe they're not back yet! They went to pick up some munchies ages ago."

"You must notice that when I give Leslie a compliment, and I try to often, she's completely flustered. Her face reads like a book. It's almost the same face she gets when she's lying. I've never met anyone else who cannot hide embarrassment or deceit at all."

"It's made her life easier in some ways but harder in others. She'd never have taken so long to break up with John. He would have seen right through her."

"Yeah, Yeah, Yeah! And in high school she always had to sleep at my house cos she knew she couldn't go home and tell a lie. I hope I have kids that will be that transparent."

"I don't think there'll ever be another character like Leslie!"

"And there'll never be another you or me either! How's that for oozing self-confidence?"

Leslie and Izzy are finally back.

"What took you girls so long? One day we'll all have one of those *Get Smart* cell phones and we won't have to sit and worry anymore. Who could've predicted that Max's shoe phone would be real some day?!"

"They don't look like a shoe!"

"No shit Sherlock! I was merely referring to the size not the shape!"

"Well the *'ship of love'* just got a new battle wound."

Leslie's first car is a big old piece of shit, but never fails to get her from A to B. To listen to her talk about her car, one might think it was her boyfriend. She speaks of it with a twinkle in her eye and a smile in her voice, therefore its nickname, *'ship of love'*. Most everyone assumes it is after her passionate escapades within!

"This guy was driving too fast and hit some black ice and didn't stop in time. Since I have a huge motherfucking bumper the size of half his car there was only a dent. His car … not so lucky. Of course it had to happen on the busiest street, so we pulled over to a side street to assess things. Izzy ain't budging, so I roll down my window and crawl out of the car. Well the dude is looking at me like I am from another planet and I shout at him, 'Yes, I would have used the door if it worked. There's a lot worse shit going on in the world … this isn't a big deal!' He actually laughs, but he can't be very happy. Then we have to wait for the cops because he insisted on running up to the first house and asking them to call. Then I realize … the cops are coming, YES … a man in uniform … yummy! So I quickly applied fresh lipstick!"

Izzy pipes in, "So then she invites him in the car to kill the time waiting for the cops. He could have been some crazy fuck. And 'the ship' is a two door so I had to get out and let him in the back."

"Well he was too big to crawl through the window."

"Well he could have waited in his own car."

"Well he had more fun waiting with us … or I should say me because you didn't have much to say."

"Because I don't care. I'm never going to see this guy again and I know way too much about him."

"He did go on about his kids. They all had the flu and one of them puked on him, so all in all he was having a really crummy day. Then the cops finally arrive and did the accident report. I was so excited, because he was a double yummy. Just the uniform guarantees some level of yummy … then when they're actually good looking, that's double the pleasure! I tried to drag it out for as long as I could. I learned that you need a police report for insurance purposes so always call the cops. The whole experience was worth it just for that information!"

"Leslie is insane and that's why we're so late. But we did get some good munchies for all you stoners."

"Izzy one of these nights you'll smoke a reefer with us."

"No I won't. It just doesn't agree with me. It's not like I haven't tried."

"Sam's always smoking. I suppose if you did too that would be expensive."

"His basement's in a fucking haze at all times, and he thinks his mother can't smell it. 'But I blow it out the window and leave it open a crack,' he tells me. Well they say if you stink like BO all the time you don't even smell it on yourself."

"Right, maybe his mom just thinks that's what the basement smells like. She likely wouldn't even know what hash did smell like. Either that or she just doesn't care. Her boy is a good boy and has a good job and takes good care of her and that's all that matters … if he wants to smoke hash all night so be it!"

"Leslie that's a good point … we so-called stoners get a bad rap. We're portrayed in movies and in media as some kind of lazy no-good burdens on society. I mean according to them we can't even put a structured sentence together! No wonder the people who have never smoked drugs frown on it so."

"They wouldn't frown on it so, if they just tried it."

"Well there're a lot of people who have tried it who just don't enjoy the buzz … like Izzy. And there are a ton of people who function very well and live productive lives who are pretty much stoned all the time. And then there are the people like us who use it as an unwinder at the end of the day thing."

Sharon needs to add her two cents, "This conversation here is a big hypocrisy existing in our society today."

"What? People for or against smoking pot?"

"No fuck. The fact that alcohol is totally socially acceptable, yet marijuana is illegal and completely taboo. We know tons of people who smoke, but we don't talk about it outside our own circles."

"We talk about it all the time!"

"Only on Hen Night … you wouldn't have dinner with a new date or friend or your parents and spark one up, but you sure can get pissed and sloppy on a bottle of wine and no one would give it a thought. Stoners are far more enjoyable company than drunks!"

"I, personally, love all party favours, but getting too drunk really fucking sucks in the morning, so pot wins. And, no extreme mixing!"

"It's cheaper too … you can catch a buzz so quick compared to booze. Mind altered and completely relaxed in one minute or less!"

"All this talk … stop I need to roll a joint and get another beer."

"Are we going out tonight?"

"No we're all catching up from Christmas bills."

"It's funny how things change. We used to go to bars almost every week … now we come here. Are we all getting old?"

"NO … we just don't live with our parents anymore."

"Speak for yourself… I can't believe I'm moving back there."

"We don't have to go to a bar to know we can party most people under the table. We can do that right here."

"Leslie you can party everyone I know under the table. There's no match for you."

"We gave up trying a long time ago. You try living with her. We just go to our rooms, and put on the radio just enough to drown her out and eventually she'll shut up and go to bed."

"Sharon, have you fried a few too many brain cells? I did live with her for nearly two years! All that separated us was a fucking shared closet with sliding doors that I couldn't lock or put a chair up against … nothing! Hello Leslie whenever she got the urge to chat! She just pushed her clothes over and whipped open my closet door."

"You're talking about me like I'm not even here … what the fuck! OK I get it … I need to learn when to stop. You know I actually don't like that about myself. I wish I just got tired and wanted to go to bed like normal people, I do!!! I need to learn HOW to stop."

"You have a super-power that's for sure."

"And none of the super heroes ever wanted their super power … I feel their pain."

"Well I love my super power."

"And what's yours Sharon."

"I make beer disappear!"

"So not meaning to change the subject, but doing it anyway … I'm going to box and move my sentimental possessions this weekend. John will be there, so it will be awkward, but can anyone come for moral support?"

"If you do it Saturday I'll help. Sunday I plan on making a particular someone breakfast and I don't care to rush out of the house!"

"What did you do last Saturday on the 8:00 pm date?"

"We went to the Rock N Bowl, and it was a blast. We had so much fun, and again he didn't stay, but assured me that if I would go out with him again next week he would. Maybe he got in shit from his mother or something that first time?"

"Speaking of dates, what's the scoop with Alex P since you're back at school?"

"Nothing much, but we did screw in the darkroom yesterday."

"Jesus Terri, you're going to jump from the frying pan into the fire."

"You're not kidd'n … the chemistry between us is like a hot bed of coals just waiting for the next log to ignite. All I want to do is get him back in the sack! I hate it … I'm trying to fight this girls, I really am."

"What's the latest with the other girl?"

"He tells me they're over and by the look on her face these days, I know he's telling the truth."

"You need to be single for a while. You can see him, but make it clear you want to see other men too. Just be honest with him. If he really likes you he doesn't want to be the rebound date anyway. And how do you have sex in a darkroom?"

"Well I'll tell you Colleen, very, very quietly since there's only a curtain separating us from the other classmates. If you turn the red light off its pitch black! We're definitely '*feeling*' our way. We haven't let on with anyone in school that we have been seeing each other, so it was a stealth mission."

Another Hen Night ends and I walk to my new home, which is my old home where I was raised, where I lived with Leslie, where I made friends with every neighbour I could in order to avoid having to be there. I am the youngest of nine. I had a horrible relationship with my brother Ed, who is next in age, and with my dad. Well nobody has a good relationship with our father. He is quite simply incapable of it, but mom makes up for him in many ways and hey nobody's perfect. He does the best he can considering his dysfunctional mother. It took me this long to figure that out. I do believe he loves us he just can't express it.

In one of my earliest childhood memories I realized I was home alone. It wasn't scary to me because I hadn't been brainwashed to be afraid of everything. It was just amazing. It had never happened before. I don't think it was for very long, and my sister walked in and asked who was home. I told her no one. She became agitated and I didn't understand why. Then she told me to get a jacket, and I went on the longest walk of my life. I asked her why she was taking me and she said she couldn't leave me at home alone, that I was too young. We ended up at her best girlfriend's house. As we walked back we were pulled over by a police car. The officer asked if my name was Terri Vetnor. We said yes. We were nearly home, and he told us that my family was very worried and didn't know where I was. My sister got in so much shit for taking me. I sure felt special that such a fuss was made, because I was missing. That was the first day I felt like a somebody. I was not just another mouth to feed for my parents, who only ever seemed to work, eat and sleep. I was four years old.

"There is no love without courage; there is no courage without fear."

Lynn Miles

Week 433 – About Mistakes

"Leslie I love your new place. It's the perfect scenario. The boyfriend buys the house and the girlfriend moves in. No major commitments, and you get to see if you can live together. All those years Jean-Francois lived with his parents has paid off … he's no dummy!"

"We'll see how it goes. He's such a sweetie I can't imagine he'll be difficult to live with."

"He really is. I'm so happy and excited for you."

"Holy shit don't let me become boring and domesticated."

"You will love being domesticated, but you could never be boring even if you actually made an effort!"

I walk over into the dining room, and I see that she has the poster that everyone signed at the Hen House farewell. It was a monster party and everyone we knew showed up. That was an emotional time for the girls, but I also think their time together had run its course. Stan asked Sharon to move in with him, and Izzy and Sam bought a house together. Once Jean-Francois heard about all of this he told Leslie of his plans, and asked if she would move in with him.

"You have certainly settled in well in your short time here, but then again you make the energizer bunny look like he has a thyroid problem."

"Funny … I'm having a ball decorating and moving things around, which I do almost on a daily basis."

She points over to a framed picture of a vase with flowers.

"I have moved that around to 3 different locations and I'm still not happy. What do you think of it there?"

"It looks good … I just think it's a bit high. Can you lower it without seeing the nail marks?"

Leslie runs and gets her hammer and tells me to grab the picture. She pulls the hanger out, drops it two inches, and hammers it back in. Together we do a few more things that she wanted to get done, but couldn't do on her own. She knows Izzy and Sharon aren't the helper type, but Colleen is an awesome worker bee.

"Where is everyone tonight?"

"It's just you and me tonight darling! I was so excited … I meant to call you and tell you to come early, but then I lost track of time."

"And where's Jean-Francois?"

"He went to his friend's … told me he was going to have a rooster night!"

"Well isn't that just so fortuitous!"

"Speak English fuck!"

"Sorry that's my new word from the book I'm reading. If I don't use the words then I won't remember them. It means fortunate … I'm glad we're alone because I have some shit to talk out with you … I may as well get right to it … I'm fucking pregnant! There, I just said it, and I'm so embarrassed that I can't even put it into words and I really have no idea how it happened. I've been so careful since the last time. Leslie, life as I know it … it's over."

"I need a reefer … Jesus fuck girl. You know how this happens! What are you doing? Or, better put … what you AREN'T doing … is practicing fucking birth control … that's what you AREN'T doing!!!"

"Leslie I swear I am. This is an immaculate conception. I must have gotten pregnant from wiping my crotch with a towel that Andrew must have just cleaned himself up with … I really don't get it!" I say as I begin to cry.

"Have you told him?"

"Not yet. The only thing I do know for sure with this whole mess is that I'm having this baby. Abortion as a form of birth control is not an option."

"Holy shit, yeah I get it … mommy!" Leslie says as she begins to lighten up.

"For fuck sake don't say that … you never know, anything could happen. I may miscarry!"

"I suppose … let's keep our fingers crossed."

"That sounds so horrible, but that would fix this rather large pickle I'm in. I would be so down for that."

"Do you want me to push you down the stairs when you leave?"

"Funny."

"So what'll you say to Andrew?"

"Tell me what you think of this." I say as pull myself together. "I don't want him to be with me out of obligation. I know we love each other, that's not in question, and I told him that I would never have another abortion. So, I thought I would just tell him I changed my mind, that I'll have an abortion. But, I would also love to keep the baby. I'll put the decision in his court. If he decides he wants us to have the baby we're fine … we'll figure it out. If he decides he wants me to have an abortion … I dump him, have the baby and figure it out alone. I have a good job I'll be fine."

"That's brave."

"Sometimes life doesn't present options. Some wee soul out there wants me to be its mommy. I couldn't live with the guilt of stopping that again."

"You're right it's the only thing you can do. It's a very good plan as long as you feel that if he decides he wants to have the baby that you love him, and want to be with him forever. Having a baby is a way bigger commitment than getting married girl."

"Shit I haven't even given that a thought since I found out. I don't need to get married. If he decides he wants to have the baby we can get married after ... way after. We just finished school in April and we have no money. I'm taking one day at time here."

"Let's go to the garage and smoke this."

"I'll go with you, but I won't be smoking anything ... or drinking anything. I'm officially off all vices! I may start getting the shakes!"

"Right, fuck that will take some getting used to. I can't get high with my best girl!"

"The first thing that tipped me off on the possibility of being pregnant was that smoking a cigarette made me feel sick."

"I don't know why you smoke those things. They're disgusting. I'm sure that weed is not as bad for you as those."

"I won't argue with that, but they're hard to give up. Unless of course you get yourself knocked-up, and then they make you sick. Leslie, I'm five and a half weeks pregnant. I've been drinking and smoking cigarettes and drugs during that time. What if I messed up this baby already?"

"Don't be silly, my mom smoked through two of her pregnancies and we're fine."

"Are you sure about that?"

"Funny … and they used to give new mothers beer in the maternity ward to help with breast feeding. They gave mom beer after I was born … wholly shit maybe that's why I can pound them back!"

"Speaking of breast feeding … what if I can't? I have no boobs! Don't you need those?"

"You're being ridiculous. Yes, they're tiny … really fucking small actually!" she says teasing me, "but they'll grow as the baby grows. Size does not matter … only in this case of course!"

"Girlfriend you have a one track mind."

"Just trying to lighten things up some. Are you sure you don't want me to push you down the stairs … but seriously … I wish I knew how to help you."

"Well if I'm a single mom you'll practically be its' daddy so you'll be helping don't you worry! We'll be out with the baby and people may think we're a couple!"

"Auntie Leslie … I like the sound of that."

"I'm not sure I'm ready for mommy, but I'm sure I want children and if you wait for the right time … well when is that exactly? People are waiting till they're all established now. I'll be 27 when this baby is born. That's a respectable age. If Andrew doesn't stick around I'm still young enough to find a man who is OK with a single mom. Look at your mom, she found your dad and she had three kids, and look how happy they are."

"Dad is five years younger too … the cradle robber! They're happy and dad is a real father compared to the idiot whose genes I carry."

"Those genes are a much more likely explanation why you can pound the beer back! That's something you need to be conscience of girl. Your real father was a raging alcoholic! You do get too drunk sometimes!"

"You're going to lecture me … your life is pretty sloppy right now!"

Leslie was eight years old when her mom left her drunken husband. She stepped on him as she walked out the door, piled the kids in the car with one suitcase each and drove to her sister's place in the US. They stayed there till they knew things would be good to go back to the east coast where her mom got a job nursing, and eventually met Leslie's new dad. They had a daughter together and Leslie became half-sister, half mother. Her childhood was full of turmoil compared to mine, but she rarely talks about it.

"Will you have enough time at your job that you'll get maternity leave?"

"Well I'm past my three months' probation period and the baby won't come till June. I'll have been there for over a year. I should be fine."

"How bizarre that you both work at the same place!"

"He's not a fan of working for the government at all, but he won't be quitting in a hurray if he decides to have this baby. I guess that's the down side of not being all established. We may just have to stay in these jobs that are pretty boring because we started a family."

"You got a job using exactly the skills you went to school for. You're a photographic technician for the government, not a bad gig."

"Well when I went to school for photography I was thinking more along the lines of taking pictures as art, not rendering records of government property, or working in a darkroom all day. But, don't get me wrong, it's great and I can take pictures on my own time and build up a portfolio. We shot six weddings through Andrew's network and the photographer he was apprenticing with. They're too terrifying for me to tackle on my own. I'm not built for that kind of stress. Our first meeting with a couple looking for a photographer was when I learned just how ballsy Andrew is. When they asked how many weddings he had shot he replied as cool as an ocean breeze … 'Somewhere around 30'. I just about said, 'No you haven't' … then I caught myself! Jesus he hadn't shot one on his own yet!"

"Well I could never pull that off with a straight face."

"That's why you'll never be good in business. You can't lie and sometimes you do need to. I did give him shit, and asked him why on earth he said that. Then he looks at me as if I just fell off the turnip truck and says, 'If you were getting married would you hire a photographer with no experience?' I quickly saw the necessity of his lie. Lying for survival is a different animal altogether than lying to cover up indiscretions."

"I suppose so. When are you planning on breaking the news?"

"I'll tell him this weekend and give him one week to make the decision, to give the appearance of urgency. I hate myself. He's only 24, but he's a mature 24. I'm hoping that'll make the difference."

"I bet you're thinking now that you should have gone on a few more dates before you started spending 24-7 with him."

"I tried, but after we did that trip to Florida during school break we had so much fun together, I couldn't justify keeping it casual any longer. I do just love being with him. He simply makes me happy. He's The One!"

"I know, I pretty well only see you on Hen Nights now, and you don't call me as much cos he always has something planned."

"He's not the bore John was that's for sure! I love a take-charge man! You'll have some pieces of my heart to pick up if he asks me to have an abortion!"

"That's not going to happen. He clearly worships you!"

Leslie and I reminisce for a time and she tries to keep my spirits up, but I may have a very difficult lonely road ahead of me. Not to mention the fact that I have cold turkey-ed, cigarettes, dope and drinking all in one quick moment of time when the strip turned the wrong colour. The fact that you have a real person growing in your body lends for some serious motivation. Andrew lent me his car as he often does, so I am heading back to his mom's place. He had an apartment with a friend during our last year of school so I spent most of my time there. He moved back in with his mom because he couldn't stand living with his buddy anymore. He didn't realize how much he hated cigarette smoke, and over-flowing ashtrays till he lived with it. Ironically enough that is when I started smoking again. I had quit for a year. I'm driving along listening to the radio as usual, but I feel no joy inside. I feel only terror and anguish at how stupid I have been. I realize there is no reason why I shouldn't tell Andrew right away so I resolve to do it when I get back. The next thing I need to resolve to do is to forgive myself.

"I would rather walk with a friend in the dark, than alone in the light."

Helen Keller

Week 434 - About Change

"Well aren't you just full of surprises," Sharon says as I walk through the door. "How are you feeling?"

"Are we talking physical, or emotional?"

"I would imagine that they're not very different at all!"

"I supposed you have a point there. Although, I do have some news!"

"Did I hear our new mommy arrive?" Izzy hollers from the kitchen.

"Word travels fast in these parts. And, I'm not a mommy yet. Being pregnant and being a mom are different … not to mention that I'm still hopeful that something may go wrong and I'll be able to have my first child as a planned one! It's still early!"

"Wishful thinking, and by the way that's a horrible thing to say. There're women desperate to have a child but can't conceive."

"Well, it isn't like I made the comment to them, did I? I know all about it. Andrew's sister just spent a small fortune making a baby. Now they have a beautiful healthy boy. It's fantastic. She'll flip when she finds out her baby brother is going to be a daddy … and the mother's a Shiksa … Oy Vey!" I say in my best Jewish drama queen voice.

Leslie is beside herself as she picked up on the 'daddy' right away. "So he gave you an answer and he's all hands on deck … I knew it!!!"

"He did … just last night at mom's house. I had no idea … as I was getting dressed in my room, he was upstairs asking dad for my hand in marriage. That would be a scary thing to do. If he had told me his intentions I would've saved him the horror! Dad wouldn't be excited, and he would say something like 'Why are you asking me? I'm not the one you want to marry.' Clearly he made it through, and then he came downstairs, knelt down … kissed my belly, and said let's have a baby."

"That's so sweet."

"Well yes, but then he starts talking about marriage, and I get all freaked out. I'm just trying to process having a baby, and I haven't given marriage a thought. I mean seriously if you're having a baby with someone that's a much bigger commitment than marriage. My good friend Leslie brought that to my attention! And marriage isn't like it used to be. It's just a show. You don't have to stay married and you don't have to have *grounds* for divorce. I think most people just want to have a big ass party. Why get married anymore? I really don't get it."

"You get married because you don't want your fucking kid growing up a bastard. You said it yourself … having a baby is a bigger commitment, so what's the big deal if he wants to get married … then get married for Christ sake."

"Sharon we have no money to get married. It's an expensive big ass party."

"It doesn't have to be. You can do it cheap and cheery."

"Well as much as I hold no big affection for getting married I'll do it for the sake of my baby, but I will not do it when I'm pregnant and I can't even party at my own party!"

"Well I can totally sympathize with that," Leslie says as she takes a haul on her reefer. "That's fair, did you tell him that?"

"I was taken by surprise and I didn't really articulate exactly why I didn't want to get married, but I will!"

"So now you'll start telling your families the big news."

"Well a few people in his family already know because he wanted their advice on what to do. And of course Laura knows. The first person he talked to was his mother. She's a hip lady and he values her opinion. She told him you can never go wrong having a baby. I guess he's following her advice."

"Obviously a woman who had eight fucking kids has a thing for babies. Crap your kid will have 15 aunts and uncles, just with immediate family!"

"So enough about all this … I'm here to forget my life for a while. How is everyone doing?"

We are at Sharon's house this week. Since the end of the Hen House we rotate mostly between Sharon's and Leslie's places. Colleen is too far away and I still live with my parents. Sam never leaves their basement, so we just never go to Izzy's. We still go out to the bars, but not as often since we are all in serious relationships. Once I finished school I decided it would be a good plan to stay at mom and dad's, pay off the student loan, and put some money in the bank. Living there is easy, I do my own thing. They are from the generation where as parents their purpose is to provide and any emotional connection is secondary. Actually with dad it is non-existent.

"Stan just got promoted to Director at the post office. He's pretty excited about it. I'm pretty excited about the pay increase!"

"Why? Are we trying to save up for a wedding perhaps?"

"Not yet, but he'll be my husband one day. Once we get our sex life figured out."

"You never talk about Stan in bed and none of us say too much about our partners anymore … other than yes we have sex, and yes he got a blowjob last night! It's fascinating considering when we were footloose and free we would go into great detail!"

"Leslie you go into great detail, us not so much, and now it feels like we're being horrible girlfriends if we kiss and tell."

"I'm of the opinion that it's not his stomach that is the way to a man's heart, but his cock. If you give your man regular sex, he'll not go looking for it anywhere else. It doesn't even have to be good sex, if they're getting those testies emptied they're happy! And let's face it most of the time it doesn't take too much effort!"

"Sure, but what about us. Shouldn't they be giving us consistently good sex?"

"Absolutely, but I find it very hard to vocalize what it is I want. I do it by body language, and if I don't have an orgasm then I feel it's my own fault because I know he wants me to and all I have to do is talk, and I can't and I don't know why! Maybe I should see someone about that? So Sharon, what are you doing to 'figure out' your sex life?"

"I went to an adult shop, and I got a few movies and some toys. Then you don't have to have an actual discussion you can just put the movie on and do some commentary … oh that looks like fun or holy fuck that's disgusting."

"I have never used a toy in my life and never intend to. It just seems weird. Are they useful?"

"Terri, they're necessary. What … is your name Leslie? If you want to have regular orgasms get yourself some batteries!"

"Well OK then I'll take that as a yes."

"One of the girls at work does house parties where she sells all this shit. She never mentioned it till I told her about my trip to the store! Maybe I should have one for her?"

"Sharon, Heather has been bugging me to do that for a while. I can host it at my house and call a bunch of the girls. Why don't we pick a date?"

Izzy looks around the table, "I don't know about you, but the only money I'll be spending in the next while will be for Christmas. I can see Sam's face now as he opens up my new dildo I got him for Christmas!!! Oh, and here you go mom I thought you could use this since dad has been passed a while now!"

"OK, we get it. We'll do it the first Thursday in February, and they'll be perfect Valentine's Day presents. Heather will be stoked."

"Sounds good we'll all be there. Oh … did you hear that the cast of *Family Ties* called it quits? That's one show I'll miss. At least now I have my very own little Alex P. Keaton to play with."

Colleen is cranky today and starts on Sharon. "How can Stan stand the stink of this place when you have Hen Night? Why don't you girls go outside to smoke your butts?"

"It's always the ex-smoker who's the biggest complainer."

"I just got grossed out when I was watching a show on the health effects. I quit the next day. It's been a year now and I'll never smoke cigarettes again. I can't smoke hash anymore cos of the tobacco."

"You poor thing … it tastes sooooo much better, and smells sooooo much better," Leslie says as she blows it right in Colleen's face.

"I'll admit missing that, but it's so worth it. I'd never have been successful quitting if I continued to have any tobacco. Have you all heard that they'll be banning smoking on airplanes next month? That's huge for us non-smokers. The airlines argue that they have a non-smoking section. Well that would compare to having a peeing section in a pool. It's ridiculous."

"I supposed they're afraid people won't fly anymore."

"It isn't like fucking heroin where you go all nuts, so what's the big deal? People will fly if they need to get somewhere fast. I feel for the stewardesses. They'll have some cranky customers!"

"Since I've never smoked a cigarette in my life…."

"Did too … in the basement at mom's you were so pissed at Gary and wanted a cigarette. Like that would somehow make you feel better!"

"That can't count I didn't finish it, it was so gross. As I was saying … I'm thrilled that this is becoming a thing."

"I think it's just the beginning too. Second-hand smoke is a real hazard. As I sit here tonight … breathing in all your stinky butts … I profess that one day you won't be able to smoke at a movie, or at work, and maybe even in a restaurant."

"Bite your tongue. Don't even suggest such nonsense. I wouldn't get any fucking work done if I had to go out to smoke."

"Sharon think about how much time you spend smoking at your desk. If you had to go out you would smoke way less or you would get fired."

"They wouldn't be able to fire me cos I would've quit already."

"I'm just saying be prepared. I don't know when it will come, but IT will."

"Right … like the *Field of Dreams* … build it and they will come."

"Well they did come … not a great analogy … you didn't think that one through stoner! Ten years ago who would have possibly imagined that communism would fall in Germany and in Czech and in Romania! Jesus they're taking the Berlin Wall down … did you ever see that coming? I rest my case."

"True, but then after all that was going down the Chinese youth decide to give it a try and the fucking government ran them over with tanks! So really when you think you're making progress sometimes it just isn't enough and the smokers may prevail!"

"Sharon I can't believe you're comparing some fucking non-smoking rules to the devastation of Tiananmen Square … really!!!"

"Relax that wasn't intended to sound insensitive, I was just refuting your argument about the fall of communism. It ain't over till it's over! So, Terri how are you doing on the non-smoking front? Better you than me for sure."

"It's been fine really. I keep preoccupied with all the shit I have to figure out … like somewhere to make a baby room. The only reason I stay sane through this whole mess is that we are gainfully employed."

"Have you told work?"

"Lord no … not till I start showing. I can probably stretch it till after Christmas. I want them to really, really like me. I'll keep pouring on the charm till then."

With this pregnancy my visits have been shorter! I am now walking home from Sharon's. For me Hen Night has taken on a very different atmosphere. In a way I am already the mother. I will take the girls out to a bar, and watch out for them and drive them all home. I will be an observer as I will remain straight, something that hasn't happened on Hen Night till now. My second one without a drink or a joint. It was still fun. I sat back and watched my friends, feeling somewhat like the injured player on the sidelines. I listened to their banter as a mother might hear it, and wow we all have terrible potty mouths! Up until now life has been a party. For me the party is over for a while. My body is no longer mine to do with as I please. It has been abducted by an alien. That may sound extreme, but think about it! Every emotion is different. The way people react to me will be different. My body will change in bizarre ways (I hope I get some boobs and don't get stretch marks). Then the finale, with the worst pain I will have experienced in my life, culminating in the birth of a little being, with eyes way bigger than they should be, and arms way shorter than they should be. It will be pushed out of my body, like the movie *Alien,* only a different location! Yes, I know it will be human, but for the next eight months I will wonder if it will be healthy. It could have no arms or no legs or have Downs Syndrome, and although I will love it with all my heart, others will consider it alien if it's not perfect. Pregnancy is an infliction. It is this underlying subtle disquiet until that moment when it is born, and you know for sure. The key to making it through is not to worry, and assume that you will have an easy birth with a perfect ten in the end. Simple, right?

"We'll be friends till we're old and senile … then we'll be new friends."

Anonymous

Week 435 – About a Crazy Night

"Late as usual! Why is it impossible for you to be on time?"

"I'll never be able to answer that! It is just who I am, but fear not … the Eagle has landed."

"Eagle?"

"That's the name of dad's car, an Eagle."

"Who makes it?" Izzy asks. I suppose since Sam is so into cars it has rubbed off on her.

"All I can tell you is its not foreign … dad would never buy anything foreign cos then he wouldn't feel comfortable tinkering with it. This is a man who when we were stranded in Thunder Bay and had to buy a new car we waited two more days so they could remove the power steering, power brakes and the radio before he would buy it. He just wanted to keep driving farm equipment disguised as a station wagon. It was a Rebel Rambler and man we were excited!"

"Excited about what?"

"It was our first new car."

"Well, we're going downtown to see a band at The Strand. Sam said they're amazing and he may show up with a couple of the boys."

The girls finish up their drinks and go out to have a smoke. I am sitting at Leslie's kitchen table and thinking to myself how strange and different these nights are. I worry about my baby, then I remember I am not going to do that. Worry is one wasted emotion. I look around Leslie's house and I am envious. She would have a baby room to decorate. I start to feel the trepidation in my life take hold and I struggle to fight back tears. I may very well have ruined my life, and Andrew's and this baby's. What am I thinking? Why so moralistic now? I wasn't last year. The girls come back in and are eager to get going. The timing couldn't be better as I will be completely distracted and entertained all evening.

"I read in the newspaper today that three out of five husbands will forget an important date during each year of marriage!"

"What is it about men and forgetting birthdays and anniversaries? I hear about it happening all the time. No husband of mine will forget my birthday. As soon as New Year's is over it is on to my birthday. The closer I get to the day the more excited I get, and the more I talk about it!"

"Yes, Leslie we know! You're now telling a bald man that he has no fucking hair," Sharon says as she crawls into the back seat. "By the time your birthday comes we're more excited than you … to get the fucking thing over with."

"Is everyone buckled in?"

"Yes, mommy."

"Does your dad have a radio in this car or did he have it removed too!"

"Funny you mention that. He does have a radio, mostly cos he bought this used."

"Well crank it on girl. They say music is splendid for babies in the womb."

"It better be or my kid is screwed. It's the one thing I can still do that takes me to altered states. It's my replacement for all my bad habits.

I play music and sing and for periods in the day … I'm a fucking rock star."

"This is such a pretty city. You really can take it for granted, but soon we'll be driving down Colonel By Drive along our historic canal, then we'll see the Chateau Laurier Hotel and go party in the Byward Market," Colleen says as she takes a deep breath and sighs. "I love this city."

"I saw the Chateau Laurier and the old train station and that whole area in an old movie once. I can't remember the name of it, but it was so cool. And I would completely agree with the beauty factor of this city, but it's a government town and it's boring and predictable. New York is the city that doesn't sleep and Ottawa is the city that doesn't wake up. I would've gone back to Toronto if I hadn't gotten myself knocked up. I'm in love with that city."

"It's big and dirty and has way too many people for me. I'd love to go back to the ocean and live in a small town again if I could. I love the sea!"

"I couldn't explain it if I tried, but I would take my bike over to the islands and sit and stare at the skyline and it was always spell bounding. So many people living on top of one another and knowing they're from everywhere. It's almost like a representation of each part of the world has come together to make a mini world and it's called Toronto. It just makes my heart smile. And Leslie when you're down at the waterfront it does feel like the ocean, minus the amazing scent of the salt air … replace that with a hint of dead fish … but it really looks like the ocean!"

"I've been there darling and there's no comparison, not one iota!"

We arrive in the market and start looking for parking which is an urban planning disaster in every city it seems. Why is it so hard to understand from the beginning that the city will grow and people will always want to come back to the center of it where its history and heritage are? Sometimes when I read the paper and watch the news, I feel like I am among only a handful of individuals with clear logical thought. I know I wasted my high school years away as a stoner and did the least amount of work I could in order to remain firmly planted in the cool crowd. Youth is wasted on the youth, how poignant is that! Going back to college reminded me just how smart I am and I felt denied. Denied of parents who never saw my potential. Who never pushed me to be better and never made me feel capable of doing better.

We arrive at the bar and the band is playing already and of course it is my fault since I was 'late', but then waited for them to have their smoke. You could video any given situation and I believe you would get a different story from each set of eyes seeing said situation. It is truly amazing how different people will process information. That may make a significant psychology experiment and it has likely already been done.

The band is playing the blues and I am already feeling transformed. We immediately head to the balcony because we will have a better chance of finding a seat. We huddle around a tall table and find three stools to share. The place is packed and I find I am feeling uncomfortable even though I won't be judged yet. No one here knows I am with child. The bar scene is not where most pregnant women are hanging out. It becomes crystal clear that I cannot go to a smoky bar once I am toting a big belly. It is so loud we can't really talk so we just enjoy the band till they take a break.

Sharon is returning from the bathroom and she is looking somewhere between awkward and excited. She is looking awkcited! Obviously she can't wait to get to the table. I have never seen her move so fast!

"Girls look over at that table … not all at once fuck … one at a time and be discrete."

"You should've said that before you told us to look … queer!"

We do as we are told and we immediately recognize the four boys. With the exception of Colleen because she wasn't out with us that hot summer night.

"How's it possible that they should end up here on this night?"

"It's possible because they have good taste in music!"

"Sharon did you make eye contact? Do you think they noticed you?"

"No not yet, but it's only a matter of time."

"What are you talking about, who are they?"

"You must remember us talking about that night cos it was one of our crazier ones … it was the pool night."

"They are those guys?!"

"Yip!!!" we all say together.

"They're so good looking, but they know it! I hate that type! We all had steady dates then, so we just ran with the drunken flow of the night! They probably won't remember us."

"I don't think that one guy is ever going to forget Sharon. He was all over her, and then we couldn't get her to leave."

"How did that all go down again?"

"We went to see Doug and the Slugs cos Terri begged us. It was in the west end about a half hour drive."

"Yeah, and why on earth would you have to be begged to see Doug and the Slugs? Were they not a ton of fun?"

"Yes they were good, and fun was the theme that night."

"So, we are on the dancefloor and these four guys just join us. When has any group of four guys … actually have four guys who all dance?!"

"We hung out with them all night and we all got smashed and after the show we were so hot and sweaty from dancing Leslie mentions how she would love to dive into the sea now."

Izzy takes over, "So don't the boys say they have a pool and if we want to swim just follow them in the car. So we do. I drove, and I have no idea how I managed to get there, but I did. What they neglected to mention was that the pool was a public one with an eight-foot chain link fence all around it. So one of them gets on his hands and knees and shows us there isn't that much to climb. So we climb."

I take over, "then we're all on the other side and before we know it all of them are butt naked and jumping in the pool. I was living a movie scene and the reel that kept playing was the next one where all the girls get naked and jump in the pool. Since we are women of honour … Sharon, Izzy and Leslie strip down to their bra and undies and jump in the pool. Well I'm now freaking out. I don't wear a bra. I'm clumsily standing while they're all coaxing me to take it off and jump in. I decide if I conduct myself like a prude again, as I did on the nude beach in Vancouver I'll never forgive myself, so I turn around, undress, cross my arms over my chest and jump in as quick as I can. Also, leaving my underwear on of course."

Back to Leslie, "gratefully the cold pool water sobers us all up some and it feels glorious. The boys are whining and razing us that we kept on our undergarments, and they finally realize that it isn't going to be the orgy they had hoped for. But I was thinking Sharon might just screw that guy right in front of us!"

"Funny … I don't think so, but dam he was hot."

"Except you would have broken the Hen Pact and we do not let that happen. You want to have affairs you don't have them on Hen Night. We all go home together."

"So by 3:00 am three of the boys clue in they're not getting any action so they leave … without their buddy who's still trying to make out with Sharon. Leslie, Izzy and I are out of the pool and dressed, and hollering at Sharon that we're leaving and get out of the pool. She's obviously in no hurry and enjoying all the attention. I roll a joint knowing that'll be the only ammo I can use to coax her out. It worked but now we all feel super wasted again and we look at the fence. Then we all look at one another. Then we all burst out laughing cos we're all thinking the same thing … we can't do it again. We decide to wait a while before we attempt it. Sharon's new boyfriend goes on his hands and knees again and Leslie starts. She gets over, but then catches Sharon's borrowed shirt on the fence and tears it. Izzy is next and I go at the same time so I can talk her through it step by step cos apparently it was much easier to do really drunk than somewhat sobered up."

"It was believe me. I was fuck'n terrified to scale that thing again!"

"Not as terrified as Sharon was. Colleen she was going to wait till the pool opened again, we have never been closer to leaving a Hen behind! Finally the new boyfriend got her up by practically carrying her. She got one leg hiked over and she froze. Sharon must have sat there scissoring that fence for five minutes, spewing every bit of foul language she could deliver to all of us before she finally hiked her second leg over. It was hilarious. Oh and I forgot to mention this was all going on and she was only in her bra cause if she wrecked her shirt Stan would've killed her."

"I know I took one look at Leslie's shirt and said fuck that. I can't go home with two wrecked shirts. He'd flip if I tore it … the fuck'n thing cost a small mortgage payment! Oh, sorry honey I ripped it climbing over a fence because I just decided to trespass tonight!"

"Like you would have ever told him that's what happened. What did you tell him anyway?"

"Wait," Leslie says as she has to get this last visual in. "So, we dropped Sharon off and she looked like a drowned raccoon, makeup smeared around her eyes and with her wet bra and underwear in hand. As we pulled in the laneway all the lights were out, but just as she was opening the door there was Stan to greet her. We drove away pissing ourselves."

"Well I'll tell you there was no laughter on my end. I didn't even have a good story hatched. I told him we all went swimming at this girl's house who we met at the show. I don't know if he bought it, but what can he say. It isn't like I show up like that every Hen Night!"

"Well what happened to the new boyfriend?" Colleen asks.

"He's standing just over there! He has finally tracked Sharon down and found her again ... soon we'll have the long awaited reunion ... are they destined for a torrid love affair ... or is Stan enough?

"Funny!"

"I just drove the dude home. He didn't live very far," Izzy tells Colleen. "Society really needs to start with some stricter drinking and driving laws. We need to be saved from ourselves! I'd never find his place again if my life depended on it."

It takes a certain patience to be Sharon's friend. We all wanted to leave that night and she just stayed in the pool with no regard for our pleas. Even three against one doesn't get her moving any quicker. I turn my head to see the new boyfriend on his way over. He is now leaning over Sharon and whispers something and she smiles. Sometimes there is just chemistry between two people for no other reason than there is chemistry. Some people believe it to be because they knew each other in a past life. I wouldn't rule that out because on my journey to figure out what I believe in, I decided first and foremost ... I believe in possibilities. That night last summer those two were drawn together by nearly uncontrollable forces and Sharon would have liked nothing better than to have had a one-nighter. So it would seem fate has brought him back unexpectedly for round two and she is beaming, and Sharon doesn't beam for much.

"You'll have to refresh my memory, I can't remember your name."

"Sharon, I remember yours, and I think of you from time to time. I'm glad to see you're well and looking as lovely as ever."

"I guess he didn't see what we all saw that night!"

"He was just remembering the good part, at the bar." Izzy and I banter across the table.

"Hello again ladies, I see you're all keeping up your tradition. I remember being totally blown away that you did this every week."

"Yip, eight years and going strong. I see no end in sight. Do any of you?"

"Not a chance … I'll stop going to Hen Night when I'm dead … I guess!"

"That night was some kind of fun, and I don't think we'll ever meet another group of gals quite like you. I can't believe that we get to party with you all again."

"Nothing's changed and you're not getting laid!"

"Easy girl, if we want to get laid we're quite capable! We're good with the laughs. And thank you again for driving me home…."

"Izzy."

"Right and …"

"Terri."

"Leslie."

"I don't believe you were at the concert."

"No, I'm Colleen. I hear there was more than one show that night!"

We all shake hands and make some small talk and then the band starts up again. The boys bring us over to their table and we squeeze in. They are all itching to dance so I stay back and keep an eye on things and make sure no one steals our table or purses. Eight of them head to the dance floor, but I don't know where they will fit. It is packed. Then one of the boys return and I realize who he is. He is the one who seemed intrigued with me that night.

"You know when you scaled that fence like a cop chasing a bandit I nearly got a hard-on."

"I don't quite know how to react to that," I say as I try to process his comment.

"I'm sorry sometimes I have no sensor."

"Funny, my family says that about me too."

"I just wanted to tell you that despite what you obviously think not every man is a boob man. I could see how uncomfortable you were that night."

"Well that would be a good reason to surprise me underwater and grab them."

"Don't flatter yourself girl, there was no grabbing, only touching," he says with a wink.

My expression is one he can't read because I don't know whether to laugh or punch him in the face.

"Only kidd'n … don't hit me, I thought you might have gotten a laugh there!"

"Well you may have gotten a laugh if I fuck'n knew you for more than … what … six hours!"

"Well just so you know, your body is hot, you're fit and you have a great ass! That trumps boobs any day in my books."

"Evidently you weren't that drunk. You seem to remember many details."

"I remember you."

I blush and look at him more closely. He is rather good looking and again I am surprised that he was or is the least bit interested in me. Although the older I get the more confidence I gain, and the more self-assured you are the more attractive you are to others.

"I suppose I should say thank you."

"No thanks required. So it's been over a year since we last swam naked together …"

"Correction, I had my underwear on."

"Forgive me, of course only I was naked. So you did mention a boy you were seeing then and I need to ask you if you're still together? Or, is it my lucky night and you're single?"

"Well, we're more together than ever because sometime around June 22, I'll be giving birth to our child!"

"Wow, couldn't let me down easy … just bam you're toast dude."

"Sorry, the sensor thing … you get it."

"Yeah, I get it."

We are quiet for some time and we just watch the band and the others dancing. I am so flattered, and for a moment I wish I could take him outside and find a place to hide and fuck him. No one ever hits on me. It is pretty cool! Now that would be a real one-night-stand! Izzy and Colleen come back with one of the other boys. He grabs my hand and leads me to the dance floor. Sharon is dancing with the new boyfriend and Leslie is dancing with everyone. It is times like this when I think yeah I really should have been single longer and checked out some more men. He wasn't nearly this charming that pool night or maybe I would have gone on a date with him. We all dance a few more songs and then

I have to excuse myself for a washroom break. I give the girls the signal and they both join me.

"You can't hear a thing out there and I'm dying to find out what he said when he first came up to you."

"Oh Jesus he just said, 'Too bad the pool is closed for the season'."

"This guy really wants to dip his sausage and you be careful girl."

"There's something about that man, but Stan and I are doing great, I won't mess with that. Just make sure I get in the car!!!"

"We will! So the other buddy came back to the table to hit on me! This is a good night! He had some rather complimentary things to say, in between the thoughtless inappropriate ones! It kind of makes you feel special."

"It usually just drives me crazy because 95% of them I'm not the least bit interested in."

"If we got hit on as much as you Leslie it would drive us crazy too! What did he say to you?"

"I'll tell you later, now let's skedaddle, it stinks in here."

"Wasn't me!"

The chance of running into these boys again was highly unlikely. I know Andrew's brother criticizes my Hen Nights. He doesn't understand them. He is one of those insecure people who would never let his wife go out every week. His kind think the only reason you should be in a bar is to get picked up. Sure many people are there for that reason, but it doesn't mean we are. Now Colleen is the only single one so we are date bait for her. We keep our eyes out for an older guy who looks alone, but other than that the boys come to us and we will flirt and have fun, but they will be 100% aware that they will not be given a phone number. It is better to just lay that on the table right away and they can decide if they want to move on or just have some laughs. Some are pretty cocky and will hang on till the bitter end because they think they are irresistible … just like these boys that summer night. What is guaranteed from our outings is a good time … nothing more. And who doesn't love a good time?

I pile all my tipsy boisterous friends in the car and drop everyone off. Although no one has smoked in the car it smells from everyone's clothing. I roll down my window and breathe the cool night air trying to get the smell of the smoky bar off of me and out of the car. If I don't succeed my dad is going to kill me! I hope Colleen is right and someday there will not be any smoking in the bars. Even as a smoker when I am eating I do not want to smell a cigarette! Now in my delicate condition I had to go outside for several hits of fresh air. I started smoking to be cool. I would snitch cigarettes from my mother's pack at first. Then when I smoked too many and it was obvious, I started buying them. I had steady employment as a babysitter. I was 14.

"First you're sowin'… then you're growin'
Then you reap … until you sleep."

Bryan Ferry

Week 436 – About Progress

"Leslie, I love the colour you painted your bedroom. You did an excellent job. You know I would have come to help. Just say the word."

"I'll not have my pregnant best friend smelling paint fumes when she feels sick most of the time … not happening."

"As long as I have my trusty soda crackers I'm good. Just keep feeding the little bugger and it's happy. Where are the other girls?"

"They went to get a bite to eat together and I just wanted to finish a couple last touch-ups on the room."

"So we went to see a place on the weekend only it wasn't anything that I expected. We went from renting something in the city to now trying to buy something in the country since we can't afford the city!"

"What? You're joking!"

"Never a dull moment with Andrew!"

"I could see you living in the country."

"Really? You're talking to the girl who would have loved to move back to Toronto! Although, I do have this split personality cos when I'm in the country I love it too. It's on the Quebec side near a town called Perkins … can't sound any more French than that! At least if I'm going to live there let it sound exotic like Vals-Des-Bois. It's on a little lake called Barnes, again so *francais*. The lake is the only reason I'm considering it."

"Well did you like it?"

"I did, I mean for the price point it just makes more sense than renting. It's very much a cottage. The main heating source is a wood stove."

"How much are we talking here?"

"They're asking $49,900, and mom and dad said they could lend us the down payment. Which is completely depressing, but Andrew's mom would not be able to. Who has all those kids and a wife and doesn't buy any life insurance? Andrew says they couldn't afford it. I can never figure that one out because my dad washes trucks for a living and his dad worked in the House of Commons as a Hansard for Pierre Trudeau. How could they not afford life insurance but we could?"

"Andrew's mom didn't work and yours does. That could have been the difference."

"I suppose so … well she sure has to work now to support herself! You know my crazy boyfriend told me he wants to have five kids. It must be coming from a big family. I think you either want lots, or none at all depending on your placement. I figure the older ones end up not wanting children because they practically raised the younger ones. They know all the hard work it is, so it's the younger ones who have the babies."

"Your eyes are wide open, you have enough nieces and nephews, you know what you're getting into to."

"Jesus that brings me back to that summer I spent taking care of my niece and nephew. Did I ever tell you about that day when I lost them both?"

"Yes, and I have heard the story a dozen times! I can't fathom how terrifying it must have been … I've never lost my baby sister!"

"Funny! I think it would be better to lose your own children than someone else's! That was the worse day of my life."

We hear the door and the rest of the girls have arrived. It has been a cold fall. It is the middle of November and it barely makes it above -10C. We all say hello and settle into the kitchen.

"I need to warm my bones." Sharon says as she puts on the kettle. "How is that baby growing?

"Fine I guess. I had my first appointment with the OBGYN. Dr. Deep … I was expecting him to have a couch and try to get inside my head instead of my belly."

"Was he nice?"

"He was fine, but I would've preferred a woman. It's just weird spreading your legs for a stranger."

"Not if you're Leslie," Sharon says as Leslie walks by her and gives her a punch. "Honey you may as well get used to spreading your legs for a ton of strangers for the next year."

"I know, right, then they bring in the residents to show them this and that. I'll just be one more hairy vagina and growing belly to examine. I have thought of going with the midwife home birth thing, but if we're living in the country and something goes wrong …."

"Who's living in the country … what're you talking about?"

"Yes, a twist in the plans girls. I have given this a lot of thought and we'll put an offer in on this cottage in the country. I can make it a home instead of renting. It isn't perfect, but it's a start."

"Most important question here … how long will it take you to get to my house?"

"Without traffic, door to door, I'd say an hour."

"That isn't terrible, but it isn't good either."

"I would seriously love to base all my life decisions on the proximity to, and the ability to attend Hen Night Leslie, but that just isn't possible!"

"I don't see why not!" She says with a smirk.

"I'll have to face the fact that I won't be here every week, but you know I'll try really hard. And I wish not to think about this any longer."

"I have to back up a minute," Izzy says. "Did I hear you right when you said, 'hairy vagina'? Did you not go to that appointment that we set up with Sharon's friend to get waxed?"

"I did and I told her to start with my mustache. Well after that I said thank you very much, paid her and left. Are you girls fucking crazy doing that shit to your pussies? You can't call it a pussy anymore, a pussy has hair. You all have turned your privates into clams for Christ sake and there is nothing warm and inviting about a clam."

"Well our men aren't complaining one iota."

"I'll do lots for a man, but that'll never be one of them. I will be squeezing a little human out of it, and yes, it will be hairy."

"She's really good and it doesn't hurt that much."

"Hurt is the key word. I figure genetically the hair shows up, it must be there for a reason."

Colleen pipes in, "I believe it's there to filter dirt from entering that orifice, whereby keeping it cleaner. And I'm with you Terri. I'm a trimmer not a waxer."

"We're in modern time's now girls," Sharon says. "We have hot and cold running water to keep it clean. No more use for the muff!"

"Men must like it because on some subconscious level they think they are fucking a child. Not that any of your men want to do that, but what's the appeal really?"

"It's clean and pretty and they don't get hair in their mouths!" Leslie says while she sticks out her tongue and starts licking the air by Sharon's crotch.

"Why on earth is it so important to you girls that I get waxed? Give it up it's never going to happen."

"I'm still curious about this cottage thing. If you do it, when will you move?"

"It's empty so we would ask to move in on December 1. I would have my own place to celebrate Christmas. I would love to have my family up on Christmas Eve."

"How will you furnish it?"

"That's the most amazing part of all this. You know Andrew's mom sold her place and is moving into that little house in the market. Well she has a ton of furniture that will not fit and we can have whatever she doesn't take. It's all great antiques and totally my style ... not that it would matter since beggars can't be choosers."

"Timing is everything isn't it."

"Or not, since I haven't timed any of this nonsense in my life, but I get you. I'll keep you posted. I should know next week if it's a go."

Leslie is in her fridge getting a beer and she hollers up to Jean-Francois to see if he wants one. The men are not expected to leave on Hen Night, but they usually keep themselves scarce. He is upstairs watching TV in their bedroom and so she runs him up a beer. The music is on but not as loud as she would normally have it. She enters the kitchen excited. I believe Leslie lives in a perpetual state of excitement. Her brain races from one thought to the next at the speed of sound. That is why her attention span is more or less non-existent.

"I had this crazy conversation with one of our purchasers at the office. I had just walked in with a coffee and a donut and he was waiting for me to sign his papers. Then out of nowhere he asks if I know why there are holes in donuts. So I say no and then he tells me … 'It's to make it sexual and therefore more appealing to eat'. I tell him that I had never considered a donut sexual, but it's true, the ones without the hole don't seem to sell as well. Their trays are always more full. I don't say anything for a minute and then he asks me if I've heard the expression 'glory hole'. I say no, but I'll bet it has something do with donuts because you seem like an expert. He then tells me what the fuck it means and I'm so embarrassed … I turn lobster red and I don't know what to say. Any guesses?"

"Well it's clearly sexual so I would say a vagina."

"Um … how about a toilet … Lord knows everyone loves a good poop."

Colleen says, "I know what it is, but I won't steal your thunder."

"Bullshit, you tell them then cos I don't even believe you."

"Why wouldn't you believe me, why on earth would I lie about this?"

"Sorry, sorry … I just can't believe someone else has ever heard of this. You go ahead and tell them."

"Why me … now you're testing me to see if I really know."

"Jesus Christ are we really starting a fight over this? Just tell them!!!"

"Fine, so back in the brothel days there were many prominent men who didn't want to be seen at all so there was this special room and it had a hole in the wall. The prostitutes would be on the other side of the wall. Their customers would stick their dicks in the whole and get a blow job."

"Isn't that just crazy? It makes me want to open up a donut shop and call it The Glory Hole!"

"Which is more crazy, the actual definition of a glory hole, or your purchaser telling you about it? Do you think he's a few bricks short of a load?"

"I don't know … it seemed innocent enough. I think he saw the donut and was just making conversation!"

"I think maybe you're being a bit thick, and a bit naive here … just make sure this guy doesn't find out anything about you please."

"Relax … so I'm laughing to myself in the car on the way home, picturing the prostitutes drinking wine and talking quietly, having a great old time while some trained goat is doing all the work. That would serve e'm right!"

"Or, they're drinking their wine and knitting sweaters to make some more cash on the side…"

"Knitting sweaters, really? They would likely be turning another trick."

"Then word gets around that the blow jobs are so great they expand with two holes and three goats rotating because it's so busy they need a rest."

"Or maybe they have other animals in there to adjust to penis size. They may need a cow or a little lamb."

"You're disgusting … and I really need to start writing this shit down and someday write a book about all this nonsense."

"Yes you should be doing that or better yet video record them."

"Nobody is video recording me smoking drugs and getting drunk. What if work ever found it somehow?"

"And how would that happen Sharon … unless you totally piss me off one day and I mailed them the tape."

"Fine if you want to video Hen Night then do it."

"Nah, I feel like it would alter the vibe and we wouldn't be ourselves … I'm really going to start a journal though … this is a genius idea. People would buy a book of our stories … wouldn't they?"

"Well if anyone would pull it off it would be you."

"Thanks Colleen that's sweet of you to say, that gives me inspiration. I'm going to make like a baby and head out ladies."

"Well I hope for your sake it's 'head out' cos I've heard those breech births can be a bitch."

"Bite your tongue queer."

"You set yourself up for that one sista."

"Why are you leaving so early? Just cos you're pregnant doesn't mean you have to be a pussy waa waa!" Leslie says and emulates wiping tears from her eyes.

"I need to get the car back for Andrew."

"Where's he going at this late hour?"

"What, 20 questions? I don't know, he just asked for the car at 11:00 pm. I can't wait till you're pregnant one day! You won't be miss party animal and for once you will be kicking us out of the house so you can go to bed!"

"That'll never happen."

"We'll see!"

I give all the girls a hug and say my goodbyes. I am driving (a standard!) back to Andrew's mom's because I took his car. I told the girls a white lie because sometimes it is just easier to do that. Leslie would do her utmost to keep me there longer. I can hear her before it comes out of her mouth. C'mon let's dance … you love this song! Are you hungry? I'll make you something … don't leave yet you big queer! And, Leslie is serious. I have seen her start the oven and put food in at midnight. I have never been sure if it is due to her need for munchies, or her need to prolong the night. Andrew doesn't need the car, but I feel tired and I just need to go to bed. I am ten weeks and making a baby is exhausting. What the hell am I going to do in the middle of nowhere when I am alone with a baby? Go for walks, pick berries. Go for walks, pick berries. Go for walks … stop, it will be fine I'll be so busy with the baby I won't even notice that I'm in the middle of nowhere surrounded by French neighbours who don't take kindly to English folk moving in on their territory. The baby is due in June, which is perfect timing. I will swim like mad and get back in shape, and it will be the best time of year to be in the country on a lake. I am going crazy already and I don't even know if we will get the house. Despite all my reservations I want to make a home for my man and my new baby, and this is the only way to do it.

Andrew is young and he has committed himself to be forever responsible for this new life. He must be terrified. I am two years older, plus one day. I feel like those two years may as well be ten for how prepared and resolved I am to be a fantastic mother. For years I have watched my siblings as they raised their kids. I have been forming my own set of rules and ideas about how I will raise mine. I have also received some good reading material on the subject that I will devour through my pregnancy. I will be ready to do right by this little life.

"I still believe in the Holy Trinity, except now it's Target, Trader Joe's and IKEA."

Jen Lancaster

Week 437 – About Shopping

"Izzy's coming soon with the van and we're going to Charlotte's at 7:00 pm. You know she likes us to be there early."

"That's because she's not the party animal you are. Some people need to get their sleep and by the end of a long day they're tired! Not everyone has your stamina!"

"Funny."

"You know you're very hard to stop once you get going! It's also the best part of being your best friend, who doesn't love to laugh … all night long! I heard about some guy who was diagnosed with terminal cancer, and he decided to just watch funny movies and apparently he cured himself. I don't know how true that is, but it's a good story. Hanging around with you may bring longevity to all Hens!"

"Whatever … is Laura going too? Didn't you say she was in town?"

"Yeah I told her to meet us there cos the van is full. I think she may have gone already to have dinner with Charlotte. I'm sure she's the one thing Laura misses the most about Ottawa."

Izzy arrives with Sharon, Denise, Ruth and Meagan. Denise is Izzy's friend from work. Ruth is the wife of Mark. Mark was good friends with the boy I lost my virginity to and that is how I got to know her. She is a fairly frequent Hen. Meagan is a friend from high school who we rarely see. Charlotte's store called Pawley's is an old house in a small town about 25 KM outside of Ottawa. She renovated it and she has the most wonderful gift shop in half of the house. We always have better attendance on this annual Christmas shopping night. You can tell Charlotte who you need to buy for, a bit about them and then she seems to pick you out a perfect present. It is her talent, and she obviously has a great eye for what to stock. The store is jam packed with treasures.

"I suppose Colleen isn't coming as per usual."

"Nope, that house is haunted. She says the ghosts know she can see them and it makes them uncomfortable."

"Izzy do you want me to drive?"

"I'll drive there and if you drive home then I can have a few cocktails. It's so great that Charlotte does this for us."

"No need to be too grateful. Think about how much money she makes off of Leslie alone in one night. She is a shrewd business woman too."

"I'm not going to go crazy this year!"

After the before travel joint, we all pile into the van and head out on our road trip.

"Did anything bad happen to Colleen when she was there? Who cares if the house is haunted, it isn't like *Amityville Horror* … I mean Charlotte lives there happily with her ghosts. She has some great stories about them," Denise says.

"Nope, she just doesn't want to disturb the girls. I obviously have no radar in that department. I always feel happy there. I sense nothing at all. Which is your favourite ghost story?"

"Well the one when she was trying to write something down and the pen kept flying out of her hand is the scariest. In that situation it directly affected her ability to function! Wasn't she with a customer?"

"Actually, she was with a real estate agent and she was going to put the house and business for sale! I would say that that was a clear plea from her ghosts for her to stay!"

"That was some intervention!"

"The doll house story could just be coincidence however bizarre it is."

"What's that story?" Meagan asks as this is her first visit.

"Her dad made her a perfect replica of the house. One night during a bad storm a branch fell and cracked the front of the roof. The next time Charlotte was dusting she noticed the doll house had a crack in the exact same spot!"

"I don't know whether to believe in ghosts."

"How can you not when you hear these kind of stories from a trusted source?"

"I suppose, but it creeps me out to think that my dad may be in my room when Sam and I are screwing. So I just decided that wasn't an option. You go somewhere after death, but you can't come back to spy on your kids."

"Izzy that's a gross thought. I'm so glad my parents are still alive. I may never have sex again after they pass."

"Every shopping experience should be as good as this one. I propose we all open a clothing store with a liquor license! People can shop and try things on while having a beer or wine. We'll all work there and give great fashion advice to our clients. Guys, it's perfect."

"Leslie I think there are rules we may be breaking, but you may have something there. I have no doubt if you ever have the cash to get one of your ideas flying, you may end up rich one day."

"No really though, we all go to Charlotte's and bring our own booze and some food. We drive a half hour for the experience to shop, eat and drink at the same time. What if we just converted the basement in my house and did house parties?"

"That's already been done girl."

"No, you actually have your basement as the clothing store. At house parties you have to order it all and get it later. And you have to listen to the god forsaken presenter drone on forever about the products."

"Oh, like we'll have to do at the sex toys Hen Night! Did you guys know that Leslie's having a sex toys night on the Thursday before Valentine's?"

"Thanks for mentioning that Terri, now I can take you kids off my call list."

"Are you kidd'n, that's two months away … still call."

"So, I haven't seen you since the big news. How's your pregnancy going?"

"I would say terrifying and awe inspiring at the same time. I do miss my vices … other than that, I've been lucky so far, no puking!"

"Do you have a place yet?"

"Well now that you mention it … girls, we're just waiting on financing to go through and we'll move into the lake house, which is actually a love shack, but that sounds so much better! I don't anticipate any problems and we'll take possession on December 1st!"

"Do you have any pics or the listing sheet?"

"I just happen to have the sheet in my purse. Izzy can you turn on the overhead light?"

"Wow you have a lot of property."

"It looks deceiving because all this space down to the water is the public access. People can launch their boats and such."

"Will people be swimming or picnicking? Who knows, but I would probably welcome it."

"It looks very cute."

"It's a good start and it's only 30 minutes to the market where my mother-in-law moved and 45 minutes to moms. In LA people commute for two hours."

"I would move, what a waste of time!"

"I'm sure they would move if they could. Nobody wants to commute for four hours of their day. Shit I don't want to commute 45 minutes, but I'll have to! It just makes more sense than renting."

We arrive at our destination. Wandering around Charlotte's house is like being on a movie set for a rich Victorian family home. She has a collection for everything: a plate collection, purse collection, teacup collection, doll collection and on and on. Everything is arranged and displayed to perfection and you cannot stop taking it all in. Her antique furniture is redone and updated with exquisite taste. I love the energy here ghost and all. We all settle in the kitchen and get drinks in hand before we go shopping. We shop for an hour and then retreat to the barn. In there we find Don, her perfect partner of ten years. The barn is his sanctuary out back … the envy of any man-shed ever built. It is his place to get away from all things girly in the house. It is a cold night, but there is a roaring fire in the woodstove and all the girls can smoke inside so they are happy.

There we all are … nine girls and Don. You can well image that he is in his glory! Smiling and ever the gracious host he is taking it all in.

"So did you ladies find some good stuff?"

"Of course, that's a guarantee here."

"Did Charlotte show you the new shelves I put up for her?"

"Of course I did."

"But you can't really see the shelf for all the product it's loaded with."

"Sharon did you get to the Christmas cards yet? You have to see the Merry Fucking Everything one. It's you."

"I save those for last, so I can spend the rest of the time reading them once I've finished shopping. Charlotte, you have the best greeting cards period. Girls, I drive out sometimes on a weekend just to stock up on cards."

"Leslie are you a little off tonight? Not a single inappropriate moment."

"I haven't warmed up yet Donnie. I'm working on the new me. I'm going to drink less and exercise more and improve on the potty mouth." Leslie says as she starts to stretch. Then she drops down and does a few push-ups and hollers 'motherfucker' as she does the last one.

"Leslie, every Thursday you're starting the new you. How's that working for you? It's funny since you're in good shape and can still run like a deer whenever you just decide to do it."

"So what's the gossip in the Hen World?" Laura asks.

"Not much to report really. We're mostly going to Leslie's or Sharon's and we don't go out nearly as much. We're all getting so domesticated!"

"You girls are getting down right boring. I have a new crush on the young boy I met."

"How young?"

"Only seven years younger, and what a little honey! I may have this huge crush based solely on sex. He's such a good lay!"

"And you have had your share!"

"Laura you look so good I'm sure no one would notice any age difference. Sis, we have such a great gene pool for youth. I still have to make sure I have ID when I go out."

"Terri your baby face will take a while yet to catch up to you."

"You hate looking young when you're young, but that sure changes. I'm in love with looking young now."

"We typically hate whatever it is we have. If we have curly hair, we want straight, small boobs want big boobs, big boobs hate the weight of them and want smaller ones. There's just no making us happy."

"Speak for yourself Denise, I'm happy with my gene pool!"

"Fuck no kidd'n Ruth, cos you're perfect! I'm speaking generally here. So there isn't one single thing you would change about yourself if it was free?"

"Nope, got a man who loves me, I love him, I'm all good."

"You are a lucky girl. Leslie what about you?"

"My nose! I would get rid of the bump."

"Sharon?"

"My nose! Rhinoplasty all the way. Oh, and if I could get rid of all my fucking excess hair too. I'm a goddam female sasquatch."

"Terri?"

"If you asked me that five years ago I would've said boob job in a heartbeat. Nobody should make any major life decisions before they're 25. Now I would never get a boob job, but if it was free I might liposuction my upper thighs some … that spot where they rub together! It's very annoying and my pants get worn out too quickly."

"Laura … Charlotte?"

"Nope … nothing here. Anyone who would have a voluntary surgical procedure is downright crazy."

"Well I had my tubes tied ages ago if that counts … I guess I'm downright crazy!"

"That doesn't count as plastic surgery."

"OK Meagan … and Don, what about you?"

"From the only man in the room I'll say all you ladies look marvelous to me and I wouldn't change a thing. Men don't think about that kind of shit!"

"I'm good with my gene pool as you call it," Meagan says.

"I guess since I'm the chubby one I don't have a voice because obviously I would want to change myself!!!"

"Izzy I'm so sorry I didn't mean a thing by that. So would you like to be thinner or are you comfortable!"

"Of course I would like to be thinner. Hanging around with all you skinny queers takes its toll."

"Well Izzy you know how to do it, and if you really want to we can help. It takes a hell of a lot of will power. You know my mom would automatically go on a 'diet' the minute she went five pounds over her comfortable weight. You should go home and weigh yourself and resolve not to gain another pound. That would be a great start! Just a suggestion."

"That's a good one because it gets harder and harder to lose it the more you have."

"Ok, I can't stand the smell in here anymore so I'm going back to shop."

"Yes, girls go and get that all done so it's not midnight when I'm ringing you all out!"

Eventually we all end up back in the store and keep up our Christmas shopping. The girls are getting a bit drunk, and I am nervous. I see Meagan teetering with her wine glass near some breakables. Let's face it, nearly everything in the store is a breakable. I quickly offer my arm to steady her. She says she is done so I walk her up to the cash and give Charlotte the eye. The let's-get-her-out-of-here-and-sit-her-in-the-kitchen eye.

"I can't find my drink. Has anyone seen the wine glass with the red grapes?" Leslie hollers from somewhere in the store. "There's too much shit in here… sorry Charlotte I didn't mean shit in the shitty way!"

"I see your glass, I'll bring it over." I walk to the back of the store and Leslie is looking at all the prints that line the back wall. I hand her the wine glass.

"Thanks girlfriend … look at this picture. Isn't it precious?"

"Who would you buy that for?"

"Me silly, buying art for someone else is way too personal. You have to treat yourself sometimes too!"

"Unless you're about to spend every penny on a cottage that you sincerely hope you'll be able to live in during the winter! It's beautiful. It will look great in your house."

"I'm afraid to get rung up tonight. I have spent a fortune, but I'm going to get this because it'll make me smile every time I look at it. So much for not going crazy this year!"

"Good. Now come and look at this stained glass window piece. I'm thinking of it for mom."

"That's perfect … she'll love it. Oh look at these. How fun… that's one way to have some boobs at least while you're cooking!"

Leslie is looking at an apron that is done up with a 36x24x36 body wearing a sexy bra and undies.

"She has them as his and hers … so fun."

"That would be the kind of gift to give the couple that has everything. Leslie your parents would be perfect. They cook together."

"Actually that isn't a bad idea. I'll put this vase back. Yes, this is fun!"

"Sharon, have you found the perfect cards yet?"

"This one is cute." There is a girl in lingerie sitting on Santa's lap and the text bubble says, 'Define Good, Santa'. The best cards Charlotte keeps under the cash so her older customers don't get offended. She already has these X-rated ones out for us on the counter. There is something about making fun of Christmas that makes it even funnier. The first one I read is a picture of a 1950's looking girl and guy. She is standing under the mistletoe and her text bubble reads, 'How about a Christmas kiss?' His bubble reads, 'Sorry I love cock'. The next one is two reindeer sitting on a rooftop and smoking a bong. Rudolf says, 'It's the only way I can get through the night'.

"Ok I have it narrowed down to these two ... HAVE A JOLLY FABULOUS CHRISTMAS. IT IS JUST ABOUT POSSIBLE IF YOU DRINK ENOUGH. Or this one ... YOU CAN TAKE YOUR NAUSIATING CHRISTMAS CHEER AND SHOVE IT UP YOUR ARSE. I'll get both."

"I have to get one of those too, just to prove to Andrew that arse is a word. I guess it's a Hen thing, but I rarely say ass. It's almost always arsehole! Then he always tells me there's no such word and here it is on a Christmas card! I'm going to mail it to us for a gag! It will likely be our first card at the new place ... perfect."

"Arse isn't a Hen thing it's a Leslie thing. We're all just so used of hearing it we all use it now ... so I guess you're right it's a Hen thing!"

Charlotte cashes us all out and it is our usual late hour. It is 11:00 pm before we are all finished and bringing our bags to the car. It is a very long day for her and I can tell she is exhausted. The night is not over yet. It always ends with a night cap in the barn. By this time most of the girls are tipsy and the conversation turns to bras. The girls are debating the brand with the best support for the price and it is getting animated and Leslie decides she needs to show us hers because she cannot remember the brand and can someone read it. Before long Sharon and Laura are comparing their bras and Charlotte grabs her camera and the girls pose for a picture. She tries to coax us all to pose in our bras and then she could make Don a poster for the barn. All of the girls oblige except for me because I don't wear them. I take the picture and do a very good job arranging them all around Don who is front and center. All that schooling has paid off!

Leslie always wins the largest receipt award. We have a fun ride home talking about all the awesome presents we purchased. Then a wave of brilliance hits me as I turn the corner onto a long straight-away. I throw the van in neutral and cut the engine. Izzy freaks out.

"What the fuck, did the car just break down!!!"

"Yeah, I didn't do a thing the engine just stopped. I have to signal and pull over girls."

"We're in the middle of nowhere and it's freezing out there. This can't be happening!"

"Don't worry I'm sure someone will be glad to pick up seven good looking girls even if six of them are drunk!"

"Jesus Christ this isn't going to be fun!"

"Izzy do you keep any emergency shit in your car … like a candle so we don't freeze to death?"

"We still have a half bottle of wine Charlotte made me bring back. We can always keep drinking."

"Leslie really, this is serious."

"No shit Sherlock, but if we can't fix the car we may as well numb ourselves a wee bit more! Someone roll a reefer!"

"If we don't open the doors our body heat will keep us going for a while!"

"If we don't open the door how will we flag someone down to help? That's a bad idea!"

The car is at the side of the road. The engine quiet but nothing is quiet about the interior.

"If we take turns trying to flag some help, then only one person freezes at a time!"

"OK, who's going first?"

"Well I'm busy rolling a reefer."

"I'm busy drinking wine."

"Fine let me out and I'll get us some help, you bunch of ..."

"Yes, Ruth you're perfect, any guy would stop for you."

I am feeling like I would love to act out this role a little longer, but fear the girls might kill.

"Wait before you go, Terri, why don't you try to start it again?"

"Oh look here the car is in neutral. Let's see what happens if I put it in park. Voila, all systems go."

The girls nearly blew my eardrums with squeals of jubilation and relief. I thought Izzy might even start crying.

"I wonder why it cut out in the first place. I'll get Sam to bring it in to the shop tomorrow. Thank God."

I cannot contain my laughter anymore, and the girls make the realization pretty quick.

"You queer ... it isn't fucking April Fools you know. I have that gross adrenaline rush panicky feeling."

"I'm sorry ladies, but when you're the only straight one, sometimes you just have to take advantage of that place of power and amuse oneself."

This is such a high five moment, but I have only myself to high five with. I receive much verbal abuse and a playful swat to the head as I pull the van back onto the highway. I executed that to perfection. The girls eventually saw some humour in it all, as I pointed out that no harm was done, and I deserved a little laugh at their expense for driving them back safe and sound. I move into my own cold car and head out still feeling very proud of my epic prank.

"When I'm good, I'm very good, but when I'm bad, I'm better."

Mae West

Week 448 - About Sex Toys

"Hey girlfriend, I see the presentation girl has arrived!"

"Oh yes, and I've gotten a sneak preview of some of the shit. I guess I'll purchase my first ever sex toy! Don't know that I'll ever use it, but I have to buy something."

"Why wouldn't you use it? We may as well get some assistance. If I'm particularly horny some time I would use these things, but it will be a first for me too. It turns on the guys like crazy. It will take some time in order to feel comfortable with the whole idea of it."

"I'm not so sure I would ever feel comfortable using these. Come and meet Heather. Heather, Terri, Terri, Heather!"

"Hi, nice to meet you."

"Same."

"So Heather, with all the products you can promote at house parties … why sex toys? I don't mean to be forward, but I'm wildly curious."

"I'm just trying to do my bit to bring North America out of its sexual repression one woman at a time. Sex and nudity are very delicate issues for most people. Women especially are very uncomfortable with their sexuality. I personally think a good orgasm is as beneficial for keeping you young and youthful as healthy eating and regular exercise! Most women I speak with think of sex as one of their many chores. I would love to see them love having sex."

"Well we can't all be Leslie!" I say as I wink at her. "I do feel revitalized after a good orgasm. It's like I get a second wind. Sometimes I get up and read or do a wee chore I missed doing."

"I just feel like starting all over again."

"Leslie you're one of the lucky ones. Many women have very low libidos … especially at this age."

"Yeah they say we peak in our 40's. God help my husband if this ain't peaking. He'll be all worn out … provided I even have a husband then!"

"I'm sure you will. I saw Izzy's van pull in the driveway. She has a load of girls."

The girls file into the house almost robotic like. They are all on guard because there is a new face tonight. It takes some time to all get settled. I haven't seen Ruth since Charlotte's place and she comes over to give me a huge hug.

"Look at you, looking a little pregnant. I'm sorry I didn't send you a card or anything."

"Don't be silly. I'm sorry I couldn't invite you or most of my friends for that matter. Did you know that Andrew's immediate family plus mine amounts to 35 people? We figured we could get away with 10 friends each. Mom's house is pretty tiny."

"We all thought you were going to wait till after the baby was born."

"Believe me I wanted to. My dress was pretty in a peasant sort of way. But, I never intended to get married in an elastic waistband. I really did it for mom. Every time I made my argument on why I can't possibly get married now, she had a solution. Andrew's sister was pretty neurotic about the whole thing too. Since it wasn't the getting married I didn't want to do it was just the timing. I decided mom deserved her happiness. We had a minister come in at 6:00 pm, and then a potluck dinner. It was different!"

"That sounds lovely!"

"It was good. I really wouldn't have changed much other than the dress and the time of year … and the location! I've never dreamed of a big wedding anyway, but it would have been in the fall at some quaint rustic inn and I would have worn a dead sexy dress … and partied my fucking arse off!"

"Now you won't have a bastard child. Do you know if it's a boy or girl?"

"Nope didn't ask. I want the element of surprise."

"Have you worked on the baby room yet?"

"That's another story. I'll tell you later. I think she wants to start."

Heather thanks us all for coming, but I am thinking in her head she means cumming, so I laugh out loud and everyone looks at me. Then a few of the others start to giggle like we are back in high school. She goes over all of the items and their benefits, mentioning a few pitfalls of various products. Better to not sell them than have them returned. I am in shock at some of the engineering gone into these apparatuses. I mean, there are entrepreneurs who make a business of manufacturing and selling sex toys. I feel like a prude as she talks, and come to the realization that I, too, am sexually repressed.

"This one is so small Heather what is it used for?"

"It's a vibrator specifically for the clitoris. I have some customers who wear it in their underwear when they go out and they put the controls in their pocket."

"No fucking way?"

"I guess we don't have to worry about a bulging crotch, we can get horny and have an orgasm and be pretty unnoticed."

"So these girls are walking around the office and everyone is trying to figure out where that ever so slight buzzing sound is coming from!"

Leslie is overhearing all this and having a heyday with the possibilities.

"You could find her easy cos she's slouched down in her chair rubbing her nipples. Or look in the bathroom and she's splashing her face trying to cool off and look normal. Or maybe you'd find her in the kitchen making out with the new guy. I much prefer an orgasm in the privacy of my home where I can make all the noise and faces I want! And a cock needs to show up to that party! Wow, these girls are wacked!"

"I guess this isn't for you then Leslie. I'm just telling you what it's used for."

"Sorry, sorry… I didn't mean to sound insulting there."

"No, not at all … Leslie I work with you, I think I have you pegged by now. Something tells me your personality is the same at work as on Hen Night! So what does interest you?"

"I like the card game when you take turns scratching his and hers nights. The powders and body oils are nice."

"So no batteries."

"I don't know? I feel like I don't really need the extra help!"

"Maybe you don't, but your man will get totally turned on if you pull out a vibrator and start with it, guaranteed."

"Well if my man had any trouble getting it up I may take your advice, but that just isn't an issue. My Porsche boy is firing on all eight cylinders baby!!!" Leslie says as she does her little pelvic thrust.

The girls peruse all the goods and buy this and that. I get something called a silver bullet. You can use it as a small vibrator, or insert it and supposedly it is totally amazing. Heather packs up and joins us for the rest of the night. Leslie puts on tea for me, and all the girls are rather curious about how I am surviving since my whole world seems to be falling apart. The regulars know all the gory details, but the other girls want to hear about it.

"So Terri what's the story on the baby's room?"

"The story is that on Christmas Eve our water froze. I was going to host my whole family for a dinner, and I had to call in the morning and cancel. We have no running water, so we will have to wait till spring to paint."

"How do you manage?"

"We have it all figured out except for the showering. We do that somewhere … usually at Andrew's moms, or my folks' house when we visit."

"Well how do you flush?"

"Fortunately we have trained ourselves not to piss or shit so we don't need to flush!"

"Funny."

"We bought an auger, found three large pails and got a toboggan. We go on the lake and drill a hole. Then we scoop out water to fill our pails, and bring them back to the house on the toboggan. It's quite amazing how a toilet still works when you just pour a bunch of water into the hole. So far the septic system is fine … fingers crossed."

"So it really is true that bad luck comes in three's cos I heard about your jobs too."

"Yip department closed on January 15th and we both lost our jobs. I would have rather not known till after the wedding, but what can you do. I got a job through a temp agency. I can work till the baby comes and max out my UI."

"Well that's only two things," Izzy says trying to improve my life situation with some positive expression.

"I would hazard a guess that Ruth is referring to the fact that I got pregnant as the first piece of bad luck. I get knocked up, move to the money pit where my water freezes and then my husband and I lose our jobs. Life can be a real fucking bitch."

"Now why isn't life a fucking bastard? Why is it we always go to the female gender automatically?" asks Colleen.

"Maybe it's because we just hear it more often."

Colleen continues, "And think about it, when you insult a man and you call him a son-of-a-bitch it's still derogatory toward women … you're just cutting down his mom! I'm sure someone has done some study on the subject."

"Someone has done a study on pretty well everything. I lose my mind when I read headlines like: Studies show a correlation between looking good and self-esteem. No shit Sherlock … they do studies in what I consider common fucking sense! I could have told them that before they started their stupid study."

"Sharon I read one the other day … a government study spending our hard earned dollars on stress in the workplace. I mean people are getting doctors certificates to leave work for months at a time cos they're stressed!!! Live my life for a month … I'll show you what fucking stress is. These people need to focus on what is good in their lives and if there isn't anything good then change it."

"Was it just government or private sector too?"

"They talked about both, but the stress leave thing hasn't caught on in the private sector yet. They mentioned Canada Post too. Maybe Stan could take a 'stress' sabbatical!"

"Ladies the government will always spend our money on a certain amount of nonsense. It's a fact of life so get used to it."

"Yes, that's the Canadian way. Just accept … no push back."

"Well in the big picture we're doing just fine. We're always rated one of the best countries to live in."

"Well why not go for THE BEST I say!"

"OK … once you push that baby out you can start your career in politics! In the mean time we get what we get."

"Sharon you're just lazy! I've had thoughts of politics, but now I feel it will be limited to a school's parent council!"

"Shit, have you thought of that … in Quebec the only school in English is in Hull. That's a hell of a morning commute for a five year old!"

"Izzy, I'll cross that bridge when I get there … just working on survival right now. Living in the country is like a full time job. Splitting wood, cleaning the chimney, getting water, boiling water to wash dishes … I'm *Little House on the Prairie* or should I say *Little Love Shack in the Gatineau's*. I would be staying at mom's more often through all of this if it weren't for Max."

"Who's Max? What now?"

"She's my Christmas present from Andrew, an adorable mutt that looks like a border collie. She is awesome, but Jesus Christ, I only had five months of freedom left and that disappeared as soon as he brought her home. I really tried to seem excited, but my heart sank. I knew exactly what that meant and it's all come true. Cleaning piss and shit in the house. Getting woken up to let her out at 5:00 am and coming straight home from work. Maybe he thought it would be a good warm up to the real deal, but he thought wrong. After three days with a puppy I wanted to kill him! If she wasn't so adorable I might have brought her back!"

"Speaking of him, did he find work?"

"Andrew will take a whirl at being a full time photographer. He'll get some shoots through the guy he apprenticed with after first year. He's super passionate about it so we'll see how it goes."

"I have to hand it to you. All this going on and you're not even drugged to survive. I'm really enjoying listening to you ladies. In perspective my life is really quite uncomplicated," Heather says.

"Oh, how I would love uncomplicated!"

"I have some news to share," Meagan pipes in. "I'm getting married this August."

We all make a fuss and congratulate her, but deep down inside we all know that it is likely the dumbest thing she will ever do and we will pray that she comes to her senses before the big day. Her boyfriend is a bully and mentally abuses her constantly. She is beautiful and lovely and deserves so much better. She needs an Andrew to sweep her off her feet so she too can realize there are plenty of really nice guys out there, and we don't have to take their shit if shit is what they are dishing out most of the time. Is she settling, or does she really think she will be happy with this guy for a lifetime? Everyone says relationships are a lot of work. I work enough! I don't want to come home to a man who I have to work at being with. I've been there and done that … never again!

"So give us the details!"

"It was a total surprise. We had a trip to Toronto planned, just a weekend get-away and he took me to dinner up in the CN Tower. It was really cute. The waiter brought me the ring on a dessert plate with chocolate sauce around it that said, 'Will you marry me.'"

"So when's the big day?"

"August 25, we'll have a small wedding."

"Thank Christ you're not doing one of those two year engagements. If you want to get married just do it or wait to get engaged till you can get married!"

"Sharon there's preparation to be done."

"Nothing that can't be done in six months to a year, that's all you need. Meagan is doing it. Fuck, Terri got married in three months!"

"Well, how well I manage has yet to be determined!"

"It will be beautiful and perfect because you planned it. I'll just give my husband of two weeks a plug here, because he really is a wonderful photographer if you don't have someone in mind…"

"I'll definitely look at his work. If I like it, he'll have the job."

"Fair enough."

"I did remind you all it is my birthday on Monday right!"

"Only fifty or so times, Leslie."

"Well are we going to go out on Saturday, or are you queers just trying to drive me crazy? No one has said a word."

"We have a bit of a night organized, so just plan on being ready for a seven o'clock departure."

"You had me going for a while there. I'm so excited! Where are we going?

"You'll know when we get there now enough of that. Oh, but you'll need to dress warm and bring your skates."

"I love it already!"

For Leslie's birthdays we always do something special since she is the Grand Poobah of the Hens … Cwack Cwack Adack! We have some great debate at times on how we will celebrate, because she loves to be active yet some of the girls aren't as sporty as others. This year Colleen and I will skate down the canal with her, and meet the other girls for drinks at the bar at the end of the canal. We will have tequila shots ready in our knapsacks for us to do at each hut, and a flask full of beer for a chaser. Since it will be Saturday night, all the boyfriends have been invited. We have it all figured out.

"I'll be packing my things in the car if anyone has any last requests. Leslie maybe you want to change your mind on the vibrator. You know what they say … once you've had vibrating rubber you will never go back!"

"You can't be serious, maybe one day if I don't have a real live yummy cock I may change my mind." Leslie says in her animated way as she is holding her hands in a circle down by her crotch and thrusting toward them.

"Leslie if you ever left work I might have to quit. It would be so boring there without you."

"Not everyone appreciates my sense of humour you know."

"Really, I can't imagine why."

"Because some people feel I can be inappropriate."

"Yeah, I would be one of them … sometimes you are. There's a time and place … it's Thursdays. Sometimes at work I shake my head," Sharon says.

"I can vouch for the ladies at work that we're just fine with Leslie just the way she is!"

"Well good cos if she got fired I would have to take the bus and when the 'ship of love' rolls into my driveway every morning I'm very grateful."

"Well you could show your gratitude by being ready to leave when the ship arrives! One of these days I'm going to leave without you."

"Speaking of leaving I really do have to pack up and go."

"I'll help, and be on my way too."

I say my good byes and help Heather pack her car. As my car heats up I sit and think about the evening. How brave she is … how unrepressed to be able to do this. Why can't sex just be a comfortable conversation within a family, not just the Hens? I know it was taboo in my house growing up. Anything personal was taboo. I remember going to my mother and telling her how someone in the house was wasting toilet paper, and bunches of it were wrapped up and put in the garbage. No one needs that much toilet paper to blow their nose, I said. Why was it impossible for her to explain about a menstrual cycle and that my older sisters were throwing away their pads. She told me that it was fine and I left puzzled. Nothing about that answer made any sense! It broke all the rules. You do not waste! But this time it was OK. Why? I needed to know so I asked my sister Laura and she told me without hesitation. I was 11 years old.

"When life gives you a hundred reasons to cry, show life that you have a thousand reasons to smile."

Anonymous

Week 474 - About a Birth

"Come in, the girls are so excited to see you, and the new little gaff of course. I'll get the other stuff in the car. Terri's here with the baby!" Leslie shouts out as she heads outside.

Izzy and Sharon have seen him, but the others haven't. The change in a baby in the course of three weeks is surprising. He wasn't very pretty upon arrival, but now he is lovely. I am the first one in the group to have a child and I feel like it is unfair to tell them how truly vile childbirth is. It is miraculous and all, but I don't think you can prepare yourself for that kind of pain, or for the complete game changer a baby is.

"He's beautiful Terri."

"Finally! Yes he is!"

"What are you talking about?"

"It's just that when he was born he was really quite odd looking. Yoda-ish but Yoda has a wise cuteness about him. He just looked wrong because he was stuck in the birth canal for so long. If I could have had a video of Andrew's face when they handed him his son I would win a contest. It was a look in the middle of horror and disgust. It was pure *horrgust*! I don't think it ever crossed his mind that childbirth would be a bloody gross affair! I was impressed that he didn't faint!"

"We did hear you had a hard time of it."

"When the highlight of the whole experience is puking on your husband's arm, you could say it all sucked. It's just that they can't do a thing for you and everything they try soon becomes so irritating that you want them to go away. It's true what they say … you sort of blame them for the pain and wonder why in hell we're stuck with this job."

"You know the answer to that one! If birthing babies were up to men we wouldn't have much of a population," we all say this in unison because we have had this discussion before.

"I'll note that my original desire to have four kids has drastically changed. I'll have another, but that may be it! It was a very good decision not to have the home birth or it could have been tragic."

"Yah think? A 24 hour labour ending in a c-section … you can't do that at home."

"Right … but really only the last 15 hours were hellish. At the beginning I was all 'this isn't so bad!'"

"But look at the by-product. He's so sweet and helpless."

"Or, smelly and useless, depending on how you're feeling any given day. I think I finally understand post-partum depression. I mean I have never suffered from any kind of depression, but wow you can feel blue after a baby."

"I would love to have a kid that comes out at around the year and half stage. You plop it out and it's ready for daycare. Infants are so … well you said it, useless but I think what you may have meant is that they're so damn dependent on you."

"Sharon, that's a much better way to put it. I've done a ton of reading on this stuff and they say the first six years are super important, but the first two are critical to how their brain gets wired."

"Please don't tell me you'll be one of those holier-than-thou mothers who take everything there is to know about mothering from a book. I didn't have a perfect mom and I don't plan on being a perfect mom … you just do the best you can … just like everything else in life."

"I won't be a preacher on mothering, but I really don't see any down side to reading about it and taking what I like from books and using the information. You have to take a course on how to birth, but once the little Yoda is out no one has to learn about how best to raise it!"

"That's because there is no right way … what's good for one mom may not be good for another, and at the end of the day you have to do what's right for you."

"I get that … I do, but there's a lot you can learn about the wrong way to do things that I think is pretty universally accepted now. Like you really shouldn't hit your children! I think we've all been smacked by our parents at one time or another."

"Yeah and we're all just fine. I plan on daily beatings myself … one good swat upside the head just to get my kids out of bed!"

"Funny … but you know what I mean. The one thing I know for sure is I don't want to be all work and no play, like my mom. Gratefully Andrew is nothing like dad!"

Izzy comes over and takes the baby and looks very comfortable with a newborn. She has nieces and nephews as I have. She has a big smile on her face and you know she will want to have kids one day soon. Then she surprises me with her next comment.

"What's up with the name you chose? I mean I sort of like it. It's growing on me … very, very slowly. But it's so biblical for the one Hen who hates anything to do with the Bible and religion."

"I don't hate the Bible and religion. I just think the Bible was severely edited in order to change its actual meaning and religion is simply not necessary. Besides I didn't choose his name he did."

"What do you mean by that? Babies don't talk."

"Well I was walking in the grocery store when I was about six months pregnant and I saw a woman with a newborn in a snuggly. She had this huge smile on her face as she was walking toward me, but her smile was for the woman in front of me. They greeted and hadn't seen each other for some time it seemed. I wanted to catch a better look at the baby so I slowed down to sneak a peek. As I was doing this the new mom told her friend that she named the baby Noah. The next moment I received the biggest kick in my belly that I had ever felt. Me being me, I took it as a sign that my baby was a boy and he wanted to be named Noah. When I brought this story home to Andrew he was having nothing to do with that name, so I didn't really have it on my list of possibilities. It wasn't till I puked on him that he relented. As he was wiping himself off he says to me, 'Honey after all this you just name the baby whatever you want and I'll just hope it's a girl.'"

"Izzy, I hated it at first too. Actually, I'm still trying to embrace it!"

"Which I knew right away cos your face is such an open book. You can't even pretend to like your best friends' baby's name. I mean that's not a life altering lie, a little support would have been nice … it was a good bonding moment for Leslie and Andrew. He saw the look on her face and says to me … 'see no one likes this name.'"

"I said it's growing on me and I mean that … look at my face … not lying. Really and truly it does suit him. He looks like a wise old soul."

"I think he is."

"You look great," Colleen says with a big smile.

"Thanks sista, but I've been blessed with very good genes, my sisters were the same. Not a stretch mark on me either. I didn't realize what a big deal this was till I saw a bunch of mothers comparing theirs in the hospital. That was the worst five days of my life. Just when you think you've been through enough pain to last a lifetime … then you need to turn into the Dairy Queen and holy mother-fucker that hurts. After about day four it actually started to feel like nursing may be a natural act between a mother and her baby. I was quite simply more motivated than most to continue, since I wasn't about to give up these jugs I have for the first time in my life!!!" I say as I grab my tits and proudly push them up.

"So they do work after all. All that worry for nothing."

"Yes, I'm a capable nursing mother … go figure!"

"By the size of him I would say you are."

"He came out that big … that has nothing to do with my quality breast milk!"

"Ok now the last baby question and we can get on with other more interesting topics," Meagan says.

"I know you had a big debate with Andrew on the whole circumcision thing. Who won?"

"His Jewish roots run deeper than I had anticipated. I told him if he wanted to do it so badly to arrange it and go with him because I would have nothing to do with it. So he did. What I didn't realize was that he then gets to go to work after and I ended up with a screaming baby for two days. It was just a horrible experience for me and Noah. If we ever have another boy, that won't be happening again."

"What was so bad? I've heard that the babies barely notice."

"I think it was just one of those things where we ended up with the old doctor who didn't give a shit. I think he used a fucking meat cleaver and took more than he should have! Noah bled a lot and then his bandages would stick and I had to soak him in baths to get them off and then we would wrap him up again and he would bleed again.

I asked the nurse if it was always like this, and she said not at all. She couldn't come right out and tell me that the doctor who did it was so old he shakes, but that was the impression I got. There was another mom in my room and her baby was just fine after it."

We passed Noah around from Hen to Hen. I had such a great break from holding him all the time. I do believe a baby needs a transition period. How can we expect them to go from the warmth and vibrations in utero to sleep in a bed all alone? It just doesn't seem fair to me. So I am the mom who most times has her baby sleeping in bed with her and her husband, at least for a little while till he gets used to the great outdoors. I can stare at Noah for hours and feel nothing but contentment and curiosity.

The one book that stood out above the others was *The Magical Child*. It is based on theories by some doctor whose studies are not mainstream, therefore not widely accepted. His research suggests that a baby's brain isn't fully developed at birth … that there are connections made for years … somewhat like growing your teeth in. If certain connections are not able to be made then certain parts of the brain are unable to work well, or just don't connect. It was fascinating and what I took away from it was that whatever baggage we carry around, it isn't fair to pass it on to our kids. We have to let them explore and make mistakes and get dirty. Stop saying NO all the time and let them get hurt. My whole life I have been terrified of spiders, but I do not intend to share this fear with my child. I will suck it up and pretend as best I can.

"So I'm about as ready for a rye and ginger and a little toke as any one person could possibly be. But, I'll have a beer cos it's not so strong and apparently really good for lactating mothers!"

"Yeah 20 years ago … what do the experts say about those carrying on's while nursing now?" Izzy asks.

"Ask me if I give a rat's ass girl. I've been through hell and back again and my life motto is everything in moderation and I'm going with that. I haven't partaken of any of my vices for over nine months, and they have been the hardest nine months of my life!!! So, I'll start with a beer and see how it goes! Quite frankly if it puts the tyke out for a while it may become part of my regular routine! You may even have to pick me up off the floor tonight and stick that baby on my ever so big voluptuous booby once he starts screaming for food!!!"

"OK, settle down … point taken!"

Leslie goes right away and pours me a beer … clearly she's very excited for me.

"This tastes like the golden nectar of the Gods! I don't know if I'll be able to cold turkey when I have kids?"

"You will, life quickly becomes about the baby growing inside and you'll always want to do what's right. I know you … Jesus this does taste soooo good. This is the best I've felt in months! I feel like I can have my body back. It's no longer abducted."

"Well technically it is till you're done nursing."

"Jesus, you too? Colleen you sound like my mother! Between you and Izzy … relax! A little moderation will be fine. I may only get to Hen Night once a month … let me fucking enjoy it … please!"

"OK, OK!"

"So while you've been off doing the mommy thing we found a new bar that we've been to a few times." Leslie says. "We've had a blast there. Once your abduction is completely over we'll take you out for a good roar."

"What's so great about this new bar?"

"Nothing in particular really, sometimes you just go somewhere and it has a really good atmosphere."

"Sharon likes the baseball team that shows up every Thursday for drinks."

"OK … I get it now … you go for the eye candy."

"Not only, they also have a house band, and it's just busier and closer to my place than the other pub."

"So Leslie, what are your latest escapades?"

"None, just having a good time on my Thursday night out."

"Last week Terri, she was hilarious. We were chatting with all the boys and some of their girlfriends and the conversation turned to movies and everyone's favourites. One of the guys was talking about *Star Wars*, and he stops and excuses himself as he sticks his hand down his pants and removes his jock. He apologizes and says it's just super uncomfortable and maybe he was trying to be sexy … who knows? But I have to say he doesn't have to try too hard because he's as hot as a habanero. Anyway the conversation remained on *Star Wars* and doesn't Leslie grab his jock and put it over her mouth and nose. Then she does the perfect breathing and goes into a *Darth Vader* rant starting with, 'Luc, I am your father.' None of us know exactly what she's saying because we were killing ourselves laughing."

"Oh right, I did that didn't I! Well he's so hot and that will be the closest I'll ever get to his cock now that I'm living in sin!"

"Oh my I miss Hen Night. Last week while you were all having a strapping good time I was with mom on my porch waiting for dad to come back from driving my nephew and his dad to the Oka reserve."

"Why on earth would anyone be going there considering the conflict going on? The Natives shot a cop a couple of weeks ago."

"I know that's why mom was losing her mind when dad was supposed to be back around 7:00 pm but didn't show up till 11:00 pm."

"Excuse me, but we all don't get up early to read the paper and I have no idea what the fuck you're talking about? Izzy says with mild irritation.

"Well in a nut shell they want to build a golf course on the Mohawk land that these poor buggers have been trying to claim as their own, and rightly so. I mean if you want to be technical most of the land in this great country should be native, and they've already been pushed to the north where nobody else wants to live anyway. I say give it to them you greedy bastards."

"And somehow that answers my question?"

"It's a start, relax. So the natives put up a road block to protect their land. Then the government sent in the coppers and one got shot and it all went to hell in a handbasket. It's a huge stand-off."

"So this is going on and your dad drives your brother-in-law and nephew to a danger zone!"

"Nothing gets by you girl … I guess they have a very good friend on the reserve. They had this trip planned long before the stand-off and his friend said it shouldn't affect where they were going."

"And your dad was four hours late because?"

"In true dad fashion he was lost. As a kid on holidays with the family, I would know we were lost, but he could be lost an hour before he would ever stop to ask. He just liked being in the car more than anything I guess. I hate being lost now. I always have my route mapped out when I go anywhere."

"Your baby is starting to squawk some. I only interact with quiet happy babies," Sharon says as she hands him over.

I take Noah and get him changed and ready to feed because once I do that, with any luck he will sleep. I can't fathom where the expression 'sleep like a baby' came from because this boy doesn't do much of that. Evenings are the fussy time and the time when you have had enough and need a break, but you don't get it. I sit in envy of my friends because they are still free. Don't get me wrong I am in love with being a mother, but it is the first all-consuming event of my life and it does take some getting used to. I practically have to bring a mini wardrobe everywhere I go … for me and the baby. I schedule my entire life around his feedings so I don't have to listen to a screaming child at an awkward time or in the car because that is so distracting. I sit and nurse my baby and listen to the continuing banter. I drift off into my own little world thinking how cool is it that I can bring my baby and nothing's changed really. Yet at the same time everything has changed. I remember back to the first time when Leslie made us all commit to Hen Night.

"The only way to have friends is to be one."

Ralph Waldo Emerson

Week 1 – About Commitment

"Leslie, if mom didn't know that we were completely fucking wasted when we came home on Saturday night then she's as dumb as a stick," I say as I take a sip of my drink at the bar.

"I don't know if I was wasted or just in a state of shock from the night's events … and what crazy ass mother is up till 3:00 am cleaning? That took me by surprise … usually 2:00 am is her latest."

"I swear that's her way of not having to have sex anymore. Nobody really wants to clean till 3:00 am." "Maybe she just keeps working till she hears your dad snoring."

"Why did you queers even go in the house? You must have seen the lights on."

"Izzy, we were so baked we didn't give it a thought."

"I was just happy we ended up walking into the right house."

"How much did you take that night? And when will you idiots learn that acid isn't your friend."

"Izzy that night was the tipping point. I've had my days of psychedelic drugs and I'm done. I can't speak for Leslie, but I think we were both freaked out."

"I'm with you Terri, we're lucky to be alive and I want to keep it that way."

"What is it we are missing in our brains that we feel the need to be brainless? I mean that's what we are. We take a hit of acid at a party and we know anything can happen and usually does."

"That was my near death experience to wake me up. I think I had an absolute blast till the incident. The night comes in and out. I remember us all blasting tunes out of the car and sitting around the bonfire at the quarry. I don't remember getting there. But I remember jumping in the water and instantly regretting it and feeling like a million water snakes were about to grab me and pull me under."

"Oh fuck I remember when you jumped in. You were talking about being baptized into the religion of sex and drugs and rock and roll. Anyone who wanted to join you should be anointed now. And you were gone. You could've drowned and I probably would've sat back and fuck'n laughed thinking you were faking."

"The only thing on my mind once I jumped was getting the fuck out of there so it was a very short time of anointment. After all I was being attacked by water snakes!"

"I sat by the bonfire and watched 15 people go temporarily insane."

"Well, were we highly entertaining or what?"

"Once I got drunk, but before that … just fucked. The worst was Robbie putting the lighter fluid on his jeans and jumping over the fire. The idiot said he wanted to test it out and see if it would work that far away from the flame. I've never seen anyone take their pants off so fast. If he had any sense he would've jumped in the water and he may have saved his pants."

"I could've lived without seeing Robbie in those bikini underwear all night. I mean who wears those? The boys were relentless with their teasing all night! I feel better knowing that I'll never let that happen to me again. It's time to grow up and have some self-respect."

The bartender finally makes his way back to us as we sit and reminisce on the night. It was completely terrifying at times … not like the other few times I did acid. Those were enjoyable, totally bizarre, but fun none the less. This time was different … no control and not aware of all my actions. You really have no way of knowing what you are taking, sometimes it is good and sometimes it is bad. As we are ordering our drinks, Sharon arrives. All three of us were in the same car that night. Izzy was lucky enough to be in a different one.

"So girls, I invited Gary's mom, Colleen to come out with us tonight," Leslie informs us.

"What did you do that for? She is sweet n' all, but she could be our fuck'n mother."

"Well Sharon, she isn't and she's really good to me and she needs some friends. You know she's hip, we've been to Gary's for enough parties and she's always totally cool."

"So true, but that's what I find a bit odd. Parents don't usually party harder than their kids! It's not natural."

"Well Terri your parents are fuck'n ancient … Colleen is like 30 years younger."

"That's a good point. Maybe I'm just jealous that Gary can go home and be himself.

"Whatever, the fact remains that she's coming and wants to hang out with us. We pretty much do girls night every week and it would be good for her. Her husband is a bit of a nutjob."

"It was kind of you to invite her … you're a sweetheart! Oh, there she is now."

We all wave at her and she heads over. Leslie gives her a big hug and makes her feel welcome. I have been joined at the hip with Leslie since that first party I brought her to. We have had some fun and crazy times and I know she will always have many more friends than I will. Colleen will be her latest addition.

"Gary filled me in on some of the details of the party at the quarry. It sounds like that night was over the top. I thought you kids would've learned your lesson after your graduation night."

"You can't blame me for my excess that night, after all, I was stood up. I went to my high school grad with Leslie and Gary. So fitting to end my high school career that way … dateless! I should have seen it coming! Did he think I wanted to be his fuck'n girlfriend or something? I just wanted a date for the dinner."

"Well it didn't take long for Bill to move in on you."

"Yip … he was keen and I finally got laid two dates later. Sex is way over rated … I don't know if he's normal? He doesn't get very hard and I wasn't even sure if he was in there… he was having a good time though."

"He smokes a ton of dope so maybe he can't get a solid hard on. They say that dope can affect that."

"It isn't affecting Sam none I can tell you that."

"We know we've seen the picture … and he'll always be affectionately known as 'springboard.'"

"Well forget Bill and Terri …"

"Fuck! Forget me and Bill? I finally got laid girlfriend … that isn't something to be tossed aside as some non-event!!!"

"Terri, that was nearly two weeks ago now … Sharon is the news this week … what's with you and Jimmy? By Jesus, who would've predicted that could happen?"

"He's sweet and has such a nice car. That night I just felt like I needed to fuck him in his car."

"So are you dating?"

"I don't know yet. I haven't decided. There'll be at least one more date since we're going out on Saturday."

"Just don't break his heart. He's a sweetie."

"I'm not going to break his heart. He wouldn't be single if Leslie would've gone out with him. She already broke his heart."

"That's bullshit."

"No it's not … you can see it by the way he looks at you. I agree with Sharon on that one."

"Well she's dating Gary, so he's shit out of luck. If you two break up I'll sure miss seeing you around the house, but I'll be the first to admit that boy needs work."

"Well, you can see me every Thursday if you want! I think we need to make it an official pact right now. We just graduated from high school and we'll all be going in different directions soon. We absolutely need to get together every week."

"That's a little extreme, wouldn't you say. I mean wouldn't once a month be good?"

"No it wouldn't cos that's normal. It's not special. We need to do it every week!"

"Don't you mean you need to do it every week?"

"Yes, I do and I'm going to … let's just say I'll be out with my girlfriends every fucking Thursday till I die and whoever wants to join me can."

"Well that sounds like a done deal to me. But, what if none of us show up? Will you be out with your imaginary girlfriends? It's hard to go out by yourself. It's like if a tree falls in the forest, does anyone hear it? If you go out by yourself and no one you know sees you, did you really go out?"

"Funny, of course you went out. You take an hour or two if your name is Sharon, and you put on clothes and make-up and you go fuck'n out."

"You would too. You'll talk to anyone. You have fun no matter what you do. You really don't need us there!"

"I'm being very serious here. I want some commitment that you will save Thursdays for girl time."

"Guys don't take that sort of thing very well."

"Woopee Fuck'n Wooppe Wow … poor boys might get mad. If you can't just tell them that you're busy on Thursdays from the beginning maybe you should just put on your ball and chain now."

"You're right! There needs to be trust and I hate the jealous type … nothing more irritating than when they freak out cos you were talking to a guy. You could know the guy from your childhood and they're still capable of getting their cock in a knot."

"Fuck I wish I had a date that could knot his cock!"

"Why would anyone wish that? There isn't that much room up there, you'd never fit it all in … and then they wouldn't be pressing on the important part!"

"Well I could sure as hell try. Anyway, back to our commitment … every week right!"

"Well Sam is already used to my outings, so I'm fine."

"I'll gladly take a night off from my crazy husband and children. They won't even notice I'm gone. Since Pacman came out that's all they do. They're obsessed with beating each other."

"So what happens if we miss a week?"

"Then I'll pull a Ronald Reagan and fire you just like he did with all the Air Traffic controllers. What do you think happens?! We have a fuck'n good time without you!!!"

"Reagan fired the Air Traffic controllers? He can't do that … can he?"

"They all threatened to go on strike so he said fine go ahead but don't come back. They sure changed their tune."

"I love that … I had no idea he was capable of such brilliance."

"Speaking of brilliance, have any of you seen that new channel that plays music videos all day? Some of them are so cool it's worth check'n out. I was able to watch a bunch of them while my ankle was healing from the incident which so easily could have been a deadly accident! I'm so happy it wasn't broken."

"They say sprains can be more painful."

"Its times like that when you have to believe that some force out there is taking care of you. Gord crossed the line on the road and then the car came out of nowhere. I wonder if it was his drunken state that saved us."

"Now that's a stupid thing to say. It was his drunken fuck'n state that made him cross the line in the first place."

"The rest is a blur. We felt the car jerk and it did a couple of spins then came to a perfect stop just off to the side of the road. It was like we had just pulled over to take a piss."

"Sharon's the only one who got hurt, but we all tripped out like crazy after. It took a while before anyone spoke. Then Gord says, 'the only way I'll be able to drive again is if I smoke a joint. Someone roll one up.'"

"We sat at the side of the road for an hour. We all needed that joint and then we just sat and talked about how amazing it was that nothing more serious happened."

"Speak for yourselves. My ankle fucking hurt like crazy."

"Well who sits with their foot lodged between the door and the seat?"

"I do."

"Well I bet you won't anymore."

"You're probably right."

My mind wanders from the conversation. I am remembering that night on a strictly personal level. That feeling of being completely out of control. First with the drugs then with the car spinning. I definitely had an epiphany that night that there must be a God. How I hate the thought of that. On so many levels I feel like believing in God is selling out. It is like conforming to the billions who believe in Him, when I feel deep down inside that they are all wrong. Religion just doesn't make any sense to me. I haven't figured out how to express what God is. He's not our creator. He doesn't sit on a throne in the heavens and he doesn't have an archrival called the devil who sits in hell waiting for all the bad people. I feel so sure of that. But, then what happened that night? Is there a date already waiting for you and it doesn't matter what you do you'll live till then? How crazy would it be to know that date? They make movies about this stuff and people eat it up. Does everyone want to know their future? I feel there would be more disadvantages than advantages. I'll find my way on all this. One day I will make sense of what has never made sense.

"Terri, is anybody home?"

"Right, sorry I was in my own little world there. Just trying to figure out what happened that night."

"OK sista it doesn't take a genius. It's called a miracle ... that I'm especially grateful for!"

"You say that Leslie like it's written in stone and as obvious as your crooked nose."

"Hey, leave the nose out of this … well miracles are gifts from God are they not?"

"The jury is out in my books. I feel like we've all been duped by history and all these stories of Jesus. I think that all Gods were created to keep everyone in line … to keep the masses in order. What if there really is no God? I mean really, there is a lot better chance of there not being a God, than there is of one actually existing. Think about it. Zero evidence. Not once has He come to show us. I'm fuck'n here for you."

"He probably wouldn't swear."

"It's just something you feel."

"Exactly. What if we all just felt something … and that it has nothing to do with a God?

"OK, I'm so not having this conversation with you, because I just want to have another drink and enjoy the fact that I'm alive and kicking," Leslie says with her singing voice and starts kicking her feet in the air around her.

Then on queue both of us start singing the Simple Minds song *Alive and Kicking*. It doesn't take much for the direction of our banter to take a complete 180. The rest of the girls join in and we turn some heads, but we don't give a shit. I believe everyone should have a near death experience to really appreciate the fact that they are still here. It helps with the happy factor. Unless of course you were suicidal then you may be disappointed that someone didn't do it for you!

"Thank God … Oh sorry … there's no God tonight … that you know all the words and can carry us through these moments. I think the other customers were impressed."

"I think that's wishful thinking and they couldn't fuck'n wait for us to finish."

"Girls you sounded great. You add some life into this place that's for sure," the bartender adds.

"I need some advice and since that's one of your jobs as a bartender … I'll ask you. Is it too much for a guy to handle if their girlfriend goes out once a week? Now, she's with her best friends, and they have made this pact to do this. Would you freak out, or would you be OK with it?"

"I can't answer that for all men and I think it depends on the relationship. If I trust her and she doesn't give any of the signals like she wants to dump me I could handle it. But, if she's a big flirt and is always keeping me guessing, then I may have a problem with it."

"Could you get any more on the fence than that? Look fuck, if you don't trust your girlfriend you shouldn't be dating her. That is cause for a dumping for sure! The only question we need to answer here is … would you be OK with your girlfriend having a weekly girls' night out? Yes. No."

"If I'm completely honest, knowing you ladies are going to eat me alive … I have to say no."

"Jesus, what is it with men? Why are you all so fuck'n jealous? Do you not know that we hate that about you?"

"Darling you asked me a question, and I just answered honestly."

"Yeah, yeah. You're ruining my quest here to get these girls to agree to a weekly night out."

"I love seeing you ladies and listening to all your clucking."

"What in the hell is clucking?"

"You know … like chickens or hens … cluck cluck cluck … on and on, but it's hard to know what they're saying because they're all talking over one another, yet they all seem to understand instinctively what's going on!"

"Yes, yes … that's us! Now we have a name … Hen Night … I love it.

"OK, I'll make every effort to come out every Thursday with you girls."

"Colleen, Izzy and Terri confirmed. Sharon you're the last man standing. You're in, or you're out?"

"I just don't know if I would really want to see you all every week…"

"Shut up queer! OK you're out."

"Aren't we the bossy bitch? You know I'm in with almost as much enthusiasm as you."

"Right, that'll be day you exude enthusiasm girlfriend. I just know that I'm so hyper I'll need a girls' night every week to release my energy. Boys can be very boring."

"That's so true. Sam can sit in his basement and do virtually nothing for days. I start to go stir crazy."

"That's because he's one of those guys who lives for his sports. He doesn't want to play them … he'd rather smoke dope and watch them!"

"Well I don't have a 'dope in hell' of ever changing that," Izzy says in a silly voice and finger quotes.

"It does affect different people different ways. I get a boost of energy and can't sit down when I smoke. I'll clean my whole house and have dinner on for my family in record time. And of course my husband will find something about my dinner to complain about."

"Well you should stop making him dinner if he isn't grateful. My mom has made some fuck'n hideous dinners and I haven't heard my dad complain once."

"I've only been living at Terri's for three weeks now and I can attest to that!"

"Oh, and by the way was that Gary I heard sneaking in the window a few nights ago? I forgot to ask you. And you know if dad catches you, Gary will die."

"He was so stressed out he decided that he would never do it again … not even sex was worth that amount of fright. He could barely get it up he was so nervous."

"Holy shit it's late, and I start my new job tomorrow."

"Was Laura pissed when you quit the craft store?"

"Not at all, she was thrilled I got on at Eaton's as there'll be more room for advancement. The Rideau Centre is gorgeous and it'll be so much fun working downtown."

"I guess that means you're leaving."

"Yeah, so if you want a ride home so are you."

"I can drive you Leslie, it's not far out of the way if you want to stay."

"I actually never want Thursdays to end."

"We know … well sistas I'm off. Have a great weekend."

All the girls wish me good luck on my new gig and I head to the car. My brothers are always in awe about how much dad lends me the car. Well it's only me and him who drive it now so why should it sit in the driveway? It isn't like my mom and dad ever do anything! It is so great to have Leslie there now. Her persistence on a weekly outing is a great idea. Bill is a push-over so I just tell him what I am doing and he agrees with everything. Women need to stick together and stay in touch for our mental health. We need to have a sounding board and to vent our troubles and frustrations, as well as share our joys and accomplishments. My friends listen and are genuinely interested in me. Why should that ever change just because we get married and have kids one day? I asked my mother a couple of years ago if she thought I was pretty. I guess since I had never really asked anything that personal before I shouldn't have expected anything personal back. She told me that she couldn't be a good judge of that because I am her daughter, and she sees me every day. I took that as a no. How else was I supposed to decipher that? Leslie and the girls tell me I am beautiful frequently. I still have difficulties believing it, but I am working on it. My girlfriends make me feel good. A weekly fix is a very good idea.

"Once again you're the song … I'm the one who turns the pages.
There you go flying high … Here am I, rock of ages."
Bryan Ferry

Week 96 – About the Coop

"Now that was a busy weekend and week. I'm so happy to have a fucking break from moving and organizing and painting. Look at us! Now we have actual homes to host Hen Nights. We won't always have to go out."

"Alleluia! It's bloody expensive moving out! I won't be able to afford going out anymore!"

"At lease you have John to share the rent."

"Yes, but it's all relative because our rent is quite a bit more. My Hope Chest that Carmen started for me all those years ago has saved me big bucks."

"How's she doing?"

"She's great and she must be saving a fortune because even after they got married they still live at Carmen's mom and dad's. Some parents you can do that with and some you can't. She did say she was looking for a place so I'm sure it won't be much longer. I feel closer to that family than my own sometimes. I'm so grateful to have had their place as my sanctuary growing up."

The Speirs lived just up the street and had four children whose ages all matched up with one of my siblings. Carmen is seven years older than me and she always brags that she held me when mom brought me home from the hospital. None of their ages matched up with mine, but I adopted them as my second family. I visited frequently ... always uninvited. I just showed up and they treated me like one of their own. I always felt love there. Even in high school after my visits Carmen would always watch out the window to make sure I was heading up the driveway before she left her post.

"Leslie this place is so amazing. Are the girls coming here?"

"Of course dummy ... my first time hosting a Hen Night. The couple who own the house are great. They brought me food on my first day. It was thoughtful, but it comes with a price."

"A price?"

"Yeah, I had to listen to him go on and on about how we are on the brink of nuclear war and every country is doing testing. Then he told me all about Reagan and his Star Wars thingy that will protect us from any bombs that come our way and then I lost all focus and I don't even know what he said after that. Who really wants to hear all that? Once I have something to worry about I will. Until then I live in blissful ignorance."

"I'm with you. Reality is too depressing. I'll turn on the news to see if there's anything interesting. Last time I did a suicide bomber drove into the US Embassy in Beirut and 63 people died. I think we should start our own news channel that's only happy, positive, enlightening stories. Our current media fuck'n sucks."

"And speaking of sucking, just before I left your mom and dad's, I had a one-afternoon-stand with Peter Burns!"

"From school, who lives across the street, Peter?"

"That would be the one."

"And why did you do that?"

"Like all my episodes … it just happened. I was cutting the grass for the townhouses, as you know I do for a side job, and he saw me and invited me in for a glass of water. I took him up on it and before I knew it I was giving him a blow job."

"God dammit girl it's amazing you don't have some disease by now!"

"No it isn't!!! I haven't actually had that many men you know! But, if sperm had some kind of health benefit I would love to know because I may just be the healthiest girl on the planet! Maybe we should be rubbing it on our faces for a mask or something and it would cure acne … who knows? There could be endless possibilities."

"I have no doubt you should be the one testing all this. Swallowing is only necessary at the beginning of a relationship and I sure as hell wouldn't be swallowing for some random rendezvous … not that I have ever had one!"

"It's not so bad. I personally have no issue with it, not one iota."

"No shit! I wish I loved sex as much as you. Sperm gives me a bit of a gag reflex. It can be completely awesome when all the stars line up, but I don't crave it the way you do."

"What, sex or sperm?"

"Funny! Sex of course, I don't know a soul who craves sperm … or, do I?

"No, crave wouldn't be the word I would choose."

"I'll suck a dick and it can cum in my mouth, and I'm totally fine with it, but it just doesn't taste very good. Why would a guy even care if you swallow or not? I mean once you've finished him off, is the swallowing really so important?! Once John complained that I wasn't swallowing anymore so I told him if he really needed it swallowed I could pass it over to him and he can see if he likes it! I wasn't built like you. You were built for men to worship. You must have the nicest tits they've ever seen. You do have the nicest tits I've ever seen!"

"Enough already … fuck if I could give you some of my breasts you know I would in a heartbeat, besides your breasts are sweet as pie."

"Yeah, raisin pie!"

John and I decided to move in together so Leslie decided to get her own place. She landed a much better job at a law office so she will be able to manage it fine. I was so happy she got out of the retail life. It is way better having the weekends off. I too have left retail and now have a full time office job. Sometimes I want to pinch myself to make sure that I am not in a dream and my gorgeous adorable man really does love me. I am having the time of my life setting up our place together. He is so great, but I have noticed that if he is without any of his vices, he tends to be on the crabby side. Leslie thinks he gets too angry when he drinks and that it's uncomfortable. He does change after a few, but as long as I don't rock the boat he is fine.

"Careful on the stairs girls," Leslie shouts out her door. She saw the girls walking up the laneway from her third storey loft apartment located smack in the heart of The Glebe. It's the perfect first apartment.

"I hope the landlord has good insurance because I'm already worried about walking down those once inebriated!"

"I hadn't thought of that, but you make a good point. There're two railings … we'll all be fine. There's no need to get that drunk either."

"I know there's no NEED, but shitfaced happens … mostly to you … so you may want to take some of your own advice!"

"Funny!"

"Oh and don't you say a word about Peter," Leslie quickly adds before they arrive at the top. She is trying to break up with Gary, but it has been a process. He is not in favour of it.

"Izzy, Sharon, sistas, come in … welcome to the first mother-fuck'n Hen House.

"Jesus Leslie, by the size of it I think you should be calling it the first mother-fuck'n Hen Coop."

"Fine Hen Coop it is. Coop, house, who cares … the Hens have a home base for Thursdays! Girls I'm so excited to have my own place it could be a mother-fuck'n Hen Nest!"

"It's awesome, what a find. It has so much character … way better than an apartment building. But those stairs could be problematic."

"Don't buy too many groceries at any one time. That's a long haul up."

Leslie shows us all the things she has done and gives us the tour. The other room is the bedroom with a bathroom attached. It takes all of one minute then we settle into our usual ritual of rolling up a couple of joints and fixing a drink. The main room is an open concept with a galley kitchen and Leslie has a small table and chairs set up beside it. She has the cat litter in the bathroom … as soon as she moved in she got Reggie. He is a white, super fluffy cat and I actually like him very much and I am not a cat person … dogs all the way.

"Is Colleen coming tonight?"

"No she's with the kids cos Hank had something going on tonight."

"Probably some crazy drug deal! How has she been while you're trying to break up with her son?"

"She gets it and she's fine. She was here last weekend helping me clean and do some stuff."

"Next week I want to host at my place. I'll have it all set up by then. I wanted to finish painting first."

"Girls only … get rid of the old man!"

"He has plenty of notice. He'll plan something with a buddy. So do you remember how pissed I was when my boss didn't give me the office manager position. I mean I wasn't even going to apply until all the reps encouraged me."

"Yeah, you were the same amount of pissed that your mum was at dinner last week."

"Don't remind me. I still feel awful … it just comes out sometimes."

"What happened?"

"Jesus girls, I had to fuck'n kick her under the table to wake her up to what she was saying. Mr. Vetnor's sister was visiting and she's a nun and not a cool one like Terri's sister. So when she's there she wants to say Grace. So she starts, 'Thank you Lord for your many blessings. Thank you for this beautiful dinner.' Then Terri interrupts her and says, 'I think we should thank mom for this beautiful dinner.' Then auntie says all uncomfortable, 'OK, then let us thank the Lord for the food your mother used for this beautiful dinner.' Then Terri says, 'No, let us thank the farmers and all their hard work for the food' … and that's when I kicked her. Mrs. Vetnor looked mortified, but I do believe Mr. Vetnor had a wee smirk on his face. I don't think he fancies that sister much!"

"Terri, Jesus Christ there's a time and a place for your constant challenging of religion and that wasn't it. You should have let her say grace and shut the fuck up!"

"I wish someone had told me that … believe me. I just can't stand when He gets all this credit for shit He doesn't do! If I could rewind that moment in time I would. So can I finish my much better story about work?"

"Yes, you didn't get the position and I saw who he hired when I picked you up. She's beautiful and much older."

"Yes she is. I have no doubt the pervert was hoping for a fling, but a twist of fate has changed everything. She has only been there for one month and she quit today. She isn't giving him two weeks either. So as of tomorrow my evening girl will be starting as receptionist full time and I'm officially the office manager. I'm the Chosen One out of desperation, but I'll show him."

"But who will train you?"

"I'll learn with many phone calls to other offices in the city and to Head Office."

"I just love a good redemption story. Your boss doesn't deserve you."

"No kidding! He's a slime bucket, and he has no impact on me. I work more closely with all the sales reps and they all love me. I really like the girl taking over my job and we'll work great together. I'm in one happy party place tonight!"

"Congrats girl! That's great news."

We have all settled into to our new Hen Coop quite nicely. We could go out and find a bar close by, but all we want to do is chat and catch up on our week. A lot can happen in a week. I'm a prime example. I moved in with my amazing boyfriend and got a promotion!

Izzy has this expression between concern and laughter and asks us if we heard about what happened to Bruce. Bruce is my friend from grade school and he is amazing. He has a genetic degenerative disease that will render him in a wheelchair eventually. He will struggle with his speech and motor skills, and his life expectancy is shorter than ours. I have watched Bruce go from a completely normal healthy child to a weeble. He doesn't need a wheelchair yet, but when he walks you are waiting for him to fall down … but he doesn't. He just wobbles … just like in the commercial … weebles wobble but they don't fall down. That seems like a terrible thing to say, but Bruce is so cool you can say anything to him. He knows his fate. Bruce is special and he has special friends who take care of him. I only see him at parties now and Izzy told me about his girlfriend. I was so excited to hear that. Izzy is a gossip hound. Bruce is a fighter, and he is never down … except at times in the literal sense!

"So we were at Sam's on the weekend and Robbie brought Bruce on his motorcycle."

"No doubt they were all smoking dubbies in the basement."

"Well everyone but me. So we're having a good time and then Robbie and Bruce decided to head out. I went to see them off and make sure Bruce got on the motorcycle and was holding on and good to go. They take off and not 50 feet down the road doesn't Bruce fall right off the fuck'n back. I thought Robbie would notice straight away, but he doesn't come back. I can't even express how funny the whole scene played out. It was just the way he fell … he didn't look real … he looked like a crash test dummy or something. I tried so hard not to laugh, but I couldn't stop. I ran up the street to check on him and he was laughing too. Then finally five minutes later Robbie returned!"

"Jesus how was Bruce? I could see how Robbie didn't notice right away the man weighs 90 pounds soaking wet."

"His pride took most of the bruising. I think the laughter was more cos he was in a bit of shock."

"That guy has a rough road ahead of him."

"No shit! If anyone of us starts feeling sorry for ourselves we should just think of him."

"I'm so not feeling sorry for myself … not one iota! I booked a flight today to go see my family. Newfoundland and the sea, here I come baby."

"That's the best news."

"I haven't seen them for two years. Ellie looks so grown up from the pictures I got. She better remember me. I so miss them at times I feel my heart breaking when I talk to her. I can hardly keep composed! She's 11 now!"

"Leslie you're one tough cookie. I think I may have followed my family, even if it was to Newfoundland. You've made the most of life without them here and you should be very proud of yourself."

"I have worked as a waitress and in a jean store … don't know why I should be so proud of that?"

"Give yourself some credit and learn to take a compliment will you! You're great at budgeting and now you have your own apartment and a new job."

"A car is next. I hope by the winter so I don't have to wait for a godforsaken bus again. The transit here is fucking brutal!"

"Tell me about it. I got frostbite on my face when I was bussing to John's in February during that cold snap. That fucking bus driver saw me running to him and he just closed the door and kept on going. Who does that when it's -20 C out?! I was so mad I walked from Baseline and it took 30 minutes, but that was warmer than standing and waiting 30 minutes for the next fuck'n bus."

"That boyfriend of yours should be picking you up girl!"

"He was driving all day and didn't want to get in the car again. I can sympathize with that."

"Well I can't."

"Well you don't have to cos he isn't your boyfriend."

"Whatever ... let's change the subject. I think I'll change it to wrestle time ... you need some sense knocked into you!"

So up Leslie gets and puts me in a headlock and pulls me off the couch. Izzy and Sharon move some of the furniture quickly so we don't split our heads open or break anything. I pull Leslie's arm away and get my head free. We are now on the floor and some room has been created, so I grab Leslie and get her down for just a moment. Our arms and legs are flailing around and there is much grunting and laughter. She is wiry and strong and always a challenge. It surprises me because I can do like thirty male push-ups to her five, if she is on a good day. We have been doing random wrestling since that party when we tried to convince all our guy friends that we had mud-wrestled at the bar in Hull. They wouldn't fully believe us so Leslie just says, 'no really, watch' and jumps on me out of the blue. These wrestles only last a few minutes and end once I stop fighting back. I learned that they'd go on way too long because she will not give up. She has more UPI's (unidentified party injuries) than anyone I've known. You see I am not the only person she wrestles with. She stirs it up with anyone and everyone who will respond to her subtle pokes or nudges or a shove here or there.

"Are you boneheads finished yet?"

"I'm so done, Leslie you're a brute!"

"That was a good round. For once I felt like I had to work a little!"

"Funny! One day we will do that straight and I will kicky your assy!"

"Anytime baby, bring it on!"

"Well it won't be today ... cos I'm going to roll a joint."

"Oh wasn't that the saddest day when *M*A*S*H* ended? I love that show." Izzy states as she helps with moving the furniture back into place.

"I think it was nearly everyone's favourite and it'll be in reruns forever, so it's not like you can't watch it again and again."

"I know, but they won't be new. I've always had a thing for Hawkeye. What is it about him? He's not particularly good looking but so yummy!"

"It's his sense of humour that makes him so yummy cos I totally agree."

"Me too!"

"He's too scrawny and his nose is too big!"

"Well your nose is too big and you're still yummy!"

"Yeah right, and leave my nose out of this!"

Leslie goes over to her radio and turns up *Thriller* by Michael Jackson. "Don't you guys love this song? C'mon let's dance."

"I'm not dancing, and if I wasn't so polite I would pick up your radio and smash it! I'm so tired of hearing this fucking song!"

"That's because it's been number one on the charts forever!"

"Am I the only one sick of it?"

"Well Sharon baby, you get to hear it again because I'm dancing to this great beat."

"Yeah … well beat this Michael," Sharon says as she makes the motion of giving a hand job to her imaginary dick.

Finally a song Sharon likes come on … *Mustang Sally*, and she and Izzy join us for a dance. That song gets so much airtime since Sally Ride became the first female in space. After the dancing I say my goodbye's as I will have my first day as Office Manager tomorrow! I walk down the skinny staircase and over to my bicycle. I finally bought myself a really nice one, and now I worry that it will be stolen. It may be the first thing I own worth stealing. My new apartment is only about a ten minute ride away. The night air smells like laundry from the clothes line. When you capture that smell onto your clothes it is a very different scent than actual air. But, every once in a while in the late spring or early fall the air actually smells like it does on your clothes from the line. I don't know if there is a smell I like better on this great planet. And what moment is better than crawling into bed, after a long day, into fresh sheets from the clothesline. Mom hangs her clothes up all the time and I will miss that. I ride slowly through the streets lined with great big old homes that define the neighbourhood. Affluent ... I respect them, but I know I will never be one of them. I have been told never to dream big. I have been told that poor stay poor, middle class stay middle class and the rich stay rich. They are probably right, but damn it would be cool to not live paycheque to paycheque. I hope they are wrong. If I don't get myself back to school I don't have a hope of changing anything. I arrive at my new apartment and I admire my red and white paint job in the kitchen. There is something so happy about the colour red. Carmen knows it is my favourite colour, so she filled my hope chest with everything red and white for the kitchen. I am happy as I head into the living room to catch up on the day with John. I am 20 years old.

"Late at night I park my car, stake my place in the singles bar;

Face to face, toe to toe, heart to heart as we hit the floor."

Ferry/MacKay

Week 150 – About Sex in the Coop

"Look at you with your new CD player. So you finally saved up enough. Somehow it seemed crazy to me that you kept buying CD's, but had nothing to play them on."

"You know me and my budgeting, and what's the point of having a CD player ... and not being able to use it? Or, have one CD that you get tired of listening to again and again. I now have a good selection and we'll fuck'n rock tonight!"

"I know right! Now it makes total sense! So did you girls sign the papers? Is it really official?"

"It is and I'll miss this place sooooo much. It just makes sense financially, and I'll have more living space."

"I'm jealous. You, Izzy and Sharon living together. How fun will that be? And you won't be my neighbour anymore."

"You can dump John and move in with us."

"You know for the first time since I met him I have had the odd feeling that he may not be the one."

"Anything specific happen?"

"He's just so cranky if he doesn't have dope. Then he snaps at me and we'll fight about the dumbest shit. I guess I have always thought that at some point he would grow out of smoking dope, but he's a lifer, I'm sure of that. It gets expensive, and do I want a man who changes so much when he doesn't get his fix? I mean what if all drugs just disappeared … I couldn't live with that man! You and I can go days without getting high, and we don't get all crabby."

"Well I was pretty miserable when we had that two week drought."

"Well that time I really wanted to kill him. I just stopped talking to him cos nothing made him happy. So when are the girls coming?"

"They're grabbing a bite to eat and should be here soon. I think Ruth is coming too."

"I can't believe this is our last Hen Night in the Coop. I'll sure miss having you close by. Oh yeah … when I came up to the house there was a totally gorgeous stud muffin on the porch smoking. Is that your new landlord?"

"If it was I wouldn't be moving. He's their nephew from California. I can't even remember his name so I just call him the California Kid. He loves that."

"Has he not tried to take you to bed yet?"

"Jesus Terri, he's their nephew. If I got caught how awkward would that be?"

"Since when do you care about something like that … you're moving out."

"Speaking of 'moving out'…" Leslie jumps up and bounces over to her new player. "I am putting on my Billy Joel CD that I've had for a month now! I'll save Madonna for later."

The door opens and the four girls walk in. They are huffing and puffing from the climb up. This is Ruth's first time here. She didn't want to miss seeing the apartment where so many Hen stories happened. Ruth went to the French high school close to ours and we met when I was dating Bill right after graduation. Her boyfriend Mark and Bill are good friends. I dated Bill for two months until he left for Vancouver. We all have a fresh beverage and the rest of the drinks are put in the fridge. It seems that there is only alcohol in there at the moment because Leslie placed out the nibblies we bought for the night. Sometimes Hen Night is as much about the food as it is drugs and alcohol … oh and friendship of course!

"Bill says 'hi' Terri. You know he'll always have a thing for you!"

"Well the feeling is not mutual. But, I do miss the free drugs! How's Mark doing?"

"Well, excellent because he's now an official Firefighter!!! It took him two years to finally get in."

"So Ruth the big day is approaching. You must be excited!"

"I just hope the weather's good. It's the one thing you have no control over and I hate when people say that a rainy day is an omen of a bad marriage."

"I say getting married is an omen of a bad marriage!"

"Now Sharon, is that anything to say while in the company of this bride to be?"

"Yeah Sharon! Good thing you're not invited to be a negative nelly through it all!"

"I'm just not a fan of the institution, because those vows mean nothing now that you really don't have to keep them."

"Of course they mean something. I think every couple that exchanges vows really means them when they do it. At least I hope they do! And it's not a bad thing that you can get rid of your husband if he turns out to be an arsehole. Men can change once they get that ring on your finger. There's no shortage of stories of women whose marriages started off great and then things got ugly. My mother is a perfect example," Leslie says in nearly one breath.

"We all know you and Mark are the perfect couple. You two ooze lovey dovey all the time. I'm sure you'll have a great life together. I personally don't know if I ever want to get married."

"You will if Mr. Right comes along … you're softer inside than your outside appears."

"Don't tell anyone Ruth, I have a reputation to uphold!"

"I hope you girls do understand that we just wanted a really small wedding."

"Yes, of course we do. Don't give it a thought."

"So what's our agenda for the night?"

"We'll go out to the neighbourhood pub in a bit because it'll be the last time we can all stumble back to the Hen Coop."

"Will Steve, your bartender crush be there?"

"I got to do more than crush on him finally! He was a tough case. I have been flirting with him for months. No wonder he took a while … I found out he likes the natural look. About a month back I had gotten myself all done up with gel in my hair, and my makeup all perfect and I smoked a quick reefer, then walked in for a drink and a visit and he says to me, 'Hey how are you? Have you just come from a swim?' I say, no why? And then to my *horror* he says, 'because your hair is wet and your eyes are all red.' I nearly cried! I toned it down for the while, and he finally walked me home on the weekend and came up and yum, yum, yummie. It was excellent. He is sooooo beautiful and has the most beautiful penis I have ever seen! He won't be my new boyfriend … we have a mutual understanding that it would only be a fling."

"Yeah, but you think he has a great ass, and I think it's big and square and I don't think I can trust your judgement. Maybe I should do him too!"

"Sharon, you'll stay away and you'll have to take my word for it. He was a great lay."

"Even better than Mr. Police officer, who I never met!"

"Terry, you never met Roger? How did that not happen?"

"I don't know Izzy. We just never crossed paths and it isn't like they dated for very long."

"I know that was a sad, sad, sad, day. There's nothing sexier than a man in uniform. I knew it couldn't work out, but it was hot while it lasted!"

"Yeah, well not being able to smoke drugs around him may have been a problem. He never got to see the real Leslie."

"It wouldn't have lasted as long as it did if that were the case. OK, I've thought about it and Steve the bartender wins for best lay yet!"

"Man that bedroom of yours has been busy."

"No not really. I was away last weekend with Colleen at the trailer."

"Yes you were and we had a blast! The rest of you girls missed a good time."

"I didn't really want to tell you this, but I feel I must confess. While you were away and so generously let me use your sweet apartment ... I slept with the California Kid."

"WWHHAAAT?" We all say in unison.

"Sharon you lucky, lucky bitch. They don't come any hotter than him!"

"Just tell me the landlord didn't find out."

"He definitely found out! Yes, when buddy didn't come home they were freaking out in the morning, and this was the first place they called on. The only real surprise he got was that I answered the door not you!"

"Shit Sharon, you bonehead, why didn't you kick him out and send him downstairs after?"

"Because there was no 'after' … he just kept coming back for more! It was a wonder I could even fuck'n walk to the door to greet him!"

We are all surprised by this news and enjoying the story immensely. As Leslie puffs on her reefer she is now making sense of the big happy face on California Kid all week and why her landlord seemed awkward. We are all giddy watching Leslie's irritation with Sharon when there is no need. Who cares if she slept with him, he is a grown man. I think she may be jealous.

"I don't know why you have that crooked nose even more bent out of shape. I'm the one they think is a slut not you."

"I don't know why. It's fine really. Well it'll have to be cos it's already done. So how was he?"

"Active! I've never met another guy who could get it up again that quickly. I was getting a tad sore, but you don't get to bed down with someone that hot everyday so whatever he was giving I was receiving."

"Just like you to not really answer my question."

"Well if you're asking if I had a great big beautiful orgasm, yeeeessss sireee Bob and more than once. He didn't need to do much, Jesus just looking at him would make any girl horny."

"You got that right! I just saw him for the first time when I arrived. I did a double-take and I don't double-take many boys. I'm very jealous."

"Jesus, if he's that good … why the hell didn't I sleep with him? He's going back home this weekend and offered to help load the truck on Saturday."

"That gives you a two day window to get him to bed! He could leave Canada having bagged two Hens!"

"I'll not take sloppy seconds, however temping it is. My God look at all these boxes around … it's so final."

"Just look on the bright side … we have a great townhouse and its back in the old neighbourhood. We are going to have a blast there. Think of it as an upgrade from coop to house."

"I know it's all good. Let's split when everyone's finished their drinks."

We all arrive at the bar which we have frequented for nearly a year. We only go out once a month or so since the arrival of the Hen Coop. It is busy and we can only grab a few chairs at the bar. Leslie's boytoy is bartending tonight and she is happy about that. We say hi to some of the regulars we have gotten to know. This is the first time they have heard about the move.

"We aren't going that far away … we'll be back on occasion."

"You better. This place isn't the same when you girls are absent. I'll always stop in for a drink just to see if you ladies arrive. If you don't show up by 10:00 pm I know you're not coming."

"Well that's so sweet. We love that. Girls, we have a fan club."

"I don't think you can call one bachelor a fan club."

"Well you can add me to it also and make it official."

"Thanks Steve … we are a jolly good time aren't we!"

"I always tell your hamster story to my customers.

"I haven't heard the hamster story."

"Really?"

"Really, or I wouldn't have said that!"

"I guess you are making lovey dovey with your man most of the time you're out of the loop girl."

"That's OK, I like it that way."

"It must have been four months ago and I noticed he was acting weird. I was keeping an eye on him, and it just got worse. I had him out all the time. I would put my hoodie on and put him in the pocket. I was freaking out that he was going to die on me. Well after a few days I woke up to find him stiff as a board in his cage. I shed a few tears, and then got me arse to work. I had plans that night so I didn't do anything about a burial. The next morning I go to the cage and take a pen and poke him hoping he might be OK, nothing! Of course I don't have any time again and I have to get me arse to work. At work I called Terri and asked her to come over and help me bury Newman. So we meet at my place and we have a bite to eat and we make a toast to the best hamster ever and we go over to the cage. I take my pen for one last prod to make sure, and doesn't the little fucker wake up. Stiff as a board for two days and he comes back to life. It gave me quite the fright."

"That's crazy. Maybe he was in some kind of hibernation? Is that a hamster thing?"

"Not that I know of."

"Personally I think he had one too many trips down the stairs in his hamster ball. Leslie you never closed those stairs off to the main house and he went flying more than once!"

"Izzy he did it on purpose. He loved that ride!"

"You're delusional. That hamster just drove himself down the stairs cos he thought it was fun!!! He had his body so beaten up in that ball he needed to pretend to be dead to make it stop!"

"Well we'll never know what actually happened, but he won't be balling down the stairs anymore at the new place. They're hardwood. Now that would be nasty."

"One of my favourite stories from the Hen Coop was last month when you had the final party. It was so great to see everyone and especially Bruce. It had been a while and I sure noticed the difference in his body. He seems to be progressing fast. I thought it was so cute how the boys all took turns carrying him up. Each of them positioned themselves on a landing and handed him off. I'm so grateful that they're still including him and taking care of him."

"Now how's that a highlight? The night was so much fun and they bring Bruce to all the parties."

"Because I have a soft spot for him. I have known him since kindergarten. And watching the way our friends haven't given up on him … well it just makes my heart smile!"

"Well my highlight of the night was when Natasha stepped on Monte's head after he passed out. He was such a dick to her. That high heal mark may be there for life."

"That's so Sharon to have Monte's head stepped on as the highlight … I know you're not his biggest fan!"

We reminisce about all the great times we had at Leslie's and how much we will miss it. We close the bar down and begin our stumble back. Ruth left the bar by 12:00 am and the rest of us are tired when we arrive. As per usual, Leslie is still full of piss and vinegar. She puts on her new Madonna CD and cranks *Holiday* and somehow we all find the energy to dance to it. We dance till 3:00 am and no one wants to leave because this night is special. This night is a chapter ending in our weekly excursions. This night is a sleep on the couch or floor night even when it hasn't been cleared with the boyfriend. This night is a night that is worth dealing with the consequences of said actions. This night is an epic Hen Night and I am not going anywhere.

"Worry never robs tomorrow of its sorrow. It only saps today of its joy."

Leo Buscaglia

Week 676 - About a Family

"Thank you so much for coming here girls. I know it isn't exactly the perfect Hen Night scene, but I was so excited for you all to see my house in the city!!! I live in the city, I live in the city, I'm over the moon, I'm over the moon!!!" I say in a little song and dance.

"You're not the only one! You're not the only one!!! It took us 15 minutes to drive here! Welcome back sista."

"I'm not completely settled in so don't mind the boxes. Things take time with three young ones about."

"Hand over that baby please. Terri she looks so much like Andrew's side of the family."

"I know right! I can't find me in there anywhere, but maybe her lips."

"This is a wicked location girl."

"Well once I give you the tour you'll see that we bought the place on location. It does need some work but it has a fucking furnace and I will not be freezing this winter. And it has neighbours and it has a store I can walk to and … well you get it. I'm in love with everything about it!!!"

"Have you noticed any kids in the neighbourhood?"

"Not so far, but I've been in way too much getting settled."

So after six years of living in Quebec and never feeling like it was home I have my family back in Ottawa. While living in The Love Shack trying to keep warm we made two more babies. Noah is four now, Tobias/Toby is two and our daughter Sophie is six weeks old. For the past few years Andrew has been the regional manager of a photographic retail chain. He loves the owner who has become a mentor of sorts. After a year of doing just photography the feast or famine lifestyle wasn't working for me. He was hired on the spot to oversee eight stores and a steady paycheque is king. We do photography part time. He is working hard to provide for his family, and life isn't easy, but we have lots of love and we live life knowing things could always be worse and you must be happy with what you have. Andrew is always happy and naturally good-tempered and loves us all so much that that seems to be all he needs to keep on truck'n. I have never seen him lose his temper yet. I am ranting and raging frequently. I wish he would yell some so I would not feel so bad about doing it. My venting seems like it feels good at the time, but he is right when he says it doesn't accomplish anything. The kids tune out. Now, instead of hollering at them I am trying some new techniques that his mom suggested! Distraction is working quite well.

"Hi Noah, how do you like your new house?"

"It's good. Look I have my very own room. Mom let me pick the colour and help paint it."

"I sure hope it was you who picked out the colour! It's a beautiful room Noah."

"I'll let Toby sleep with me cos mom says he won't bug her so much tonight if I do that!"

"That's very kind of you. Well goodnight and sweet dreams. Can I have a hug?"

"Noah we all want a hug. It's so good to see you again little man." Noah obliges all the girls and then we move on to the next room.

"Hey Toby, nice room you have. Is that a Power Ranger you have there?"

"Yup, it's Wed Wanger and I have Bue and Geen, see…" Toby jumps out of bed to show the girls. He lights up with excitement having visitors in the house!

"OK bud back to bed. Remember our talk and we made a deal! Mommy is having friends tonight and downstairs is off limits unless there's an emergency. You can go jump in with Noah if you want to later."

I finish giving the girls the full tour of my new 100 year old palace and we gather around the kitchen table. I put Sophie in the swing and crank it up. I have a large country kitchen that is an addition built in the 50's. It has a side door out onto a small porch where I have a few chairs and some ashtrays out for the girls when they need to smoke. I have all my nibblies ready and I am set to entertain.

"Girl you must have let Toby pick the colour of his room too! You couldn't have chosen that colour?"

"Well he did better than Noah wouldn't you say!"

"It was hard to find a purple that Noah and I could compromise on, and Toby wanted bright orange, but I persuaded him into that burnt orange."

"Good for you. I wish I had let my kid's paint their own rooms and maybe they wouldn't be such a pain in my arse today!"

"What is Gary up to these days?"

"The older two aren't the problem. I never see them anymore anyway. It became less and less once I left Hank. Emma is doing fine, but Brent is a lazy arse and I can't keep subsidizing him. He's putting me in the poor house."

"I didn't realize Gary and Colin weren't in touch. That's really crummy of them."

"Well stop giving Brent money and that should fix the problem?"

"You girls wait till your kids are teenagers … you'll see."

"We do seem to be creating monsters with this generation."

"Yes, they're overprotected and spend too much time in front of the TV and computer playing video games."

"My boys have a couple of good computer games and I know I won't be able to keep them from the TV videos forever, but I'll keep it out for as long as I can. I caved and got a Gameboy for Noah for the commute to the country."

"Do you have any music in this house yet?"

"I have a ghetto blaster and the CD's are unpacked so go pick what you want. I have a couple here that I chose if you want to see them. Once the boys are sleeping we can move into the living room and put on the stereo if you guys want. I have all my albums still!"

"You're kidding!"

"Andrew won't part with anything, you know that. Have you seen his mother's house? He comes by it honestly."

"Izzy, how are you doing these days? When's your due date again?"

"The 18th of December."

"You have six months to go! Isn't it fun being pregnant?"

"I feel great. I've been lucky. I can't stop eating … it's scaring me."

"Oh thanks for reminding me I have some food for the night. I even have hors d'oeuvres"

"Great cos I'm about to pass out any minute!"

"Just speak up will you!"

Leslie has the music going. Sophie is fast asleep in the swing and Noah is doing a great job keeping Toby upstairs. Noah is very much the wise old soul. And he is as smart as a whip. He started out looking like Yoda for a reason. He is fucking Yoda! This is the evolution of Hen Night … married hens, separated hen, pregnant hen, and mother hens.

"I inserted a new first in Abbey's baby book this week!"

"She's walking isn't she Leslie? I could see the other day she was so close. Thanks again for taking the boys, it was very helpful."

"It's funny watching her teeter all around, and terrifying. I can't take my eyes off her. I'm just waiting for the major tumble!"

"Now you have to be on all the time!"

"Isn't that what play pens are for? Just stick her in there and then you can get things done."

"I can't wait till you have a baby. You're so gonna get constant razing from us."

"I'm not in a hurry and it may never happen."

"Stan wants a baby and you love Stan and you'll be having a baby; that I would bet a lot of money on."

"Well don't put it in the bank yet. Stan was ready on the wedding night for Christ sake. I understand why, but the old man may just have to wait a while."

"Well if you wait to be ready that'll never happen. Did you not hug those two adorable boys upstairs? How can you not want one of those?"

"It's soooo much work."

"I can't argue with that and you're not exactly a get-things-done kinda girl!"

"Funny. Now who's coming outside with me?"

"That depends, what are you smoking?"

"I'm having a reefer then I'm smoking a butt. I pre-rolled a few so we didn't have to worry about the kids busting us."

"Smart thinking!"

Leslie and I join Sharon for a joint and Colleen stays back with Izzy to keep an eye on the baby. I haven't heard a peep from the boys. I'm afraid if I check on them I may ruin it, but I know I will go up shortly.

"Meagan wants me to take care of her daughter once she starts back at work so I'm going to do it. We've had some play dates already. Kids love kids. You get them together and they're happier."

"How do people afford putting their kids in daycare? Finances are tight cos there's always month left at the end of the money, but I'd rather go into debt in order to stay home with my kids. In my situation the idea of paying for daycare is rather counter-productive!"

"Meagan has a very good job with the city. Her university diploma will take her far."

"Or maybe her politician father had something to do with it!"

"Good point Sharon. So Leslie, I'm going to do the same thing. Andrew's mom is running a daycare through an agency and I have already put a call in to them. They said they could fill me up if I wanted."

"I could never ever run a daycare! I know I'll be the type of mother who really only likes her own kids. Not that your kids aren't great!"

"Terri aren't you worried about your neighbours smelling this?"

"I'm not a hypocrite like you my dear. I don't believe there's anything wrong with smoking hash and I don't care if they know."

"I'm not a hypocrite!"

"Well not in any other aspect of your life, but you hide your smoking as much as you possibly can. I was so happy when you moved into that house with a garage! Now we don't have to walk around the block to smoke a joint so your neighbours won't smell it! Now we just stink up your garage!"

"Do I detect a note of sarcasm there?" Sharon asks.

"Well if it were me I would just smoke in the great outdoors. Have you seen how big your back yard is? I don't know if the smell could travel that far and through all those cedars to land on your neighbours' noses for them to misguidedly judge you."

"I'm heading in now. You have given me this lecture before. I'm just not comfortable being open about doing something illegal when they know I have a child."

"Whatever works for you darling, I'm not judging. I'm just calling you a hypocrite that's all. If you think something is OK you should shout it out! That's how it will hopefully get decriminalized someday."

"Fuck that … I want it legalized!"

"Like that'll every happen! I'm just thinking baby steps here Sharon."

"Terri this food is just what the doctor ordered."

"Glad you approve, but just remember it isn't really true that you're eating for two and the more you pack on now the more you have to unpack after!"

"You sound like my sisters."

"Cos I am your sista."

"Izzy do you know if it's a boy or a girl?"

"I haven't asked yet but I may not make it through. I'm so curious. It's only Leslie and Terri going on that makes me hold off. I'll admit during their pregnancies it was much more exciting when the birth happened."

"I was sure Sophie was going to be a girl even though I didn't ask. Her pregnancy was so different. Andrew never had so little sex in our whole marriage. After sex I would get so itchy I could have scratched the lips off my ocean pearl."

"Your what?"

"That's our new word for my bird! We were high and listing to that new song by 54-40 and dancing after the kids were all in bed. Suddenly it struck me toward the end of the song that they could be singing about a vagina. You know ... the whole smells like fish tastes like chicken thing! So I just did a little thrusting motion when they sang ... 'I got an ocean pearl' and pointed to my crotch. Well he found it hilarious and that's what he calls it now if we are talking code around the kids. I guess you had to be there!"

"I guess so. Oh you just made me think of this! Did you all realize that Kurt Cobain was 27 when he committed suicide?"

"So."

"Just that it was same age as Brian Jones, Janis Joplin, Jimi Hendrix and Jim Morrison! Quite the coincidence wouldn't you say ... all famous rock stars!"

"Really? I have no clue who Brian Jones is!"

"Wow, your level of not being a Rolling Stones fan is going off the charts here. He was a singer and guitar player with them, until they found him floating in a pool at a party."

"I bet we would all be drug addicts if we were famous!"

"Well you need to get us and the Hen story on Oprah like you keep promising. After all, you are The Grand Poobah. We're just your adoring chicks."

"Funny, I don't think so. Why don't you get that book you keep talking about written?"

"I'm keeping my notes. Timing is all wrong right now. I need to be able to sit down and not fall asleep. I was reading the boys a story last night and I just fell asleep half way through. Then Noah says rather loudly, 'Mom what happens next?' Well I wake up and read a few more pages and bam, I'm out again. Then Noah says, 'Moms aren't supposed to go to sleep till after you put the kids to bed.'"

"You need to get yourself some sleep or teach that boy to read."

"If I live through three children under five it'll be a miracle."

"The miracle happened by moving to the city and not commuting anymore. I don't think you would've made it through another year there without some kind of tragedy."

"Girls you have no idea. I haven't even told you all of the stories of me dozing at the wheel. They're too embarrassing. Andrew knew I just couldn't drive it anymore and we had to move, but he needed a little push. I can't even believe that I have this house. We had five weeks left to find a place. I was packing and had nowhere to move to!"

"You got very lucky."

"Or … is my husband just amazing at putting what he wants 'out there' and then making it happen! He was having nothing to do with a townhouse."

"Well he also stressed the shit out of you in the meantime."

"I know, believe me I know, but I admire him. He wouldn't settle and I'm really starting to trust that this positive energy stuff works. When I doubt it then it takes longer for things to 'happen'. I mean I did will the neighbour's dog to die. I don't even know why I second-guess this stuff. It is a real thing!"

"You know it is. Everyone in this room knows it is. It's just that really and truly believing in yourself is the most difficult thing you'll do. Andrew does it."

"But Colleen he's over the top sometimes. There has to be compromise."

"Leslie you're not his biggest fan because he's a risk taker and it hasn't always worked out. But in this situation compromise would have them living in a neighbourhood they didn't want in a townhouse they didn't want."

"Hey I would've been fine with a townhouse. Just moving back to the city was so euphoric I would live in a shoebox. But I don't because everything worked out and I'm learning to relax and trust that my husband may just have a super power! The seemingly impossible keeps happening. It's very remarkable. That day he just said let's drive through this neighbourhood and I was cranky and negative and said we can't afford this neighbourhood and two weeks later we own this house."

"Maybe we should start calling him Mast'r Splinter."

"I think you could for sure. He's very Zen without even embracing all my spiritual thoughts, but he respects them and he's fine with the no religion upbringing. I can't even tell you how many people ask us which religion we're going to raise the kids with … are you going to raise them Jewish or Catholic? I say neither … the reactions are interesting to say the least. Like a deer in the headlights … frozen surprise."

"Well I know Jean-Francois will be sending Abby to a French-Catholic school and there'll be no compromising there."

"They have all kinds of French immersion programs now and that way you could be involved with her at school. If you don't speak French you won't even be able to go on a field trip. When the time comes you need to have a serious discussion about that. I'm just pregnant and I've already started to check this stuff out."

"We never really looked at the schools in the area because we moved on the house so fast. One of Andrew's mom's friends told me that the public school here is dreadful and I should send them to the Catholic school."

"So why don't you?"

"Because I chose to be secular. I don't believe religion is necessary to raise children with morality. I think the reason she said the public school was awful is only because it's very multicultural. The school is in the rent-to-income housing area where there are many immigrant families who are trying to make it in this country. I want my kids to have the experience of having classmates who are from various backgrounds."

"Well it could be problematic if the kids can't speak English. It could slow down the teaching process."

"It may, I don't know, but I'll have a better idea in September when Noah starts school. We'll soon find out."

"I can get the no religion thing when I hear about Ireland and the Catholics and Protestants. Don't they realize how close their religions are? Why are they still killing each other?"

"I know right ... that isn't even a race issue. I mean in South Africa they just had their first interracial elections and now the dude who spent over 20 years in jail is the leader of the country."

"The dude is Nelson Mandela and that's a beautiful thing that has happened in this world lately. That is progress!!"

"Yeah well it's a sad world we live in when O.J. Simpson gets crazy media coverage and you barely hear about the massacre in Rwanda. I mean they followed him down the road for hours. It was media frenzy over two deaths. That's infinitely more gripping than 800,000 deaths that we barely hear about!!!"

"It's Hollywood Colleen. People love celebrity. The average person watches five hours of television a day. I don't get how that's fuck'n possible! When I heard that stat I figured they must have made an error. That makes me lose respect for the Western World."

"Listen to how lame we've become. Jesus we make a few babies and now we're all worldly and concerned citizens. My hemorrhoids are killing me or I would've gotten us up and boogying. Fuck Hen Night is going to the dogs!"

"No it's not, it's just evolving with us. I need to have some intelligent adult conversation."

"I'm so starving of adult company I stalked one of the mothers in the park yesterday. I followed her home so I know where she lives. I can do frequent walk-by's and maybe make a friend! All you need is one in the neighbourhood for a play date once in a while. Maybe I'm a bit too anxious … after all I managed with just one neighbour for the last five years. It's when they told us they were moving that Andrew finally agreed to sell. It may have had more to do with losing my income from taking care of their daughter. But who cares why … now I'm liv'n the dream."

"I have you beat. I had the mailman in for coffee yesterday!"

"Are they allowed to do that?"

"I don't know, but he came in and we had a nice visit. We have small talk nearly every day … it isn't like we're strangers. He's always so sweet to Abby too. He just looked so tired I thought I would offer him a coffee! I didn't actually think he was going to say yes. He was very appreciative … turns out he was hungover. Something I can relate to."

"There's my girl! Look at you stretching and yawning. I bet you could use a diaper change. Oh, how I love disposable diapers. We used those fancy cloth ones for Noah. I lasted six months and that was that. I didn't even empty and rinse that last pail full. After two weeks I threw the whole thing in the dumpster. I bet it kept even the animals away that week!"

I take Sophie upstairs to change her and check on the boys. They are curled up together on Noah's bed with the light on a book open on their laps. Noah will make up some fantastical stories while flipping through the pages. It is highly entertaining especially for Toby. I turn out the light, put the book away, and get the baby ready for the 11:00 pm feeding and with any luck she will last till 3:00 or 4:00 am. I head back down with a baby blanket and a screaming hungry infant.

"That child can wail."

"Tell me about it! As soon as these jugs hit her there'll be silence. Then she'll reach up and twirl my hair the entire time. Maybe she'll be a hair stylist? It's fun to think about who your kids will turn out to be."

"Well I pray for all you new moms that your kids don't turn out like mine. Believe me, healthy is not the only requirement. That's all you hope for when you give birth but then the list gets much longer ... caring, respectful, motivated and I've been ultimately disappointed on all those fronts. I know he has some real demons he's struggled with, and I've been patient, but at some point doesn't love conquer all?"

"Not for everyone Colleen. Some people are just stronger than others. Mental health is a very tricky thing. My mom doesn't even believe in mental illness, how insensitive is that?"

"That's because Mrs. Vetnor is an island, nothing breaks her shoreline down ... she's so tough, she just doesn't get weakness."

"Gratefully all of her kids are reasonably together. She would not have had a clue how to deal with any mental instability. I think if she was better equipped to deal with Ed's temper I may not have been his punching bag all those years."

"Personally I think it's time for some tough love. Kick him out and see how he changes his tune."

"Sharon you know I can't do that."

"Well as a friend I'm telling you ... you should."

"I've said it before and I'll say it again ... I can't wait till you all have freaking teenagers!"

We all talk till Sophie is done feeding and the girls prepare to leave. The new fines for drunk driving (which were long overdue) have all the girls car-pooling and Izzy is DD as she's now the pregnant one. I have a sleeping baby in my arms so I blow a kiss to everyone and thank them profusely for coming. Andrew is at the Photo Marketing Association conference with his boss till Sunday. I close the door with a bigger than big smile on my face. The thought of a screaming baby and two rug rats running around didn't keep them away. They were impressed with the boys and the fact that they didn't come down once. I didn't tell them that I had lemonade and chips up there and that I told Noah I would buy him a new game for his Gameboy if he managed to keep Toby upstairs. I guess I will have to find that in the budget now. I didn't think he could pull it off. He must have been very resourceful. The complete joy I feel now living in the city overwhelms me. We have been here for two weeks and I haven't stopped smiling. It is a nice change because I was crabby and bored and frustrated in the country. Andrew called me one day about a year ago and listened to me rant for a bit and then in his very calm demeanor tells me that just once it would be great if he called and I had something good to say. His words resonated like a constant distant echo and I stewed on them for days. He didn't deserve my anger or frustration. I have a lot to be thankful for and I was not very appreciative or nice sometimes. I would like to think that his phone call was a turning point in my behavior although I know it wasn't as pivotal as I lead myself to believe. Living there was hard. It got better once Satin died. Before that I lived in fear when I was outside, and I love to be outside. He was the neighbours' Doberman who used to come over and growl at us all the time. He would run beside the car growling and barking till we rolled down the window and said the magic words. Once I was working outside and Noah was sitting on the ground beside me teething on dirty sticks and I didn't even hear the dog. I looked over and there he was, inches away, baring his teeth to Noah. Of course I had already asked them to keep him tied up and they refused. They just told me to tell him 'a maison' (translated it means 'to the house') in a very firm voice. It always worked and it worked then … yet for a few seconds I thought my baby was about to be dog food. Satin dropped dead in the middle of a bitter winter day while he was running nonstop in circles around their house on his self-made racetrack (the dog was clearly a few fries short of a happy meal). When they came to tell us of his demise it was more about probing to see if we had poisoned him. I could barely hide my elation. I really had to work at seeming somber and sympathetic. That was the first day where I really started too believed that my thoughts could have an impact on real life. I had never wished as hard for anything as I wished for that dog's death. I was 28.

"Never give up on what you really want to do. The person with big dreams is more powerful than one with all the facts."

Albert Einstein

Week 950 – About Embarrassment

"Before we head out I just need to confirm that you're all coming to the Halloween Party. Abbey's so excited. She helped me put together Gracie's costume and we made pumpkin sugar cookies today."

"Where are those pumpkin sugar cookies?"

"Nowhere you'll find them!"

"I guess I can wait till Saturday. Yes we're going to be there. I'll speak for everyone. If I'm wrong pipe up."

"We do need to get going soon if we want to see the first set."

"Yes mother."

"I'm a mamma, but I ain't your mamma. We paid good money for these tickets and I want my money's worth!"

"You're starting to sound like you're married to a Jew! Speaking of tickets do you have them?"

"Yes, and bite your tongue! Andrew's the most generous person I know!!! Believe me, I wish he had that careful with money thing! Oh and Colleen isn't coming she had plans with Emma this evening."

"I'm surprised they're playing in such a small venue. Maybe we'll get to party with them!"

"If anyone can catch their eye it will be you. You look fantastic … love the outfit."

Leslie blushes at the sound of a compliment and goes to give her children a big hug and kiss goodbye. She loves to plan parties where we get all our families together. She has a good house for entertaining and the yard is so big there is lots of room for the kids to run around. We have started to go out for more of our Thursday's now that the children are older. They are much harder to keep out of sight. Our husbands are more than capable and they knew it was coming one day. Sharon finally had a baby boy. Kyle is two. Izzy had Hannah first and her second child Cole is also two. Abbey is six and her baby sister Gracie … also two. My kids are now nine, seven and five. It is a wonderful thing that our children are growing up together. Abbey and Sophie are the best of friends just like their moms. We have gathered here so we can all cab together. I am very grateful for the new drinking and driving laws now that I am a mother.

"Everyone grab a cocktail and we can go to the Hen Den before we head out. Jean-Francois took the kids up to bed."

"After we smoke those I can call the cab on my new cell phone! Andrew bought it for me once he sold his portion of the business! He's officially out!"

"That's massive news. Does that mean he won't be working 24 hours a day and you won't be late for every single Hen Night?"

"He only worked 24 hours a couple of times … let's not exaggerate. I think that his digital imaging company was a bit ahead of its time.

The equipment he and his partners bought three years ago is now half the price! Owning your own business is not all it's cracked up to be."

"It's hard as hell from all your stories. I'm so excited for you … but I hope he has a plan B."

"Of course he does … my husband is no slouch."

"Well … where will those monogrammed shirts be showing up for work? You know if he had a middle name … like everyone else on the planet, and it was Steven or Stewart his shirts would have A.S.S on them instead of A.S!"

"Easy Leslie it's a happy day. Andrew's largest client has hired him at the newspaper where he works now. We had dinner with him and his wife a couple weeks back and they're super awesome. I broke the ice on the 'I wonder if they smoke dope question' really quickly once I saw the huge Zappa poster in his basement."

"What, did you just say, 'Hey since you like Zappa you must like pot?'"

"Pretty much and Andrew gave me the death stare, then we all smoked a joint together. His stare of death turned into him grinning ear to ear. And that night he got a job offer!"

"Wait a minute … is that the same client that your husband was golfing with while you were in the hospital getting your tubes tied?"

"You need to let that one go girlfriend … I made Andrew go that day. I didn't realize that I was going to be so sick, or that I was going to have to call my dad to pick me up. None of that was his fault. I made a huge mistake in telling him to go ahead and play, that I realize … and is it fucking pick on my husband night or what?"

"It's just that sometimes he makes it so easy!"

"You're all just jealous because you know he worships the ground I walk on."

"And so he should! You put up with all his crazy shit."

"Everything he does is in the name of love and with his family's best interest at heart. None of you can argue with that!"

"No, we can't. We just question some of his decisions that's all."

"And I DON'T! But it comes back around to trusting that life works out even when it doesn't seem probable. That happens all the time. The bottom line is I trust him. He always figures it out. All of your husbands have good jobs with pensions and it's all very normal. My life will never be like that. I have to accept it, or I'll die young from worry," I say as I call the taxi.

"Sometimes too normal and too boring!"

"Leslie ... is Jean-Francois not coming around?"

"I want a partner for everything not just for domestic duties. I've now gone on two holidays with my children and no husband. When is the last time you've seen him at a party? Likely a year."

"Give him some time ... it was only a month ago that you packed his bags and read him the riot act."

"And since then we've gone out ONCE! You'd think he'd put a little more effort in! If he doesn't come with us next March break I don't know what I'll do? Being a single mother isn't on my top ten list of accomplishments."

"You two will be fine," Izzy says as we all go pile in the cab.

"Hello Mr. Cab Driver. How are you this evening?"

"I'm good ladies. And you?" We all reply with varying degrees of good to awesome and give him the address of the club.

"Did anyone have a chance to talk to Bruce at the last party?"

"We all did for a bit I think."

"Did he tell you about his world travels alone in his wheelchair?"

"That's mostly what Bruce talks about. He has remarkable stories."

"The one he told me was about trying to take a piss at Heathrow airport. It's the way he tells it that kills me. He's so animated and it takes him so long to get his thoughts out at times. I get impatient waiting for the next line, but he tells them all like they're comedies when in fact some of them are heart-wrenching!"

"Well what's the story?"

"He was at the front of the men's room trying to get someone to undo his belt buckle and then he could do the rest … i.e. stand up and take a piss, and no one would help him. He tried for ten minutes asking every stuffy Brit around. Since no one would help he went to the info/ help desk and asked there and do you know what they did?"

"No…"

"What they did was call an ambulance to take him to the fuck'n hospital and by the time he got there he'd already pissed himself. Then he nearly missed his connection. It's just ghastly, yet I died laughing through the whole story!"

"Bruce should have gone to the girls' bathroom and I bet he would've had success there. Hey Mr. Cab Driver can you turn up the volume please?"

"I have such a huge amount of respect for that guy. He's sort of my hero!"

"Did you know that he's writing a book for the handicapped on the best and worst places to travel?"

"He didn't tell me that Izzy."

"Well I heard it from Robbie."

"You are our gossip girl!"

There is a pause in the conversation as we all start singing Bon Jovi getting ourselves in the party mood.

"Terri I heard on the radio that your school will survive another year."

"Yes it will, but frankly if our council has to go through that battle every year it's too exhausting. They should just close the fuck'n thing … but it's been an amazing place for my kids. I wish they weren't such good kids because the principal is so hot I would love to be called into his office daily!!!"

"So that's why you joined the school council."

"He wasn't there when I joined. My motives were pure. Oh, and speaking of kids I have a classic Toby story. Every night as a family we do our *highs* and *lows* of the day at the dinner table and I had just taken them all for their physicals. Toby's turn arrives and he tells us that his low of the day was the doctor touching his testicles. Then he ponders for a minute and tells us that his high of the day was the doctor touching his testicles. His voice was nothing but pure innocence and when Andrew and I started laughing he was embarrassed because he had no idea just how funny that was."

"He's starting to show a nice natural sense of humour. Nothing like your sick sense of humour."

"What do you mean by that Sharon? I don't even have a sense of humour!"

"I mean you've been hanging around Leslie for too long. I called you the other day and Noah answered, and told me a story about you."

"Oh, sorry I missed you … what did he say?"

"He said that you were playing the Cruella game … whatever that is … with all the kids after school and then you caught Toby and flung him over your back till his face was pointing right into your arse, and then you let one rip."

"I did, and the kids thought it was the funniest thing they'd ever seen, and they all wanted a turn. I had to explain that I can't toot on command and it was a one shot deal."

"What's the Cruella game?"

"I'm Cruella Deville and they're all the puppies and I have to catch them all. Of course they keep escaping. It's good exercise."

"How many kids do you have after school?"

"I have three all day and then five more show up after school … but three of them are mine. Having the extra kids about keeps mine distracted. Sophie has such a crush on the neighbours' son. When he's around she's bound to do something inappropriate."

"That last story when she frantically wanted her dress removed because he showed up was something else."

"Where does that behaviour come from?! I mean she was four years old. It isn't like she'd been watching *Nine and a Half Weeks*. I used to think she would be a hairdresser. I'm now leaning towards stripper."

We arrive at the club and exit the cab and the driver says, "No need for a tip ladies … that was most fun I've had all day!" We laugh and give him a good tip. We present our tickets and head into the club. We find some stand up chairs around the edge of the third storey balcony. They are close to the bathrooms, the upper bar, AND we have a good view of the band. This place is such an icon of the Ottawa music scene. I have many memories … it feels great to be here. The last time I was here I fell asleep by the speakers and I was not drugged or drunk … I just made the fatal mistake of sitting down! I was DD and Sophie was a baby. Leslie is already talking with the group of people beside us and Sharon has gone to buy the first round.

"I thought I recognized you! Terri do you remember Craig from the occasional high school party!"

"Sorry, but I don't."

"Whatever … this is Craig … and I already can't remember your name, sorry, sorry."

"Hi, I'm Paul."

"Hi, I'm Terri and this is Izzy."

"I pegged you for another Zappa guy. I'm surprised to see you here."

"Well we did get free tickets!"

"That explains it. We grew up dancing to these guys and you have to support a good old Canadian band."

"They had some good commercial success in the 80's."

"And here they are playing Lordy's and we're going to dance the night away."

"Sharon did you get me a tall glass?"

"Does it look like it's a fucking tall glass? It's right in front of you."

"Oh … no it doesn't."

"Then it's not a fucking tall glass. If you want a tall glass, go get your own!"

"No need to be snarky. I just thought that you knew that I like a tall glass. This is perfect, thank you."

"You're right it's perfect."

"I think you need some loosening up girl. Sit down and I'll give you a little head and shoulder rub."

"I'd never say no to that."

"You're lucky I'm still talking to you let alone giving you a rub."

"I did have a crummy day and oh my god that feels good. Terri, you do have magic hands."

"So I've heard from various recipients."

"Terri you must know I give a better shoulder rub than you."

"Yeah, yeah, just like you roll better reefers than me ... NOT....
and maybe double NOT NOT!

"Funny!"

"I would be happy to give my honest opinion on the quality of your
shoulder rubs!" Craig says.

"Do I sense a little friendly competition starting? I would be more
than happy to rate you as well," his friend says.

"Here comes the band ... at the break you are on sista."

The rumble of an excited crowd takes over the club and the band
waits till the hooting and hollering slows down. Leslie is killing my
eardrums with her whistling ... the shrieking thumb and index finger
whistling. The crowd quiets down and Alan thanks everyone for
coming and at the quietest moment in the club so far Leslie shouts as
loud as she can, "GIANT TIGER WE LOVE YOU." Paul and Craig
are just about on the floor laughing. We don't know whether to laugh
or to hide because every person in our vicinity is staring at us. Some are
laughing ... some are sneering.

"Fuck Leslie, the band is GLASS TIGER ... you're going to get us
kicked out."

"Jesus, didn't I say that?"

"No bonehead you said ... no you YELLED, 'Giant Tiger' and the
whole place heard you," Izzy said.

Leslie starts to laugh with everyone else and really can't believe
that she said it. The brain works in mysterious ways sometime. We all
shop at GT Boutique and she must have been there recently! There are
a number of real serious fans staring at us, but the music diffuses their
irritation quickly. How fortunate that we are high up in the balcony.
The band won't have been able to tell who shouted it ... so dance

floor … here we come. We leave all our stuff with Craig and Paul and they keep our seats for us. At the break we head back upstairs.

"I could be wrong, but I think you may have hollered Giant Tiger again. You need to stop saying their name now and don't utter it again for the rest of the night."

"I did not say it again … 110% I did not."

"So glad you girls are back, I'm feeling a little stiff and looking forward to this massage-off."

"Right, but first I need a drink. My turn I'll be back in a minute."

"We need to do this right," Izzy says as she pulls a scarf out of her sleeve. "We can't know who's giving the massage … to remove any bias, because I get the feeling you'll say anything to get into Leslie's pants … which you won't, because she's married. You do know that?"

"Woah, I have no intention of trying to get into her pants. That doesn't mean that I wouldn't like to, but of course I know she's married."

"OK good, we understand each other."

Leslie arrives back with our drinks. Izzy has the whole competition organized. We will massage her, Paul and Craig. Each will be blind folded with the scarf by Sharon and she will keep track of who each one picks as the best. This is insane, I get it, but we have bantered back and forth about this for years and Izzy wants a definite winner so the subject will be closed for good. During the break we massage the three contestants. I am declared the winner as I knew I would be. Leslie is too pinchy, she uses too much finger and not enough palm. We have all received many massages from Leslie and I have given many massages over the years. It is all part of the Hen experience. We have a great night at the concert and it is obvious that Craig has a real crush on Leslie. It is also obvious that she is very attracted to him as well. She would never cheat, but just the fact that Jean-Francois has disappointed her so many times lends itself to a wondering eye. If you are not happy in a relationship of course you will start looking around. I am always hoping that he smartens up so she will not have to be a single mom. Once Leslie is in un-love she will never go back to love. That is because it will take barrels of disappointments for her to get to that point of actually breaking up her family. Since she is incapable of pretending she will have to leave her husband. All he needs to do is be with her … the dummy.

"Holy shit it's after 1:00 am. I totally forgot that we can party till 2:00 am now."

"It's about time Ontario woke up. Our bars would clear out to head to Hull by 12:30 am."

"Well in Quebec the drinking age is just a suggestion!"

"We partied there when we were 16 no questions asked."

"Speak for yourself. I tried to get in and my baby face was stopped right away. I spent the night in the car waiting for 3:00 am so I could go home. I never bothered going back."

"We didn't have to go to Hull cos Laura and Charlotte took us out."

"True enough."

"Paul and I are heading out. Do you ladies want a lift back to the hood?"

"Funny how none of us left."

"Well Colleen and I did. I'm not far but it isn't officially the hood."

"You need to do some tests before we'll leave with you. You need to walk a straight line and then extend your arms and bring your finger to your nose."

"I'm fine. I would never have offered otherwise. I have precious cargo," he says as he winks at Leslie.

"Craig, I'm on the way, could you drop me first? Anywhere close … you don't have to drive right to the house."

"No problem."

We all head to his car and squeeze six into five spots.

"Did you know that they're having a huge Millennium Bash there? It will be the place to be when 2000 hits."

"I don't think we'll go out because who knows what'll happen?"

"Izzy have your head read … girls, girls, this should be the biggest party of our lives, c'mon. I'll have a party if all you queers are worried the world will blow at midnight!"

"We'll be there if you want to do that Leslie."

"I do and you can all pitch in."

"The stuff people are doing is crazy. A friend of ours is planning on maxing out his credit cards and lines of credit and bringing all the cash home."

"Why?"

"He thinks that once the clock strikes twelve some bank glitch will make all his debts go away! I mean he can return it on the second, but that seems like a lot of effort."

"Well I plan on having some provisions in the house. I'd rather play it safe than sorry."

"Then I'm going to your house if the world goes wonky. Don't forget to get enough for five extra."

"No seriously, have some extra stuff in the house."

"I will just for you Sharon."

"You sound so convincing … now get out."

I get out of the car and walk into the house. Some of its charm has worn off since the move. We had to get our basement sealed in order to keep the water out and our pipes in the kitchen freeze if it hits -25 C overnight. We just have to keep water running those cold nights and we are golden. Even when it does freeze I only have to walk to the bathroom to get all the water I need. It is all relative right! I used to have to go to the lake and drill a hole! I reflect on our conversation about the turn of the millennium. It isn't everyone who gets to witness that kind of year change! When we were younger it was often the year we would ponder. When you are 18 the thought of being 36 means you're old. It was a lifetime away and now it is around the corner. The kitchen is tidy and I know Andrew made the extra effort to please me. He is simply a warm hug that never leaves you. In my nine years of marriage I have never wondered what life would have looked like if I hadn't married him. I certainly have questioned why he hasn't made his fortune yet. He has such confidence and loves business and is willing to take the risks required to succeed. He has never had control of his destiny, as his portion of the partnership was 48%. So many times he would disagree with decisions made, but could not do anything about it. He is going to work for a paycheque again and that makes me happy, but I know he will always be looking for the next opportunity and I will be there, strapped in beside him, on the Andrew roller coaster ride of life.

"And I know it aches … how your heart it breaks;
And you can only take so much … walk on"

U2

Week 1,100 – About Hearts Breaking

"Guess why I'm here so early?"

"Because your husband's in between old job and new job."

"No he has so much to do to finish up at the newspaper he's still working late. It's because I've left Noah in charge."

"You didn't waste any time … he's 12 for all of two months."

"He's a grown up 12 though, and Andrew should be back anytime now."

"So you shouldn't be late for anymore Thursdays!"

"Right … I shouldn't be, you know I will. I still get the biggest smile when I think that I'm no longer running a daycare!"

"You and me both. Izzy and Meagan's kids are dream children and having all girls was a lucky break, but the bottom line is that it's really hard work."

"I have preached it before because it's sort of true … drugs saved my children's lives. I was so tired of kids by dinner … the thought of spending another minute with them, even if they were mine was inconceivable! I think when you run daycare you're harder on your own because you don't want to seem like you have favourites. Going out just before dinner for a wee puff just made me a better mom through the evening. That day when Tammy bicycled over and told me how terrible her new daycare was I nearly changed my mind. I guess I just figured that everyone plays Cruella with the kids. Are you happy back at the lawyer's office?"

"Content would be a better word. I don't love having an office job, but it pays the bills. And I may need an even better job because I'm going to have to leave Jean-Francois. Please don't say a word to anyone else yet." Leslie starts to tear up at the thought.

"You know I won't. Are you very sure? What am I saying I know you're sure and I know you've tried for nine years to make this work. You of all people deserve to be happy. I should've stopped you from marrying him, I knew deep down you shouldn't do it!"

"Don't even say that!!! He's a great dad and we have two wonderful kids. I have zero regrets, but I don't want to spend the rest of my life bored and lonely because every time I go out, or on a 'family holiday' I'm without my husband."

"Leslie you didn't answer his marriage proposal for a day. He asked you, and then you ran out the door to go find a Hen to talk to. Then you picked a Madonna song for your first dance … *Crazy for You* doesn't even have the word 'love' in it. Then we heard about the wedding day when you and your dad were circling around in the car so you could compose yourself in order to make it up the aisle without passing out! These aren't the actions of a woman 'in love'. You've always 'loved' JF … I just don't know if you've ever been 'in love' with JF. We all figured he was a great catch that you would be nuts not to marry him! I'm your best friend and I'm so, sooo sorry that I didn't believe in you enough to think that you could do better! Your divorce is partly on my shoulders and I'll get you through it!"

By this time Leslie is in full sobbing and heaving and snoting mode, just like when I found her in the high school bathroom. She can't even speak. I grab her and hug her and let her get it all out. This isn't the first time we have talked about this and every scene we have ever painted has been abstract and dark. She knows Jean-Francois will be fine. She knows they will separate without lawyers and a big battle because she will be more than fair. If there is one thing that drives the Hens crazy it is hearing about divorces where the welfare of the children is not the highest priority. The most painful part will be the nights she doesn't put her girls to bed. That's what breaks her down. She knows she will have to settle for joint custody, but hopes that by making everything easy for him he will agree to alternate nights so that her longest time without will be just one day. We are expecting the Hens soon and then JF will bring the girls back around 8:00 pm and put them to bed. I remind Leslie of this and she starts to pull herself together.

"I was telling the boys about the colonoscopy I had yesterday. I told them that the doctor puts a little camera up your bum and looks around, but first they blow air up there to open up your bowel. Toby gives me the queerest look and tells me he never wants to be a doctor. So I ask why and he says he's never going to put his face down in anyone's bum to blow air into it." I get a smile from Leslie and that's all I was hoping for.

"That boy cracks me up!"

"You and me both, but he does have a bit of the devil in him. I think for the first time in his life the idea of Karma sunk in this week. He was chasing Sophie around the living room and then he stopped just around the wall and hid. As she came running around the little bugger put his foot out to trip her. I walked in to see it all play out. She went flying and nearly cracked her head open on the speaker."

"And those speakers are hard to miss."

"Don't remind me … I have resigned myself to the fact that they're ours for life! Anyway, I look at Toby and I can't even believe he would do such a thing. I explained how dangerous that could have been and sent him for a time-out. He likes to go half way up the stairs and once his time was up, and he started down he tripped and fell!!!"

"I don't get it."

"C'mon … it was a beautiful moment. Once I checked him out and he stopped crying I said, 'Now Toby that's Karma. You did a very mean thing to your sister and then shortly after something bad happened to you. That's why you always have to be kind.' I swear I saw a big bright light go off in his brain."

"Do you really think he fell because of that?"

"I choose to believe it, and if it makes my kids stop and think before they do something mean … it's a good day. I grew up knowing I could do all the mean shit I wanted and all I had to do was confess every Sunday and my slate was clean … zero consequences. You of all people know how mean I was at times! You can thank my good Catholic upbringing for that!"

"All your kids are sweet and you're a great mom, but you need to relax on the whole anti-God, anti-religion thing."

"I'm not anti-God at all!!! Anti-religion I'll give you that. I just tell them what I think God is and I do talk about Catholicism and Andrew's family talks about Jewish holidays and such. They do learn about religion. Oh and Leslie, you are an even better mom!"

"Funny! A great mom until I tear their whole world apart."

"No more talk of that. You know how I hate reality television … it's just one more thing that makes me loose hope for Western Civilization … but I watched American Idol with the kids the other night and it was pretty good. At least it has some purpose and that Simon is a character."

"I love him. Oh there're the girls. I'll go unlock the door."

"Speaking of unlocking the door … could you maybe for one Hen Night NOT lock the door? I mean you know we're all coming and sometimes I'll have to wait and wait before someone hears me. When was the last time some crazy psycho-maniac broke into a home in Ottawa and shot down the family? Those kinds of things only happen within the family, so unless you think your husband is going to kill us all can you please leave the door open when it's your Thursday!"

"It's just habit. It didn't know it was such an irritation … if it means that much to you I'll try."

"Have any one of you travelled since 9/11? I mean it's beyond brutal."

"Other than the travel, how was your romantic getaway to New York?"

"I was good, but Stan said we may as well drive next time for all the hassle it was. You actually feel like you might be doing something wrong because now we're all fucking criminals. I can't imagine how a traveler from the Middle East gets treated."

"What did they do?"

"Just how thorough every bag was checked … and the line-up was huge. You can sense the staff are terrified … ooohh I might let a terrorist through … check, check and triple check. Then they have massive garbage bins full of water bottles and shampoo and perfume people had in their carry-ons. Then security takes their shit away and they start arguing … 'smell it … its perfume … I just spent $150 on that bottle and you're going to toss it?' And now that the US is implicating Canada for letting in so many immigrants and some of the evidence they've uncovered is linked to Canadians … let's just say I wasn't feeling the love!"

"Well I still say Bush did it all, but I know you all think I'm crazy! Bush won in the most controversial election in US history. He's a bad man I just feel it!"

"I'm still on the fence on that whole issue, but Bush does nothing for me that's for sure."

"Whatever, let's move on. I have everything ready to do our pedicures, but let's get to the Hen Den before the kids get back."

"I have a reefer ready and let me tell you we won't be bringing drugs across the border like we used to! Don't ever do that again guys it isn't worth it."

"Don't worry, we won't. I think you're the only one crazy enough to do that. I never have."

"Jesus Leslie, you smoked a joint on the plane coming back from Jamaica!"

"Well I didn't bring it back, Robbie did. And I was like 20."

"So Sharon, we need the highs of the trip too please, not just the low."

"Well the best part was screwing on a bear skin rug in front of the fire."

"I screwed Paul under cedar hedges in his back yard. That was my first time!" Leslie says like it was the best screw of her life.

"Andrew and I screwed in the handicapped bathroom at the National Arts Centre."

"Enough of the screwing talk. These days I would fuck a guy in front of a burning pack of matches laying on burlap! I just want to get laid!!!"

"Colleen sorry ... we need to find you a date!"

"Damn right you do, because I can't seem to manage it."

"Sharon you were in New York City! How can having sex in the hotel room be your highlight?!"

"It was all great. We saw *Once* and *Jersey Boys*. We loved them both. We had fantastic dinners and New York is just amazing! It is like no other place I have ever experienced!"

"That sounds more like it!"

"Little Miss Poky-hontus must have had a hard time keeping up with the fast pace there!"

"Funny."

"So, I thought maybe we could watch *Friends* while we do the pedicures. We can just hang in the basement and JF can have the house."

"Izzy you're addicted to that show. You would have us watching it every Thursday."

"Well it's no big deal if we're in for the night, and have you seen it? It's fucking funny."

"Not as funny as Hen Night! Well some anyway. Sometimes we're way too serious and downright boring."

"Yeah, like doing pedicures and watching TV."

"Honestly this is a great night for me. It's just about getting together. Sometimes going out is a chore. Once I'm there I always have a good time, but I'm happy to stay in."

"I rented *A Beautiful Mind* if you girls want to watch it after Friends. I brought it because I didn't get to it last night."

"I saw it in the theatres and it's excellent. I think Russell was robbed for his Oscar on that one. No disrespect to Denzel but really! Have you seen *Training Day*?"

"They were both great."

"Colleen, *Training Day* was good … *A Beautiful Mind* was great. It's all political, just like the Olympics and professional sports. It was Denzel's turn!"

"You just love Russell because your husband looks like him."

"Only when Andrew grows a beard. It's actually amazing how many people tell him that. I've been with him when he got free donuts because she thought he was Russell Crowe, and he actually gave another girl his autograph cos she was so insistent. He puts on a little weight, grows a beard, and Michael J. Fox morphs into Russell Crowe!"

We finish in the garage and head downstairs before JF comes back with the girls. We all call him JF now when he is not around because we are too lazy to say his whole name. Leslie has her footbath out and bought oatmeal packets to soak our feet. When she gives a pedicure it is the real deal. She could turn professional. We are each in charge of preparing the footbath and then cleaning it for the next person and she does the rest. Her perfect job would be going around and helping people … regrouping their homes, their diets, their happy factor. As is in the case with many people she's not doing what she would love because it doesn't pay enough. She would make the perfect Home Support Worker but she couldn't afford to go back to school now. Not mention the wages are atrociously low for the work they do. Leslie could enrich the lives of so many, but they would only pay her ten bucks an hour. As for me I am not doing what I want because I still don't know what that is … I am passionate about writing my book someday. I think about that often. These days I have been doing office temp contracts here and there and photography part-time. I am the lucky one who gets to have the first footbath. Leslie finishes up with my feet and I grab the bin full of water.

"Sorry, sorry, Izzy I tripped over my own two feet."

"No problem I always wanted dirty feet scum water spilled on me fuck!!!"

"Don't worry lets run upstairs and get you something to wear."

"I'll get your bath all ready for you when you're back … sooorrry," I holler as they run up the stairs.

"Well she didn't hit you."

"Only cos she didn't want me to spill any more water, but I know she wanted to."

"I heard about your hubby's new job."

"Yes we're very excited. He's never worked in radio before, but sales are sales and he can sell."

"Didn't his ex-boss Mathew go there also?"

"Yup, he may have had something to do with it, but they're both Sales Reps so he isn't his boss anymore. Andrew just keeps following Mathew around. They've become best friends and Patti is great … I like her a lot."

"His wife?"

"Yes, we went on a family camping trip this summer and had a crazy good time! And this is the first time in our lives where the month runs out before the money! Man that's a good feeling. I am much more fun and relaxed now. As much as I try not to stress about money … I do. They say that's what my bald patches are all about."

"Well they always grow back. Was that the camping trip when you made your kids use pita bread to wipe their arse?"

"Why doesn't it seem obvious that I didn't want to use up my precious napkins? We were in the middle of nowhere in the canoe when both the boys needed to poo. I happened to have a lot of pita bread and only nine napkins … one each!"

"You're silly."

"There Izzy you look all cozy now. Your footbath awaits."

"Didn't mean to snap at you. It was just my reaction to having your scummy water all over me."

"Don't give it a thought. You can't piss me off these days even if you try."

"The new job?"

"Yup."

"I heard that Sam is supervisor with the city now! And you working at that private school ... how great is that gig?"

"I love it. So why don't you put on the movie only two Hens have seen it."

"That's fine with us. We can go out to the garage if we want. It's a lovely night."

"Sharon, are you looking for work now that Kyle is full days?"

"Stan doesn't seem to want me to go back to work just yet. Besides I keep busy with all his side projects."

"Andrew knows someone looking for a bookkeeper so I thought I would ask. How's the compost business treating you?"

"The compost business is a pain in my arse!"

"But is it worth doing? ... i.e. do you make any money?"

"Some, but not enough."

"Quiet, the movie's starting."

"Relax there'll be previews."

"Stan and Andrew are very similar in many ways."

Looks like tonight is a movie night. It isn't our first ... Leslie made us watch *Shirley Valentine* one night. I made them watch *Herold and Maude*. That one didn't go over as well, which was a big disappointment for me. I decide to watch Russell again and I pick up subtleties that I missed the first time. My kids watch movies over and over again. I know every song lyric to every Disney movie made!

I drive home in our minivan, the only vehicle that makes sense when you have three kids and a dog. Sometimes it surprises me that Hen Night hasn't faded away. It is Leslie. We all just love being around her. Often it is the best part of my week and I have a great life. It has not been an easy breezy life, but I am truly loved by many and I am alive. Andrew recently lost his brother to a three year battle with cancer. When mortality hits that close to home you have to appreciate every minute that air fills your lungs. I take a deep breath and smile. I smile to myself often. Whenever I have a happy thought I smile. Noah told me once if you are in a terrible mood just smile and it will help. It does, I have tried it. My husband says I have the most beautiful smile he has ever seen and that I should wear it at all times. I think he is mad, because I have pretty crooked teeth and an overbite. I am not like him; at times I struggle to be happy. I'm pretty sure that struggle is just another curse of being a woman who is a walking bag of chemicals that are in a perpetual state of change. At 12 years of age Andrew lost his father to some rare liver disease. His father was 47. His grandfather died in the Holocaust so no male has made it to 50. Granted there were not many of them! I will have one epic party when Andrew turns 50. I am 39. Next year the Hens all turn 40 … that is going to be a good party year!

"Let us be grateful to people who make us happy, they are the charming gardeners who make our souls blossom."

Marcel Proust

Week 1,294 – About Chatter

"So you won't believe what my husband bought this week."

"I'm not even going to try to guess. It could be an ocean going sailboat, or a thoroughbred racehorse … who knows? And somehow it was free or bartered for something!"

"Not free or bartered. It's actually very expensive for a motorcycle that's 20 fucking years old."

"I love motorcycles! That's better than I expected!"

"Really he just bought another business and we have no money … AGAIN … and somehow he finds some way to get his dream bike. This is how he sells me on the whole thing … 'I made a promise to myself when I had to sell my bike to build a shed that when Noah was 16 I would buy myself another bike. I cannot break that promise to myself.' Leslie, do you have any idea how many promises I break to myself?!"

"Me too, every Thursday I promise to take better care of myself and start exercising. I break them weekly!"

"I know right … I don't get why I let him do all these things."

"Because his brother and father are dead. It's that simple."

"You're right and it'll all be fine. You should see the smile on his face when he's riding his BMW R-65, of which only 500 where ever produced … and blah, blah, blah."

"You'll always let him do what makes him happy at any cost to you. I figured that out a while ago. Once I came to that realization I could finally say that I really do love your husband. I stopped blaming him for your crazy life because you're his biggest fan. Anybody can see how much you love each other still. I envy you."

"I know you do, because you never wanted to break up your family, but it was necessary and you're happier. Things did have a way of working themselves out."

"Well life would be easier with a partner that's for sure."

"Darling you're 43 … you look 33 and sexy as ever….you'll meet the man of your dreams."

"Well I'd like him now, dating sucks big cock. Fuck I'd suck a little cock … I just want and nice guy that I'm attracted to … who happens to like sex! I've been doing the on-line scene and it just isn't me."

"We could go out to the bars more often."

"Bars are so much more fun when you're not actually looking for a date. I go to a bar now and I'm checking out every guy there. Then I may go talk to one I think is cute, and I may bring him home and get laid and we may date for a while and then it ends."

"Well maybe if they weren't 20 something! You need to look for an older guy. Young will never work, trust me."

"Your husband is younger!"

"Two years doesn't count. If you met someone 41 … I would be down with that."

"I'm just as happy to spend all my Hen Nights here."

"Yes, good planning. The ex has the girls every Thursday."

"Not like he didn't already have them then … and he has them Tuesday and Saturday. Plus he travels some for work now and I get them whenever he goes away. I love that."

"You did make it through your divorce."

"Separation, so I can stay on his benefits!"

"Right. So here's my latest family story. The other night Noah and some buddies were over and Andrew heard them talking all tough and cool and wanted to put them in their place. These guys are all actors (Noah goes to an arts' school and is in the drama program) … no jocks among them! So Andrew calls them all upstairs and teases them about how tough they are/aren't. Then he comes and grabs me out of the kitchen and sits me down at the table and says I bet not one of you can beat this here mom in an arm wrestle."

"So did you kick their butts?"

"I beat two of them and the third wouldn't wrestle me, the pansy. They won't be talking so tough for a while. The one promise I made to myself and haven't broken yet paid off that day."

"When you told me that on your 43rd birthday you were going to run for 43 minutes and do 43 sit-ups and 43 push-ups, I wasn't thinking you were actually going to do it! I've seen you run!"

"Well it isn't really running … more like shuffling. I don't have speed like you, but I've built up endurance. Isn't anyone else coming out tonight?"

"Izzy and Sharon have some end-of-the-year school stuff, but they're coming after. Colleen should have been here. I do wish she didn't sleep over every week."

"I don't blame her. When I lived in the country I sure wanted to stay the night."

"I know … I hate sounding so terrible. I never thought these words would exit my mouth, but I love waking up and having the house to myself. How is Noah doing?"

"He is amazing as always, but his scar is so fresh, he needs to put zinc on it, but doesn't! He thinks it looks like a babies butt crack. I hate to see him spend time in the sun with it unattended. It looks like someone tried to decapitate him."

"Everyone seems to be eating up the goiter story. I don't know how you keep it together."

"You just do because you have to. So … I made a large life decision this week. I decided to go and work for Andrew and Mathew. I know how Andrew is … he has zero organizational skills. I don't think Mathew is much better! They can't pay me much, but I think this business will do better if I'm around. I'm still mad that he agreed to a 50/50 split. You'd think after his last experience he would've learned."

"So why did he do that?"

"He said that the last time he had the smaller percentage and he totally loves and trusts Mathew and it's the fair thing to do."

"I suppose that makes sense."

"The problem with 50/50 is that if you're at a stalemate nothing gets done … kind of like a minority government. Mathew is stubborn and Andrew is easy going. It could be awful."

"Well they're only a few months in, no need to panic yet. Are you sure you want to work with your husband? What am I saying … you two are always together even when you're not."

"Funny! Finally the girls have arrived." All three walk in the door together.

"I know right … half of Hen Night wasted on a school event! As soon as I got the form I called and said that they really needed to change the night cos I'm busy every Thursday!"

"I'm sure you did! Funny you say that because my council changed to Wednesday's to accommodate me!!! So, will the kids be moving up a grade?"

"Cole is excellent. He breezes through everything … Hannah not so much. They're going to IPRC her."

"I hope that isn't an acronym for Interstellar Play and Recreation Centre."

"No they're not sending her to the space station although sometimes I wonder if that isn't a good place for her!"

"Izzy you're awful! What is it really?"

"I can't remember the actual name, but the teachers put processes in place that will help her out. For example they'll give her more time to write tests."

"It means Identification, Placement Review Committee."

"That's it … Colleen you're so smart!"

"It's about time that the school system recognizes not every child learns the same."

"Don't get me going on the school system. Kyle told me that his whole class had to put their heads on their desks through recess because of one kid misbehaving. He was likely only misbehaving cos he needed to get out and let off some steam!"

"I mean with childhood obesity on the rise like it is why would they be allowed to cut recess? It may just be the only exercise they get! Why don't they bring back gym class and get rid of all the crap they sell in the vending machines?"

"Kids will always pick the sugar over the healthy. If they aren't given a choice … they'll pick healthy if they're hungry enough.

"Oh girls we now have the ability to video our Hen Nights and air them to the world, for free. Abbey showed it to me. It's called YouTube … you have to check it out."

"We still have the problem of not having a video recorder and the fact that no one actually wants to be videoed."

"I get it but just one night would be fun. OK, I'm way past due for a trip to the garage."

"Really? It's beautiful out! Can't we just stay here on the porch under the trees?"

"Terri you already know the answer … it's no big deal! Leslie doesn't want her neighbours to find out she's an evil dope smoker."

"Yes I know, but it gets smoky and stinky in there."

"You all can smoke your cigarettes anywhere you want. I don't have one problem with that! I would prefer those stay out of the garage." Sharon starts to light up her reefer just to be a stinker. "I can hear the neighbours are outside … get in the garage!"

"But they're like 100 feet away with thick beautiful cedar hedges between!"

"I don't care, not one iota … get the fuck in the garage!!!"

Leslie has the Hen Den done up delightful. This is not your typical garage. It is clean and tidy and always ready for entertaining. It is a double car garage so there is plenty of room as there is rarely a car in it. She has strung Christmas lights through the rafters and has her old ghetto blaster with some CD's nearby. She always has music ready. Over time she has collected a carpet, a small love seat and a chair to make it homey. Her cooler is the coffee table. She has several pictures on the back wall (one of us at our grade 12 grad) and my favourite stitchery which depicts five black crows sitting at a bar and across the top it reads CROW BAR.

"Leslie have you had any dates lately?"

"The last shit show I had on Saturday could hardly be called a date. Every time I say I'm done with on-line … I torture myself again because I'm so bored. So I meet this guy at a coffee shop and the entire time he's talking about himself, a complete narcissist…"

"Wow, good word girl."

"I know, right. I love using big words even if I can barely say them. It took me five tries with mom and then it finally sank in."

"Back to the date please." Sharon's impatience always prevails.

"So when we're getting ready to leave he asks when we can see each other again."

"So I say never. And you won't believe what he says to me next."

"Try us …"

"He has this very matter of fact voice and obviously couldn't give a shit that I just said 'never' and then says, 'just before you leave I have to ask … are those real?' I mean I'm so dumb, I asked him… 'Are what real?' And he says, 'Your tits are they real?'"

"Please tell me you're making that up! Who could be that crass?!"

"You know I can't lie! I was stunned. I'm not going on another date unless I've met and talked to the guy or someone sets me up. Ask around girls … someone must know a single guy?"

"We're all on high alert at all times. I probed the mailman the other day, but he has a girlfriend."

"Well tell him to keep you posted if they break up and he wants to get laid! Man I miss regular sex."

"Leslie, it's time for the vibrator. At least you can get your yaya's out and won't feel the need to sleep with them on the first date."

"Colleen you're kidding, right! How can that replace a man with a hard fleshy cock that I can suck on baby," she says as she brings her beer bottle to her mouth and swallows it while taking a sip.

"Seriously you neeeeddddd a vibrator. I'll buy you one."

"I know all of you use them."

"And everyone we know. You're the only girl I know who hasn't."

"I should try it shouldn't I?"

"Leslie it's OK to give yourself sexual pleasure when you feel the need. It's healthy. Do you find it offensive or gross when men jerk-off?"

"No."

"Then what's the difference."

"Fine! I'll get one and try it out. It must be better than going on these dreadful dates. At least till Mr. Right shows up."

We all head over to the porch to enjoy the night air. Leslie and Izzy go to the kitchen to replenish all our drinks. As Leslie exits the door with drinks in hand she hollers in her best party voice, "Who's gonna roll d'ah next reeeeffffer?" Sharon and I look at each other and just start to laugh.

"What?"

"I think they may be laughing because you just told the whole neighbourhood that you wanted someone to 'roll a reeeffffer.'"

"Oh Bye Jesus I did. That was loud … wasn't it?"

"Yes it was … miss hide in the garage … I don't smoke!!!" Sharon teases as we are still laughing.

"Leslie, you must realize that they likely all know. I mean every Thursday we're here making noise and carrying on."

"Whatever, so far none have called the cops on me."

"That was a classic Hen moment I shall never forget!"

"Me too, and by the way, sorry I didn't ask earlier, but how is Noah doing since his surgery? I know it all went fine, but still it's hard to have your kid get his neck sliced open."

"The scar is healing slowly and he doesn't cover it well enough in the sun, but otherwise all systems go."

"That's a strange thing to happen. I thought they got rid of goiters once they started iodizing salt."

"Since when do you know so much about goiters?"

"I don't know I just read that somewhere."

"Speaking of reading … that war that Bush got those poor Americans into is a disaster."

"I don't think those American's are so poor. They did vote him in for a second term."

"I'm so grateful every time I see anything on that war that Chretien had the balls to stay out. That day he became my favourite Prime Minister ever."

"Leslie, why don't you let your mom come over more often?"

"For Hen Night, are you crazy?"

"That time she showed up in the French maid outfit to serve us all was hilarious."

"That was planned so I knew to wait before I smoked anything."

"Has it worn off yet, having your parents back?"

"Starting to get used to it and I love … love … love having them back … especially getting to know my baby sister again. And I can walk to their house!!!"

"I'm going in for a refill who wants a drink?"

"Colleen again? I'm sure you've downed two or three to my one tonight."

"Well sometimes the stars are all lined up and it's a party night!"

"That's so true. I think it's our hormone changes that make certain nights the perfect party night! You go girl."

"I will, and I would also like to bring to your attention that offices are now smoke-free … here it is … wait for it … I TOLD YOU SO!!!"

"Thank Christ I'm not working now! Timing is everything."

"Restaurants are just around the corner."

"I still can't believe they'll do that!"

"Really, the writing is on the wall."

"Well what'll all the 'servers' do when no one is in the restaurant?"

"What's up with that? I mean really why do all these words now have to be gender neutral? I was fine being a waitress."

"Also what if you read in the newspaper about an actor and their name is like Jamie something, you won't even know if they're a boy or a girl."

"I know right. It's just taking things farther than they need to be taken."

"It's the feminist movement ladies. We need to get on the bandwagon."

"Well if being a feminist means being like a man I won't jump on that wagon."

"No silly they're just advocating being equal to men."

"But we're from different fucking planets ... how can we possibly be equal? Not to mention we can't be equal because we're just a wee bit better! Think about it ... we can do anything they can do, and we have the one thing they'll never be able to do. Personally I feel that's what tips the scales in our favour!" Colleen says slurring her words.

"Well you won't meet a man that would agree with that, and it's more about equal pay and rising up the corporate ladder."

"Well I happen to know that Liberia and Chile have their first women as heads of the country."

"Sounds like we're getting there."

We are back and forth between the porch and the garage all night and everyone seems to be in fine form. Colleen is drunk and it won't be long before she passes out.

"Let's go for walk in the field … just a small one. It is so nice out there."

"Leslie, it's really nice in your yard and there're cocktails and chairs."

"C'mon you queers … you're all lazy. You can bring your drinks. I won't stop singing if you don't come with me and I don't know any of the words … la la la if you don't come with me … o blah de oblah da life goes on yeah la la la la life goes on … yeah, yeah life is good when you getting regular sex…la..la..life is good."

"Fine we'll go for a walk with you. But it will be short."

"I'm not going for a walk, fuck that." Sharon says decisively.

"Izzy and Terri come on, you know you want to."

"We are … can't you see us getting up. It's actually less painful than listening to you drive us crazy."

We both head to the hedges where the opening to the field is. Just as we get through Leslie leaps on Izzy and puts her in a headlock. Izzy starts to fight back, but she is no match. She drops Izzy to the ground and then grabs me. We wrestle for what seems an eternity. I want to quit, but I also want to get her down. I am way too drunk to be exerting myself this way so I let her drop me to the ground. I end up in a wet patch that was Izzy's drink. I decide I'm calling home and sleeping over. Izzy has not gotten up yet.

"You fucking queer you made me twist my ankle. It really hurts! No more sneak attacks psycho!"

"Leslie, sometimes it's best not to wrestle when we have all had a few. Izzy are you OK? Can you walk?"

"Well obviously I haven't fucking tried yet because I'm still on the ground!"

"Here, let me help you up." I grab her and Leslie goes to her left side. We get Izzy on her feet and she starts to move around.

"Now I can't go for your fucking walk so can I go back and sit?!"

"We've wrestled tons before and you never got hurt. I didn't mean to hurt you, you know that?"

"Yeah, yeah … my cocktail's somewhere on the ground."

"I'm going to run and make you another one right now."

"Run away, that's right or I may just headlock you!"

Leslie's backyard has three large maple trees, a tree house, a porch with a table and chairs and one of those two seater swing chairs which she moves around the yard depending on how she feels that day. In order to stay outside after it cools down she'll bring us blankets and sleeping bags. It is June and nobody wants to be inside. We all gather back on the porch.

"That wrestle was almost as good as the cottage one Terri."

"That cottage wrestle was nothing compared to how hilarious you were after the wrestle … all proud of yourself giving me attitude then turning around and walking right into that tree!"

"I can still picture it." Izzy says. "Just thinking about it makes me feel better."

"Then she gets up brushers herself off and runs into it again!!! We'll never get those moments back, but they'll be rewinding in the memory banks forever."

"You got that right. I peed myself that day! Things just don't work as well as they used to. I totally regret not doing more Kegels!"

"I need to pee!" Colleen excuses herself.

"I don't think she'll be coming back!"

"We'll see."

It is getting late, as we talk a while longer we start to gather all the mess from outside and bring it in. Leslie has the music on so we move to the living room and dance for a bit, because we can. Izzy and Sharon head out and Leslie and I crawl up to bed. We go to check on Colleen. The room is empty. We move into the next room. Empty also. We give each other a look and move to Leslie's room. Everyone knows if I sleep over I get Leslie's bed, it's the Hen Hierarchy. It is the most comfortable and girls don't have that homophobic problem that men do about sleeping together.

"She must have gone to the basement."

"Well I'll just crawl into bed and you go check. I may not make it back up the stairs."

Leslie runs down and I hear her scream, "She's not here! Wholly fuck what happened to her?"

I hear the back door close as Leslie goes to check in the back yard. Then the back door opens, "Terri she's not anywhere get your arse in gear … we have to find her."

I get out of bed and Leslie is in full panic mode. I check the whole house again and nothing. We then start to walk into the field at 2:00 am.

"Leslie this is crazy. We need help. What if she passed out somewhere out here? What if she just wondered off?"

"We didn't check the tree house!!!"

We race, trying to keep our balance, back to the tree house … nothing. We decide to call Izzy and get her to come back and help.

"I'm not coming over … I'll send Sam … this is too scary."

While we wait for him we are calling out for Colleen like a lost dog, again nothing. We go in to greet Sam and thank him for coming. He proceeds to check the whole house because he figures we're drunk enough to miss something. Nothing. He goes out onto the porch and sees the chair swing there with the sleeping bag on top. He goes over, peeks inside and there she is.

"You got me out of bed for this. I'm going to kill you girls!"

"Wholly crap, it didn't look like there was a body in that bag!"

"Well the cops may find two body bags here in the morning, fuck! I'm leaving and don't cry wolf again unless you have checked ALL possibilities! Fuck'n drunks!"

"Sorry Sam … we love you … thanks so much for coming to our rescue!"

We return to Colleen to try and get her up, but she won't budge. We put another blanket on her. We head upstairs laughing about Sam's face when he saw her in the sleeping bag. I crawl back into bed for the second time and within minutes I hear the sound of breathing that is low and shallow and completely comfortable. Leslie is asleep and before me … it's a miracle! I rarely sleep over because I like to be back for my family in the morning. Andrew and I have raised two teenagers and a pre-teen and what a fun time we have together. Colleen was wrong, along with just about every parent I have ever discussed teens with. Teenagers don't have to be horrible! My kids aren't, they are respectful to adults and good to each other. Not to say that they don't fight. They bicker all the time, but they don't ever want to physically hurt one another. Not like when I was growing up. My three brothers had bones broken and even a head spit open. Ron threw a fork and it missed so he took Michael's head and brought it over to the fork stuck in wall and made contact that way. Crazy right? My brother Ed threatened to take my life on an almost daily basis!

My kids have never screamed 'I Hate You' or told me to fuck off. They repeatedly tell me how lucky I am that they're nice because they hear stories about their friends' families. There was some luck involved! The boys have a genetic disposition very much like their father's. They both play hockey and neither have ever been in the penalty box! People say that's not normal. I say, "Why?" We have raised mentally healthy and morally sound individuals. Wow, even without religion attached to the upbringing … go figure … it can be done. I feel confident that I have been the best mom I could be. I have many guilt moments that I would love to take back and I am not even close to perfect, but they have always known that I love them more than anything in this world, and I have always encouraged them to dream big. I feel myself dozing off while thinking about my own big dreams. I am 43.

"The proper office of a friend is to side with you when you are wrong. Nearly anybody will side with you when you are right."

Mark Twain

Week 1,506 – About the Unexpected

"Toby you cutie patootie … get in here and say hi for a moment. You look handsome tonight do you have a big date or something?"

"No I'm just dropping mom off at your BBQ on my way to work."

"I'm so glad to hear that, it must mean she's sleeping over!"

"No, she told me to pick her up after 9:00 pm when I'm finished."

"She didn't … what are you sick or something?"

"He's pulling your leg darling, but I'm not sure if I'm sleeping over."

"Toby, good one … you had me there! You remember the girls?"

"Yes of course, hi all."

"I need a good catcher's glove for Cole. If I come in to the store can you help me out?"

"I'll hook you up."

"Toby you can hook me up anytime. Hook me up against the bed post that is!" We simultaneously stare at her in shock.

"Colleen is that necessary? Look at his face … you've damaged him for life. He'll never pop in for another Hen Night!"

"And so he should be horrified. I could be his grandmother! You know I'm only teasing! I thought it would get a laugh!"

"Well another Herold I'm not."

I start to laugh, but the girls don't get it. I explain he is referring to the movie *Herold and Maude*.

"On that note I think I'll excuse myself. I might have said, I think I'll head out, but I didn't want to open that door for all you cougars!"

"Good thinking young man. Get out while you can! It was good to see you."

"You're looking hot, keep up the good work."

"Thanks for the drive love, I'll call home later."

"Well that was fun."

"My God women are you already drunk?"

"No just high."

"I don't think he'll be in a rush to visit again. So how's everyone?"

"Not believing you're already here!"

"When we finish the mailing for the month, and it goes smoothly, which is very rare, I can get away early. I left at 2:00 pm and did my Terri shuffle home. I even took the nine kilometre route!"

"How is your … what do you call it again? Oh yes … cooperative direct mail business doing?"

"We just had our best quarter ever!"

"Good to hear, you two work very hard. I hope it all keeps going well."

It is late May and we are having our usual BBQ for Izzy and Colleen's birthdays. They are one day apart. I am keeping my fingers crossed that Sharon shows up. I miss her. Hen Nights without Sharon are what *All in the Family* would be like without Archie Bunker. They are so very different. Meagan is here and Cindy as well. You just never know when these two will show up. Cindy has hosted on occasion because she loves to bake and entertain.

"Why didn't Noah come back from university this summer?" Cindy asks.

"He didn't find anyone to sublet his apartment, so I told him he better get a job and help pay for it. I don't think he tried overly hard cos he prefers to stay in Toronto anyway."

"Does he love theatre school?"

"Totally, but sometimes I wonder why I ever encouraged that path. It could be the waste of one great brain and it's such a competitive industry."

"I would've made my kid go to the IB (International Bachelorette) Program."

"You would not Izzy. I simply asked him, 'How would you like to spend your high school years? Being creative, and acting, and making productions, or with your nose in a book for four years?'"

"None of us were ever that smart! That kind of decision never crossed our paths!"

"We could have been if we'd applied ourselves. We were in the wrong crowd for success!"

"That depends on how you define success. I'm happy. If Noah makes his living doing what he loves … isn't that success?"

"The best kind!"

"So Meagan, what brings you out this fine evening?"

"Some de-stressing … I left my husband and he's making it as hard as a fine cut diamond."

"I'm so happy for you … I mean I'm so sorry to hear that. It's just that, Meagan, that night when I told you that Andrew and I rarely fight you were gobsmacked! You couldn't wrap your head around it because you said that you two fought almost always. I felt bad for you."

"How long has it been since you told him?"

"Six months of hell on earth! We take turns sleeping in the basement."

"We're so, so sorry … that it isn't going smoother."

"I can't believe it took you so long to come out for some Hen therapy!"

"Me too … I've already smiled more than I have in six months."

"How are the girls?"

"Considering the reasons behind the separation I'm surprised they aren't more supportive. They've watched him be cruel and then some, for years."

"Wow, another marriage bites the dust. Izzy it's just you and I sticking it out with the same old men."

"Meagan, you and Sharon should get together for a drink. She's also going through hell, but she's the one dishing out the hell on Stan."

"Izzy relax, lately the only side you get is Stan's side."

"Why isn't she here?"

"She hasn't come to a Hen Night since Leslie had a heart to heart with her. She didn't like much what she had to say!"

"Which was?"

"I just told her what I thought. I mean she behaved exactly how we girls always said we never would. She played Kyle against him. If your ex-husband is busy, take your child. She would refuse just so he had to scramble for a babysitter. She hired a lawyer cos she didn't feel she was getting her fair share. I mean once you do that so much goes to the lawyer. All I can say is they must have a lot more money than we thought they had."

"I had no idea."

"I still call her and invite her when there's a larger crowd coming, just in case, but she hasn't shown up yet."

"Why did they split up?"

"She'll tell you it's because Stan was having an affair, but I think he only did because he found out about hers."

"Sharon hasn't had a good thing to say about Stan in years so it's just as well. They'll figure it out."

"Well she's gone off the deep end some from what I hear."

"Which is all from Stan … you have to keep that in mind."

"Why do you see Stan all the time?"

"Cole and Kyle still like to hang out. Once they start high school I figure that will change."

"It does … Abbey and Sophie hung out all the time till then."

"Wow lots of changes. I can't believe Sharon isn't around anymore!"

"Neither can we, but it's her choice … it isn't like I haven't tried."

"And what's new in Leslie's life these days?"

"Well I have hinted enough to Chris …"

"Affectionately known as the Hebrew Hammer! Leslie thought he was Italian and when he told her he was Jewish she came up with that one pretty quick! He could be a poster boy for the Israeli army!"

"Yeah, her poster boy with the big cock! Leslie's in heaven!"

"… as I was saying, I've told him it's been three years and maybe we should be moving forward in our relationship … like move in buddy!"

"Absolutely! Once we reach this age we can't spend tons of time on a relationship that isn't giving us what we need. What are his excuses?"

"Mostly cos of his son. Apparently he's not that comfortable around me and the girls. Maybe if the little shit would come around more he could get comfortable. Chris is too easy on him because of their messy separation he's always walking on broken glass. Sharon is a saint compared to his ex."

"That sucks."

"No kidding. I've had a crush on him since our first date. I mean this one isn't just that I'm in love with him … I have a crush on him too. That makes it soooo much better. But life would be easier if he just moved in. This single parent thing is wearing thin. I knew he was a keeper when he woke up one morning and he says, 'Am I living a scene from *The Godfather*? Will I find a dead horse at the bottom of the bed?' Aunt Flo from Red Bay had arrived and there was blood everywhere. Then after we cleaned things up he still wanted to do me. I have no problem with that, but I told him I better go get a towel. Then he says, 'Maybe a tarp is in order.' I love that he makes me laugh."

"OMG Leslie … only you. I'm so glad you're happy."

"She's always happy when she has a cock … I mean a date. Let me tell you she can be a pretty cranky single mom! I hope he moves in soon."

We all brought something to contribute for dinner and our own meat for the BBQ. Leslie has the Bee Gees playing and girls are in the kitchen and on the porch nursing the BBQ. We have all the salads and extra food displayed on the table in the dining room. Leslie's home is a center hall plan and she complains about it all the time. The living room runs the length of the house so it's a rectangle. She has a hard time configuring the furniture to her liking, so she changes it constantly. Some Hen Nights the first hour is spent rearranging her living room or basement. It is the least we can do since she welcomes us here every week. She has managed to keep her home and pay for almost all the girls' extras on her much smaller income. Since her separation her number one and only priority has been her girls. She has been taken advantage of by her ex, in so many ways. She will not ask him to chip in for a birthday party (even though he will be there), or give her any more money than has been agreed upon. She is fiercely proud and does not want to cause any tension between them. She wants the girls to have as close to a family unit as possible. She bites her tongue and just roles with it all. She overcompensates due to her guilt from breaking up her family. I wish she could stop blaming herself and just read him the riot act one day.

"So we can finally dine in comfort and I can once again say, I TOLD YOU SO!"

"What are talking about? The patio table isn't that comfortable."

"I'm talking about the restaurants. They're all non-smoking and it's amazing. Maybe by making it difficult for people to smoke the rate of smokers will go down."

"It's a wonder that anybody even starts these days."

"Oh, but the youth never change. If they're not wired well … their dumber side will rule. I'm so very grateful that my three don't smoke. I can't imagine they would start now."

"How do you handle the subject of drugs with your kids?"

"Well, Noah busted me when he was in grade eight. Not an actual sighting, but through a mere gesture I made at the dinner table. He was talking about health class and how they were learning about all the types of drugs and that marijuana was a hallucinogenic one. All I did was smirk and the little shit points at me and says, 'You've smoked pot.'"

"What did you say?"

"I just said we'll discuss it later and then I told him that I had done it a few times and that was all. I also let him know that it doesn't make you hallucinate. We don't openly smoke around them, but they know that we do it. I also know that they've all tried it. Sophie's the one who's most into it. All her little acting buddies are good kids. I believe they're responsible. Most of us have had our kids talk about their experiences smoking pot. I know Abbey has and definitely Ruth's kids. I guess the apple don't fall too far from the tree!"

"I hate that fucking expression!"

"Sorry!"

"Girls, do you remember when I told you about that $300 parking ticket?"

"Yeah, in the spring and you parked over the handicapped line by like a foot."

"I did, but there was snow on the ground and I had to make a judgement call. I was so mad I put in a request to fight the ticket and I had my court case yesterday. Colleen came for moral support because I was so nervous."

"So how did it all turn out?"

Colleen took over the story, clearly anxious to tell it, "Izzy pleaded her case finally. She was the last one. You have to sit through it all till you're called. It seemed to be going fine and then the judge said that they do not tolerate any parking in handicapped zones. Well Izzy starts to 'BUT' her and she doesn't like that. The judge says she stands by her decision. Then Izzy blows … she says in a court of law … 'you have got to be fucking kidd'n me? I did not park in the spot. I parked over the fucking line that I couldn't see due to the snow! It's not my fault the snow melted while I was shopping and that arsehole gave me a ticket.' I couldn't believe she flipped like that! I tried to shut her up." Izzy finishes her story. "Then the judge very calmly says to me, 'Are you quite finished?' And I say, 'Well that depends' and she gives me the death stare and proceeds to double my fine and kick me out. Before I could say a word Colleen gagged me and pulled me out of the court room."

"Holy shit Izzy … you need some anger management training. You don't do that in court."

"Fuck, I'm surprised they didn't throw you in jail. She probably wanted to!"

"Well my little episode sure didn't help me. Sam is freaking out about the $600 … I don't even want to go home tonight."

"When do you have to pay it by and do you even have $600 dollars?"

"I have to pay it now and we'll eat bologna and eggs for a while."

"Jesus girl you're lucky that's all she did. You were in contempt of court! You idiot!"

"You should have seen Izzy's face when the judge said that … it wasn't nearly as good as all your faces while we're telling you a whole boatload of bullshit!!! High five girlfriend we did good!" Colleen says as they both break out laughing.

"I thought I was going to lose it a couple of times … that was excellent!"

"You queers … you did that like you rehearsed it or something?"

"We did!" they say in unison, still laughing.

"Good one … you had us all completely sucked in! So what's the real story?"

"If you ever get a large fine like that it's good to contest it. If the officer who wrote the fine doesn't show up they throw it out of court! That's what happened to me."

"Good to know."

"So Cindy, do you have any gossip for sharing? We know we have to pry it out of you."

"My neighbour and his wife just split and it didn't take long for him to come knocking. I've always been attracted to him so we have gone on a couple of dates. I don't know though it's really way too soon for him. We'll take it slow. Also we only see each other when our kids aren't with us because we think they would freak!"

"That's a good bit of gossip! You're always so demure when telling your stories. It's very cute. Well ... was he good lay?"

"I don't kiss and tell."

"Well, not right away, but we'll eventually get something out of you so just spill!"

"If you must know he's no Hebrew Hammer, but I don't mind because I'm so small, it's better that way and he knows what he's doing ... he works it well! Is that good enough for you ladies?"

"Ladies? We aren't ladies, we're fucking Hens!"

"Cindy if that's all you have it will just have to do! It's just I have to live vicariously through all you because I'm so married! I need gossip ... it's in my DNA!"

We have all enjoyed dinner and chip in to clean up. When Cindy's around she'll start cleaning before we even finish. She likes things organized even when she's not in her own home. She puts on a pot of coffee because she's a lightweight when it comes to drinking. Cindy possesses zero body fat, she can't have more than a drink and she is tipsy. Meagan on the other hand is clearly trying to drown her sorrows and perhaps a bit of intervention is needed.

"Meagan do you have to go home or can you spend the night?"

"I'm staying at moms around the corner. She's dying you know, so I spend as much time there as I can."

"Shit you could have eased into that one."

"Sorry ... drunk factor. Eloquence goes out the window after a bottle of wine! It's fine. She's ready. She's had cancer for a year. Her doctor specializes in home palliative care ... I've never seen anything like it! They have a hospital bed and nurses in the house and her sister came to stay with her till the end. She's actually very lucky."

"That's amazing. She can die in her own home."

"It's been a real learning experience for all of us."

"You'll have to give me that doctor's name for future reference. Mom is in her mid-eighties now!"

"You know Meagan, I was at the airport picking up Andrew and his flight was delayed. I sat and watched all the homecomings for an hour. It was beautiful and it made me feel all warm and fuzzy. I just say that because it may do the same for you if you're really sad sometimes. You have a lot on your plate with a divorce and your mom … shit sure happens doesn't it?"

"It fuck'n does! Thanks for the suggestion. I may just try it."

Leslie is a little more relaxed on the porch-smoking thing once it is dark and she knows the area kids are in for the night. We move the table off to the side and the night turns into a dance party. Leslie runs over to the garage and returns with her hula hoops. I can't even get more than a few rotations and I'm getting frustrated. I used to do this as a kid! Leslie can go for hours if she wants and then we learn that Meagan could enter in hooping competitions she's so good! She can bring it over to her arm without stopping! We dance and sing in the cool night air. I have arranged for Toby to pick me up at 11:30 pm because let's face it I deserve a wee bit of chauffeuring around after all the years I've done it. I don't ask often, only when we are having a 'special' Thursday. As I am dancing my mind wanders. I have been working with Andrew and Mathew for four years. I have a son in University, who I know will never come back to Ottawa. Toby is graduating high school. He is staying here for post-secondary, which I am over the moon about. I imagine myself in the future all the time. I suppose it is because my present never seems to get any easier. Our business was supposed to be doing way better than it is. It was in the business plan … after two years we could hire a new office manager and I was going to run the charitable division that I dreamed of. My hopes of philanthropy are fading as each year passes much like the one before … just average. I always conceal the state of our financial reality. Andrew has basically made that part of our marriage vows. If I broke that one … now that is something he would be mad about! We manage and we are there for the kids whenever we need to be. That is the best perk of being self-employed.

"Terri I think your car is in the laneway and has been there for a bit."

"OK, that must be Toby. He's likely terrified to come in so go tell him I'll be there in a minute."

"I'll go keep him company don't you worry. Take your time!"

"Funny! Leslie go save my son from Colleen while I get my stuff."

"She's harmless and he's a big boy now. Besides I can't understand why you're leaving so early. Maybe I'll go and tell him you're sleeping and he should just head home!"

"Girls it's been a slice. Hugs to all. Meagan and Cindy great to see you. You really need to come out more often … got to go before Leslie sends my ride away!"

Leslie walks me out to say hi to Toby. I hop in the car to get perfectly driven home by my son. You gotta love that. When my children were young they couldn't grow up fast enough. I really tried to appreciate every stage and I did. But I was always looking forward to the days of freedom, where every hour wasn't attached to work or kids. I have to say now that it has arrived, it is every bit as wonderful as I ever dreamed. Yet, at the same time there is a sadness that I will never see my little ones line up for super hugs when daddy walks in the door. They would start in the kitchen, and run down the hallway and leap into his arms, and simultaneously they would holler, 'SUPERHUG!' Then all of them talking at once, competing for his attention. No more Friday night dance competitions when Noah finally figured out that the winners were in a perfect rotation every week … Sophie, then Toby, then Noah. They each danced their little hearts out in order to get the prize that Andrew would bring home. I thank Toby for the ride as we pull in the driveway.

"Sometimes the best and worst times of your life can coincide. It is a talent of the soul to discover the joy in pain."

Shannon L. Alder

Week 1,610 - About an Illness

"Leslie you left the door unlocked!" I holler as I come in. "I'm so proud of you."

"Terri you're here, yippee. We're all out back," she says as she pokes her head around the kitchen wall.

"I'm here! I guess you're getting everyone their drinks, or you're rolling a joint because it's too windy out there."

"Right on both counts. You know a bunch of the girls are going to Noah's show at Fringe and you really need to let them know what it's really about."

"I know it's on the agenda tonight. I would hate for them to go and then realize the full story while they're in the theatre."

"OK, but don't forget."

"Oh, I won't! Who needs what? I can bring the drinks out while you do that."

"Just grab the white wine and the red and there's some Guava juice shit that Francine wants."

"Will do … I brought a wonderful bottle of red tonight because I deserve it!"

"I still find it amazing that you even drink wine. I haven't gotten used to that yet!"

"I can't believe it took me so long to love it. It's by far the best thing for my digestive system and I feel so much better since I stopped drinking all that other shit. I have declared myself an official wino. I'll bring this out now and come back in for mine … Hello ladies … how are you tonight?" I get a mess of responses all at once … Sista, Chicka, Terri …

"You brought us supplies, welcome!"

"I'm just delivering and I have to run back for mine … I'll be a second."

"Leslie we have a good turn out tonight."

"I know some nights are just like that. Luckily you missed the beginning when Lynn was showing us her Facebook page with 200 pictures of her in a bathing suit. I mean that's just weird! She has every Caribbean holiday and every summer cottage and always in a bathing suit. We get it … you have a nice body fuck!"

"Well she has a jump ahead too because she never had kids."

"She and Andrea go off in their little world sometimes and I feel like kicking them."

"Well they've worked together for many, many years … and they're pretty funny!"

This is our last year being 40 something and Hen Night has expanded. There have been so many girls we knew from high school who have now divorced and reconnected. Francine was married to her high school sweetheart Tim, now a divorced single mom with two boys. Andrea is a year older and she is now divorced with one boy. Lynn is a year younger and she came with Andrea. Now Leslie's house can have two to eight girls on any given Hen Night.

"Meagan how's your family? Have you all figured out life as orphans? You know I had the biggest crush on your brother in high school! I thoroughly enjoyed seeing him again at your mom's funeral."

"Terri, really? I had no idea."

"I'm sure I wasn't the only one. He's very handsome, but very stiff and cerebral!"

"He's a smart boy."

"Izzy, I hear Cole is going to be a professional baseball player!"

"Yeah right! He's playing for the best team in his age group, but going pro is a lottery!"

"Did you hear about the lottery in the States? It's worth 640 million dollars!"

"Did someone win that?"

"I don't know, I just heard it on the news because it's the largest pot ever!"

"Why not have 640 winners who get a million bucks?" Leslie says as she lights her reefer … outside!

"Who wins this stuff? It's never any of us!"

"Sam won his sports bet last week. You have to get all three picks right and it payed $300!"

"Not quite 640 million, but that's a good day!"

"Terri how was Florida?"

"Why and when were you in Florida?"

"I get to go on three of Andrew's business trips with the Board he sits on for work. May was Florida and in October we're going to Arizona. I'm so stoked for that, I've never been."

"You've been all over with him! I don't know anyone who travels more than you!"

"It's wonderful and I'm spoiled, although we work hard for it. Work is getting increasingly frustrating as those boys seem to be at a stalemate all the time and everything just stays the same when it really needs to get shaken up!"

"Speaking of shaking things up! I finally went on a date where I'm going to actually go on a second date!"

"Leslie, that's great news! Maybe you'll get back to your happy place … getting laid on a regular basis. I guess he didn't ask you if your tits were real."

"I still can't believe you're back on the dating scene. I didn't think Chris was such an idiot."

"He isn't at all. We're still friends, and I work for him one day a week. I need the money."

"Well he didn't really spend that much time trying to woo you back once you ended it."

"Some men just don't want to be alone. I guess he's one of them."

"C'mon he started dating that girl five months later. I'm sure if he had given you just another couple of months to get that lov'n feeling back you two would be living together now."

"You just needed some time. And just like all the dumb men you've been involved with he didn't think you were serious when you read him the riot act."

"It's crazy! We were together five years and I'm not getting any younger. The minute I broke off with him he said he would move in!!! What the fuck? I had made it clear for a year that that was what I wanted. I just got tired of waiting and doing all the compromising in the relationship. Did he really think that once I made my mind up to break up that he could just move right in? I was heartbroken!"

"We know and that's why he shouldn't have dated so quickly after. He should have known that you would eventually come around. You were great together."

"That vibrator will come in handy again. You may want to change those batteries!"

"That is zero substitute for the Hebrew Hammer! I miss him! I was madly in love."

"You must feel angry with him. I have no idea how you can stay friends. But you seem to stay friends with everyone. You know there isn't a man out there who you've been involved with who isn't kicking himself for screwing it up! I can't wait to see who will be the one who finally realizes what a catch you are!"

"Funny …I'm not such a catch."

"Yes you are, and you should do yourself a favour and realize it."

"I do in some ways … I know there are some real psycho bitches out there. I bump along and when I get down I often remember this from one of Andrews's famous monologues … 'you can choose to be happy.' It takes some work, but he's right."

"Have you heard from Sharon at all?"

"She did come over about a month ago. She's still dating the married pirate."

"What?"

"After Stan and her divorced she started dating this much older man who's still married and lives with his wife, but they have an 'arrangement.'"

"Was he a sailor? I haven't heard about any of this."

"Well Francine, I guess you'll just have to come out more often," Leslie says. "Oh and we call him the pirate because he wears an eye patch."

"Have any of you met him?"

"I think I'm the only one who has, cos I think I'm the only one still in contact with her. She's coming around. She'll likely show up for the bigger gatherings. She already told me to call her whenever we go to Charlotte's for a shopping night. And she'll come to the Christmas party this year!"

"That's hopeful! Does she ever talk about why she stopped coming?"

"She says that Stan convinced her that none of us wanted her around!"

"When in fact, it's only Izzy who doesn't want her around."

"Don't drag me into this. I'm not stopping her."

"No, but you're still very pissed at her!"

"The one thing I asked of her was to please not have the pirate over when Cole was there for a sleep over. Then I find out he was there and they got totally pissed drunk. Cole said she could barely stand up. You don't do that with kids in the house."

"Sharon isn't perfect and the length of time you can hold on to a grudge isn't perfect either."

"OK, guys I didn't come to Hen Night to listen to fighting. I've had enough of that to last a lifetime!"

"Well you started it girl!"

"Oh listen ... this is a great song ... let's dance. We need to pay tribute to her. She'll never record another song. C'mon we need everyone in the moment." Leslie urges and will not take no for an answer.

We all get up and start singing Amy Winehouse ... "they tried to make me go to rehab, but I said no...no...no. Yes, I have been black, but when I come back you'll know ... know ... know!" This is a Hen favourite because we can relate. Sometimes I feel like I should be in rehab, but not seriously! I don't think they have a rehab for minor substance abuse. Are we really that much different than other mothers? Are we? We all dance around the porch which is now twice the size it used to be. Another song comes on … Adele. No one leaves the porch … we are quiet through the beginning then everyone belts out. "We could have had it all … rolling in the deep … you had my heart inside of your hand … and you played it to the beat!"

"That was awesome. I love that song!"

"You and everyone else who owns a radio."

"That song is worthy though! Some big hits you have to wonder how they happen."

"You have some great selections on your phone girl."

"I just bought the dock and speaker thingy and it's the best. No more running downstairs to change the CD! It's mind blowing … look at all the music I can carry in this little thing! Now I can concentrate on dancing. But right now I'm going to the garage."

Leslie and Francine go off to do the rolling and Andrea and I go in to get all the drinks.

"You look a little flushed girl, are you OK?"

"Menopause … one more happy dance for us to go through. You know when you break the word up it almost reads men-on-pause. I can't have sex. I'm telling you if I get a hot flash and break out in a crazy sweat the guy would just slide right off me! It's a damn good thing I'm separated."

I laugh at the picture in my head. "I've had a few night sweats. The first one freaked me out because I thought I pissed the bed. Then I realized I was wet all over and gravity doesn't work that way!"

"Everyone goes through it differently, just like birth and periods."

"And life…"

We find a tray and I grab the chips I brought and Izzy's popcorn. We head back out to the porch. The maples are in fresh bloom. The brightest greens they will be and they are stunning. The middle one creates a full canopy over half of the porch. In a light rain it will act as a sufficient umbrella. We are so lucky to have this. This is my rehab every week. We are all gathered around the table again. Meagan brought Leslie this great table and chairs when she finally sold her house. She needed to store a few things and Leslie told her to bring it all over.

Meagan took the prize for worst divorce. It was horrible and so long. When she signed the final papers she sent out an invitation to celebrate and we all showed up at the bar knowing just how momentous the occasion was.

"Did you know Amy Winehouse is another member of the 27 club? What is it about that age and rock stars."

"Coincidence I guess."

"But, interesting none the less."

"Terri, we're super excited to go see Noah's show."

"Yes, speaking of the show, I do need to tell you girls a couple of details."

"You told us it's a one man show about his experience getting his goiter out."

"It's actually a pretty genius one man show about his experience going through thyroid cancer."

"WHAT! How do we not know this?"

"Because no one knew about it except for Leslie, who was my shoulder to cry on, and Mathew who was Andrew's shoulder, to do whatever men do? When it all happened we just made the decision not to tell anyone and made up the goiter story for the surgery. After Andrew's brother's cancer experience we just didn't want all the panic of the 'C' word bringing us down. His family is certifiably neurotic. They mean well, but I think that's why Noah decided to handle it that way. Did you know once your kid is 16 they make their own medical decisions! I think it's too young!"

"WOW! This is crazy news!"

"So Noah didn't tell anyone?"

"He was in high school … I told him if he really wanted to do it this way he couldn't tell a soul. Kids can't keep a secret!"

"When you and a bunch of your family went to Toronto to see the show, did they know?"

"I called them all individually and told them the story once we knew the show was going to be produced. It was a perfect life choice, especially since his graduation and the decision to write and perform the play coincided with his five years of being cancer free. His statistic has moved to the survivor equation. Now it's just a feel good story."

"We're so happy that it all worked out for you. I just can't image sitting in a doctor's office and he tells me my kid has cancer."

"It's the worst day of any parent's life!"

"Did he not have to do any treatments after the surgery?"

"If you're going to get cancer that is the best one. Three months after the surgery they gave him a radioactive iodine pill. Essentially he was radioactive for six days. Noah had to be in isolation for three full days. We chose to do it at home. On day four he was allowed to be in the same room, but no contact. On day seven we shared the hug of a lifetime. It felt like he was a newborn again just starting out with endless possibilities ahead.

"Well how on earth did you cover up that one?"

"We booked a family camping trip. Sophie and Toby were allowed to bring one friend and Andrew took them all camping and Noah and I stayed in the house. Everyone thought we were all camping. He stayed in his room and I brought him food, left it on the floor and then went back downstairs. My role for the week was to keep him fed."

"That's a brave kid to put something so personal out there for the world."

"Yes and no. When you see it you'll understand. It's so well done and so entertaining and he gets rave reviews and standing ovations all the time. He's very proud of how it turned out."

"My God, you must be so proud too! Now I'm even more excited to see it."

"No mom could have been more proud of a child when I saw that show! You'll all get the full story throughout the play … you don't need me going on. Although he doesn't have anything about the fact that we had to do a no salt diet for six weeks preceding the pill. It was fascinating to learn that sodium is in EVERYTHING you buy … beware of the salt girls."

"This is a bit of a shocker moment … of course we're curious and want to hear all about it."

"And I just told you all about it!"

"Just one more question. Where did 'My Second Smile' come from?"

"Really, that isn't obvious? It's in reference to his very large scar on his neck … he looked at himself and then that became the title of his journal he wrote when he was in isolation. That scar did not heal the way it should have … why don't children listen to their mothers?"

"Children don't listen to their mothers because they think we're idiots. Especially teenagers! Don't try to tell them anything. Or, tell them the opposite of how you want them to behave and you may get somewhere."

"You know we have created our own mess … a generation of lazy, self-indulgent youth."

"It's my fault and I take the responsibility. I never made my kids clean the toilet. I mean when I grew up we did dishes every night and Saturday chores. You didn't leave the house until they were done."

"And women wonder why they're so exhausted all the time."

"I never wonder that. I know why I am. If I wasn't so hyper I couldn't finish all I need to do in a day. And I do get the girls to do stuff, I'm always at them."

"Technology is changing our children…"

"No shit. One of the biggest problems is they think they're so smart. Joel is so good on computers, if I ask him to show me something he has this little condescending smirk on his face. In our day our parents never asked us for help … chores don't count. I'm referring to intellectual help."

"That's an interesting point. The internet has made them smarter. They have the world at their fingertips."

"Sure, but my kids would rather play video games than explore the internet. I wish they would do more of that."

"Francine, just limit their video time."

"I have tried. Believe me. It's too large a battle and they wear me down."

"The only thing you can do is take them away. That's what worked for Toby … cold turkey man. He just came home from school one day and they were all gone. I almost enjoyed watching the catastrophic meltdown that occurred. It was all I could do not to laugh. I had been threatening it for months, I had to follow through."

"I don't think my son would survive something like that … or … I might not survive something like that … he may be just that crazy?"

"Francine you're exaggerating! Just do it. Pack it all up and disappear it. It'll be the best thing you will have ever done for yourself … and your son!"

"I'll think about it. And why is it a boy thing? Leslie, your girls didn't get into them. What about Sophie?"

"Even if she wanted to Toby wouldn't give her a turn, but she never did either. And, speaking of Sophie she just found out that she was accepted at the two best theatre schools in Toronto. Noah, graduated with a BFA, which Andrew and I tease and call it a Bachelor of Fuck All. Now, Sophie's heading down the same slippery slope."

"Two actors in the family ... you'll either be rich or stay broke supporting them for the rest of your life!"

"Bite your tongue ... they're perfectly capable of waiting tables. Rest assured we won't be supporting them post education."

"How did Abbey enjoy her first year of University?"

"Love, loves it! She's working at the car dealership for the summer. She worked there all through her first year."

"And that's another crazy thing about theatre school. They tell you at the beginning if you have to get a job to keep going financially, you won't be able to take the program ... too many late night rehearsals! If Noah didn't get a scholarship I don't think we could have pulled it off!"

"Hey look what he's done already. He'll do great."

"I hope so. But he's very generic."

"Generic?"

"Yeah, he doesn't have 'a look' and he isn't ethnic, which is also very big in the industry. It gives you a leg up just like anywhere these days, as many employers are hiring based on diversity."

"Right, they all need to catch up after being racist for all these years."

"True, but now it's our privileged white children who may be paying the price."

"There will always be enough racism out there that our kids will get jobs."

"Don't be so sure, these people are still racist, but they now have to appear not to be. I think our kids will have a tougher time getting work, but I really hope I'm wrong. I have always been a supporter of the best person for the job should get the job."

"It's change the subject time! So, Abbey got her period the other day and she says to me, ' you know mom despite the fact that I feel bloated and crampy, and I have blood pouring out of my vagina … I feel so much better. I think that God made us have PMS so that getting our period is a welcome thing. A few days ago I just wanted to kill all my friends! And now I like them again.' She makes me laugh."

"If funny is a gene then your family would be the proof of that. Your whole family and now your daughters have it too."

The song by Goyte comes on and I remember this story.

"We were out for dinner with the kids and this song was playing and we are singing along and then Andrew out of nowhere changes the words to, 'and now you're just somebody that I used to blow.' Both tables beside us gave him very disapproving looks. Maybe it was the moon or the moment, but we all burst out laughing. Toby was so jealous that he hadn't thought of it first."

"So many music hits are about a lost love. I guess that's what fires up people the most."

"Speaking of love, I have to show you all the latest pics of my granddaughter. She's five months now and gorgeous."

"She's lovely Colleen. I can't believe your baby has a baby!"

"It's unfortunate that her mommy is such a fucking head case. I hope Brent can curb some of her crazy."

"Izzy, she seems to be doing better."

"Colleen she has already had two of her children taken away from her. That is one woman who should have been neutered."

"Don't you mean spayed?"

"No I meant neutered because her temperament is more like a he than a she."

"All I can do is support and be there for the baby as much as I can. The rest is out of my control."

"I know, I'm sorry, but just hearing about her gets me all bent out of shape. The shit you have gone through dealing with that relationship is up and above any mother's duty."

"I keep paying a price for marrying Hank. His fucked-up family's scars run deep."

"I just hope that little baby doesn't end up with deep tissue scaring."

Leslie has the hula hoop out and we are all taking turns with it. I still can't do it and it really bothers me. I have never been good at accepting not being good at something. I was crushed when I realized I wasn't going to be able to play the guitar. I worked so hard on getting a good sound from each cord and then when I tried to marry the cords together my fingers couldn't do it. They wouldn't move fast enough. I played in slow motion and you couldn't even recognize the songs.

"Who wants to go for a walk in the field? Look how bright it is out there with the full moon. Don't you find it amazing that the moon moves the ocean? I wish I could jump into the sea right now."

"What I find even more amazing is that most people don't think the moon has an effect on a human body. We are mostly water and chemicals. Why wouldn't it affect us?"

"My mom worked in the maternity ward for years and she dreaded the full moon. Witcho always told us it was by far the busiest time. I notice my mood changes with the moon. Maybe that's what PMS is and they named it wrong … it stands for Pre Moon Syndrome."

"No because your period doesn't always line up with the moon."

"No it doesn't, but it does quite often. I also don't think that it's a coincidence of nature that your period is every 28 days! The moon comes around and it just starts sucking the blood out of you!"

"Interesting concept! I've never given it much thought, but I'll try to take notice of my moods before the full moon."

"Why don't we stop talking about the moon and go for a walk and enjoy those rays in the field."

"I'll go if you promise not to wrestle me. I have good clothes on for a change."

"Izzy you know I don't wrestle anymore. I've given it up in order to keep my friends!"

"OMG that time you went at Andrew at the Halloween party was so funny. He told me after that you really hurt him and he was so confused because he wanted to get you the hell off, but didn't want to hurt you, so he just took it till you stopped."

"What a pansy thing to say. He can hurt me … that's what wrestling is all about. If I start a wrestle I fully expect that I may get hurt!"

"Well I'll let him know for the next time."

"Nope … no more next time. I'm a reformed wrestler! I mean I am 49 fuck … it's time to grow up."

"You must be feeling it now, old woman, and you're just using our complaining about it as an excuse to quit."

"I'm feeling like you really want to wrestle right now cause you're getting a little irritating and I want to head lock you so bad!"

I don't know what came over me … I just snapped. Before she had a chance to move I jump up and put her in a headlock. Maybe I just wanted to be the initiator for one time? Maybe I just wanted to kick her arse to prove to myself I could do it? Leslie really has stopped with her wrestling. Maybe I miss it, but here we are, in full flailing arms and legs mode. We are grunting and cursing and the girls are cheering us on. No sides are picked just cheers. The girls quickly move things out of the way as we push closer to any danger. We are having our most epic wrestle of all time. I'm not caving this time. I'm going to finish the years of random wrestling on top. I want the gold metal and dammit I'm going for it. We fight till we are sucking wind and neither of us can move a muscle. We are weak and worn out. Sadly, it is going to end in a stalemate because the girls will not define a winner. Oh well, that's better than losing and inside I feel like a winner.

"OK, I need to sit and catch my breath."

"Now that was the wrestle I've been waiting for, for 30 fucking years. I don't know why it had to happen when we're 49 but I'll take it. High five sista!"

"Well that was it … the last stand! Don't think you can just jump on me anytime you like. I do love the non-wrestling Leslie."

"Well that was fun."

"Indeed it was."

"I wish we had a video of it we could send to Ellen. Maybe that would have gotten us on the show."

"Two old cougars wrestling … we need more than that! We know we won't be going on Oprah."

"You better put that one in your journal."

"Oh I will. I have identified two bruises now … from your knobby knees! I guess we would call that an IPI (identified party injury) considering we know the source."

"Sounds logical."

"OK chickies … I'm going to head home. It's the day after deadline tomorrow and it can be busier than deadline day sometimes."

"C'mon sucky suck. It's still early. Little baby needs to get her sleep! Or did I wrestle all the life out of her!" Leslie says as she gives me a jab.

"You know I'm going to start sneaking out so I don't have to listen to you begg'n me to stay."

"Fine little sucky girl, go home! Are you good to drive?"

"I just kicked your arse … can't do that drunk!"

"Funny! I'll talk to you soon, because you'll call me when you get home, right? Drive safe."

Since I found wine, I hardly smoke dope. I'm really a hash snob, but it never seems to be around anymore. Weed has a better buzz, but the smell and taste holds no appeal. And I have puked my guts out mixing the two, so I choose wine. I feel like I have finally reached a maturity level where I control my vices well. I am now sophisticated. I drink wine. But, I am no wine snob. I will pretty much drink anything and it all tastes fine to me. Once we opened a nice bottle of red and I was like ooohhh … yummy, and then Andrew sniffs it and says, "I think this is off," then he took a sip, and he could not believe that I could not tell that it tasted like vinegar! Sorry dude, it tasted like wine to me. Then he opened another bottle and does a taste test with me. I did notice the difference then and now I am an official connoisseur because I now know what 'off' smells and tastes like.

The drive from Leslie's is only 15 minutes, but the people who love me still worry about me. I share too many of my stories so they know just how bad I am with being sleepy behind the wheel. I have carcolepsy! Once I was driving the 15 minutes from mom's house and I stopped at a red light. The light was infinitely too long and I started to doze. My foot released the pressure on the brake and I inched my way into the car in front of me. That woke me up! I was mortified I jumped out all apologetic. The driver I hit tells me to calm down and checks his bumper and there really isn't any damage. He had a real car rather than a plastic one. I thought he was about to hug me he was so concerned. Then he asked what happened because he saw me in his rear view mirror and I was at a complete stop. I started to cry and told him I just fell asleep. I could tell he was surprised. Some people can't fathom that. Some people can't fall asleep anywhere but in their beds. Others can't even fall asleep in their beds. To minimize the hours of feeling carsick I used to sleep as much as I could on our family trips to Saskatchewan. I believe that is why a moving vehicle just knocks me out. My dad was a prairie farmer and my mom was a city girl. They met in Timmons when dad would go mine in the winter. No, Timmons isn't much of a city! Mom grew up in Ottawa when there were streetcars here. She even got hit by one. Once they married, dad brought her to his farm. She always said that the first nine months nearly killed her and she cried every day. If it weren't for the birth of Teresa she would have left. My older sisters grew up on the farm with no toilets and no running water. Their stories always make me grateful for my family position of youngest.

After moving back to the city gone a year, mom woke up feeling unwell. She was feeling like she may be pregnant again, but thought there could be no chance of that! Mom prayed for a tumor rather than another child. Once I was born they removed her uterus … it may have just fallen out along with me. Mom finally had peace. She knew she would never get pregnant again. She was back in the city she loved and that was enough for her to be complete. I never want to feel complete. I always want to feel like there is something else I need to be doing or somewhere I need to going.

I have spent 22 years in the service of my husband and family. I have worked with Andrew for seven years now. It is awesome, but I know I have my own passion that needs to be fuelled. I leave it in the background waiting for the right time. I get out of the car and walk out to the park for one last look at the moon. I take a deep breath and

I look over at the lamppost that speaks to me. It has told me more than once that the people I have loved and lost are watching out for me. My neighbour Mike, who lived across the street and became my buddy. My neighbour Lance who was dead within six weeks of his diagnosis, who sat on the porch with his wife and watched us play all the time. When the kids got a little older I would join him and his wife on the porch and chat. At his wake his daughter called me a bitch. Apparently he used to talk about me all the time and tell her what a good mom I was. I suppose that would make me jealous too. And Earl, my favourite cranky uncle. Why didn't I stay with him that night? I left at 10:00 pm and he died before morning. He was 94 and ailing and he would not sign a DNR. I would tease him that he was afraid to reunite with his wife Millie. You cannot resuscitate a 94 year old … his ribs would have all broken. My dad has passed also, but I figure since we had so little to say when he was alive, why start chatting now? Whenever I need an answer to some life issue I pray to them. I don't pray to God because I don't believe in Him that way, but I can pour my heart out to these three men.

One night walking my dog and I was in a mild turmoil about whether they really were around or not. I had prayed really hard and they let me down. I looked up and I firmly asked with great conviction, "OK … I'm tired of speculating and thinking that maybe all those other times you helped me out was just coincidence. If you are out there … make the lamp go out now!" The lamp went out. I was 46.

"'Tis the privilege of friendship to talk nonsense, and to have her nonsense respected."

Charles Lamb

Week 1,716 – About an Ending

"I can't believe so many of you came! You make me want to cry. Not that anyone ever wants to cry!"

"Sometimes a good cry feels like the best medicine!"

"I know, right. I was listening to Doug and the Slugs while working on the house there're these lyrics that go, 'And you're wondering if this move you finally made is worth what you gave.' Well at that point I had a total melt down and bawled my head off, but I felt so much better after."

"I would imagine you're hyper emotional these days. I could never do what you're doing!"

"So I don't start crying again … Izzy, has baseball started yet? I was watching a game and Cole has the hardest position by far. All that constant swatting don't his knees bother him?"

"He doesn't complain about them, but I don't know how he does it. He didn't end up with my bad knees."

"Do you know when you're getting those suckers replaced?"

"Should be early next year."

"My sister had both of her knees done and she was ecstatic with her results. Her doctor was dreamy … do have the same one?"

"Not even close. How is unemployed life treating you?"

"I'm up from dawn till dusk working on the house, but I love every second of it. No more deadlines!!!"

"Isn't it amazing how a life can change so quickly? One minute you're at this place in your life, and the next you're going somewhere else!"

"As long as that somewhere else isn't six feet under I'm good. You have to roll with it. Besides I initiated all this and I'm exhilarated. I feel like I have had some kind of re-birth!"

"Why did you put the business up for sale in the first place? I thought it was a good gig?"

"Andrea, it was a good gig, but it was the only way to break up Andrew and Mathew. The boys had their time together. They needed to move on. A business partnership is like a marriage. I just felt like if we were in control of our destiny and didn't have that 50% partner … well I needed to see what that might look like. I basically told Andrew it was Mathew or me, and I give a GREAT blow job … WINNER!"

"Which really should be called a suck job!"

"We're back to the driveway/parkway conundrum … English is a stupid language. We get it!"

Ruth walks in the door and I catch her eye so I go give her a hug and kiss. Ruth has had some serious health issues, and at times she just looks rough, but tonight she is radiant. They diagnosed her with Lupus, but then changed their minds and we are never quite sure what she has.

"Girl you look amazing! That trip to Africa was good medicine … living the high life with the elite Canadian staffers."

Ruth laughs, "Terri you have no idea how ironic that statement you just made is!"

"Do tell."

"While I was in Africa I had one of my bad puking episodes. Well Mark's brother has a best friend who's a doctor and he told us to come to the hospital now. They did a bunch of tests and I showed them all my meds and in the end they figured out that I was missing a pill that would complete the cycle that my own body won't process. They guaranteed I would feel way better. They were right!"

"You should bring your story to The Citizen ... I can see the headline now. CANADIAN GOES TO AFRICA FOR BETTER HEALTH CARE! Who would have thought? Damn you look great ... best I have seen you in years!"

"Best I've felt in years."

"It always amazes me that even with your health issues you still have a hot bath and lay your husband every night!"

"Well that's good medicine my friend!"

"And a trip to Africa...."

"Ruth!"

"Leslie!"

"Give me some love girl. Look at you. You look beautiful."

"Thanks, I feel beautiful!"

"Well I have a reefer with your name on it. C'mon outside to the Hen Den."

There are nine girls here tonight to see me off. I feel loved and grateful for their attendance, yet in the same breath I would be put out if one didn't have a damn good reason not to be here! Still no Sharon. I figured if there was one Hen Night she would come to, it would be this one. Who knows when I will get back again! Perhaps I am giving myself too much credit? I have only seen her a few times in the last two years, better than nothing I suppose. It is still early, she may show. I watch all the girls mingling with one another: Andrea and Lynn are laughing; Francine, Ruth and Leslie heading out to the garage; Colleen and Cindy are in conversation; Izzy and Meagan are looking at pictures on their phone. Next week many will be back here doing the very same thing, but I will not! This night is an end to a very long chapter in my life. I am leaving the only place I have called home (other than that year in Toronto with Laura). Since it is still early, I decide to head out to the garage and partake because I could really use a reefer right now.

"OMG this is hash! Where did it come from?"

"I decided to surprise you on your last Hen Night in who knows how long!"

"Yummy! And you know I'll always be here in spirit."

"It isn't going to be the same without you."

"We all survived without Sharon ...the show must go on! You know as long as you are here ... Hen Night will be to."

"When does the house go on the market?"

"Tomorrow and let's keep our fingers crossed for a quick sale. Francine did you ever take those games away from your son? I've been meaning to ask you."

"No, I'm too much of a suck."

"I think it's more about the guilt of breaking up your marriages that you girls are so easy on your children. Mother guilt is a powerful thing."

"Statistically, it's women who initiate most divorces. Men don't do it because they need someone to take care of them. It took Hank less than a year to get a new woman. I think a man will stay in a bad marriage forever out of shear laziness!" "You got that right and now I'm dating all the fuck'n cast offs and trust me they're brutal. I'm not looking for a prince, just a normal, nice guy ... who loves sex. Is that really too fucking much to ask? Although there's one who keeps coming back and touching base and I can't figure out why."

"Leslie, really … to get laid … and also because you're probably the only woman who has put him in his place."

"And what place is that?"

"Well Ruth this guy is pretty good looking and wealthy and so narcissistic … I love that word! All he ever does is talk about himself and how he has this and that. I spend half my time cutting him down and he laughs at all my comments! I call him out on everything! He gets in touch when he's in town cos he travels a lot. He doesn't seem to have a real home of any kind. I do feel some crazy connection to him. But, he's absolutely not life partner material. Not one iota!"

"Leslie calls him BB."

"Why?"

"Because he has the Biggest Balls of any man I've ever seen!"

"And you've seen a lot of balls…"

"Bite me … let me tell you I was grateful when he warned me the first time we had sex…."

"Which was their first date…"

"Bite me again queer … it was our second! Believe me if I didn't want to get laid too, I wouldn't bother with him!"

"How big are they?"

"They're the size of tennis balls!"

"NO WAY!"

"I don't lie!"

"Both … like two tennis balls!"

"Yup, and a wee little pencil sized dick!"

"How does he store those? He must be very uncomfortable! Like how's a guy built like that even the least bit narcissistic?"

"Because you can't see them … guys get to keep the mystery, where we wear our size on our chest! He's a piece of work. But he makes me laugh."

"You laugh more at him than with him, and for some crazy reason he loves it!"

"And there's no one else in my life so when he calls I'm like … whatever! C'mon over baby and I'll sharpen your pencil!"

"You said that!"

"Maybe, once or twice!"

"Jesus we're all starting to sound like our kids."

"So, like he called me a few weeks ago to come over, and I told him that it was like fine, but unless he was into dipping his sausage into like ketchup, he may not be wanting to get laid! Like he came anyway so it isn't just about the sex I guess."

"You never lose your flare for the English language. You sounded exactly like Abbey! Let's head back in the house."

"Terri when are you leaving?"

"I'm driving to Hog Town on Saturday."

"What area are you living in?"

"You know how most parents experience their kids moving back home? Well Sophie gets to experience her parents moving into her student ghetto! Her roommates are both gone for the summer so we said we would move in. It is just east of downtown. The neighbourhood is called Leslieville …"

"Named after me…"

"Sure it must have been … so Sophie doesn't have to live with strangers and we get a couple more months to figure out where to live. It's a win/win of sorts. I'll need the weekend to sanitize the place!"

"That bad?"

"Gross really. She says they were so busy in school they never had the time, but really whatever time they did have was obviously spent partying. Her roommates are self-proclaimed feminists and I think they just don't feel like it's their job anymore … women have progressed!"

"Well it has to be someone's job. If you're not clean you'll get bugs and mice and that's just nasty! I don't really get exactly what that whole movement has accomplished! All the really meaningful shit is still going on. Obviously not as bad, but the pay inequality and sexual harassment is still around. Oh and great job girls … now we get to work full time, take care of the kids and the house and do the cooking!!! And now no boys open the door for me anymore, and no boys stand up to give me a seat on the bus … I miss that shit!"

"Well they've accomplished hyphenated names! Did anyone give that any thought? When these kids get married are they supposed to have a fucking four word hyphenated last name?!" Sharon says as she walks through the kitchen doorway.

"Sista you came!!! Thank you so much. It's soooo good to see you." I say as I give her a bear hug and pick her up off her feet.

"You're welcome … I'm barely in the door you guys already have me all riled up."

"Bite your tongue … you just called us guys! It's just like anything people are passionate about … you get your extremist. Andrew told me he was reprimanded by a woman in the office because he used the word 'girls'. She freaked on him and said they're women now, not girls and how dare he….?"

"Fuck we call each other guys half the time … wonder how she'd feel about that?"

"She may be OK with that! Why don't we just get rid of the words boy and girl, and women and men? We can all be goys and wens!"

"I fancy myself a feminist … go easy on us!"

"Andrea we're all feminists in the dictionary sense. Of course we want to be paid equally for the same job and not sexually harassed. That goes without saying, but things have gone crazy. Society as a whole is walking on eggshells. Politically correct has a place in the world, but fuck it's extreme now! I've finally learned to sensor what comes out of my mouth. I just don't get why every word needs to be weighted in terms of how appropriate it is. I speak English now like I speak French. First I translate it in my head to make sure it's OK before I say it. If you're comfortable in your own skin and in your beliefs you shouldn't be offended by anyone who wishes you Merry Christmas. That's not an offensive salutation!"

"I don't understand why anyone would take offence to a celebration of any kind! You can choose to join the party or not. It's simple … and I choose to par-tay!"

Leslie runs over to the music station and turns up the volume. The song *Wagon Wheel* is on. She does this deliberately to drown us out and no one can talk to one another. She corrals us all into the living room and before you know it we are all dancing and singing at the top of our lungs … 'Rock me mama like the wind and the rain … Rock me mama like a southbound train … ohhhh mama rock me'. Then Miley Cyrus … 'you came on like a wrecking ball …' Then Maroon 5 and finally Steely Dan's *Hold On* before she turns the music down. She is thirsty and needs a drink and likely a trip to the Hen Den.

"I think we need to invent an automatic reefer roller!"

"They have cigarette rollers. You need to invent something everyone could use. Make sure it's something that'll make their lives easier. That's what people want … things that will enable their ability to watch five hours of TV a day! A gadget or pre-fabricated food and you're golden. Look at your new wine opener for example. No need for any muscle to screw that thing in … I'm sure it's sold like hotcakes."

"Oh and if you have a fireplace you can get packaged logs that you just light … no need to build a fire anymore … now that requires effort! I see them in every grocery store!"

"I buy those … they're great."

"What like Tony the Tiger great … cos corn flakes aren't so great? They don't even compare to the awesome look of a real flame … or the crackle of real wood … or the smell of a real fire! I'm just making a point that if we could come up with the next great gadget we could make our fortune!"

"All we need to do is post Hen Night on YouTube, but most of you queers don't want us to do that!"

"Leslie as much as you think you want to do that … you don't want to do that! You can get fired over this kind of nonsense," Francine says as she takes a haul.

"My boss would never fire me … I'm also his therapist! He'd be lost!"

"You do have a lot of years at that law office."

"Yeah, people get fired over inappropriate Facebook posts!"

"Sure, dumb arses who trash their bosses. If you're that stupid you deserve to be fired!"

"Well I'm sure they didn't think their work was going to see it."

"Don't misunderstand, ladies, you're being watched by more than your work! If you decide to take up some illegal actions make sure you have nothing about it on the internet."

"We'll keep that in mind."

"I work in the government, trust me on this."

"OK mom, note is filed." Francine says as she points to her head.

"Terri, what is Andrew's mom going to do without you?"

"We've already moved her to Toronto. We did that last month."

"How did you get her there? She has Alzheimer's doesn't she? You're not supposed to change their surroundings."

"We didn't have a choice. She has three daughters there and only Lee would be left here. I told the family not to tell her anything and just show up and take her for lunch … on the train … five hours away! They resoundingly, unanimously said I was heartless and how could I even think such a thing?!"

"Because it would be the smartest thing to do."

"I know right. I understand that woman better than her own kids do. So of course for weeks leading up to the move they had been 'preparing' her for it."

"You can't 'prepare' a woman with no short term memory recall!"

"I know! And then it was my job to go at 9:00 am and start packing her up for the movers who were arriving at 2:00 pm. She was being taken to the train at 12:00 pm by the staff. Andrew's sister would meet her at the station as she was coming from Montréal. So I bring all the boxes into the fucking lion's den. I would pick something up and she would grab it and put it back. I did try to reason with her for about ten minutes and I had her in a complete frenzy. She raged about how her family won't give her the time of day and why should she move just because they live in that city. And, all this from a woman who has done nothing but complain about how she hates it at that retirement home. I thought she would want to move! I didn't expect that amount of crazy. This little old lady telling me to fuck off! I had never seen her like that!"

"So what did you do?"

"The only thing I could do. I told her she was right and calmed her right down, and took her down for a coffee. Then I quickly talked to the staff and told them not to say a word about the move. Then I called Lee and told her to get her arse to the home and bring the baby because that would be the only way to get her in a car and on the train."

"Obviously it worked out."

"Yes, she forgot the whole conversation and when Lee arrived with the baby she was more than happy to go have lunch with them. Never in my life had I been so relieved to see someone drive away! I ran back into the room and power-packed for two hours!"

"Isn't that disease a crazy thing?"

"She thinks her whole family doesn't give her the time of day because she can't remember when we visit. I mean Andrew and I had her and mom for dinner every Sunday till mom got too sick. Then we would have just her. I don't think she ever remembered once!"

"How's your mom?"

"She's all there mentally, but her body is giving her a hard time …she's 91 and she's sad she had to go to a home. If mom is anything, she's pragmatic and she knew she could no longer take care of herself and very willingly signed herself up."

"I would much rather lose my body than my mind!"

"Hell yeah, speaking from experience where I have both types in my life. I can still have a great conversation with mom. She doesn't move much, but she can still share herself and her stories and you know every visit is appreciated and she's so grateful. All you get on the other end is a winey, miserable old lady who you can't make happy because she can't remember anything nice that you've done! I never want to be that person to my children!"

"Off topic here, but why on earth does Lee have a baby? When did that happen?"

"Ruth, she had an immaculate conception!"

"Right!"

"Well nearly! After her second child was born she had her tubes cut and cauterized. She had horrible pregnancies and didn't want to ever do it again. Their family was planning a huge trip to Europe for her

40th. Instead she was in the hospital giving birth to this one in a million baby error!"

"Don't you mean miracle!"

"Yes, yes of course miracle ... but, they're realistic in their devastation. Their other kids are 16 and 18!"

"There's no way in hell I would have had that kid!"

"You say that Sharon, but under the circumstances you would."

"Well maybe I would and then sell it. You can make some good coin with a private adoption. I mean why not? Let them do all the hard work and then the kid will probably try to find its natural mother ... then you can have a fulfilling adult relationship."

"If you're delusional maybe ... that kid would hate you for giving it up ... especially since you had no real good reason to give it up ... other than being lazy."

"Izzy are you just trying to make sure I don't come back to another Thursday?"

"OK, let's keep the love ... did you know that you can burn a hole in your underwear!"

"No Leslie this is breaking news ... what are you talking about?"

"Well I have a pair of underwear and just above the cotton lined area there's now a hole!"

"Maybe you have had your hand down there rubbing it too many times!"

"I'm sure ... me the non-masturbator of all the Hens!"

"Well how old are these underwear?"

"They're definitely third string."

"Third string?"

"Yeah, first string are sexy and for a date night. Second string are for work and errands, the kind you can be in an accident in and you won't be embarrassed at the hospital. And third string are for when you have your period or you don't plan to leave the house."

"Well maybe it wore down from you ripping pads off your underwear. God knows you won't wear a tampon so you bleed everywhere."

"I bleed everywhere because I have a flood coming every seventeen fucking days."

"I get that, but if you stick two tampons up and then a pad you might make it longer than half an hour before bleeding all over something!"

"You bled all over my car seat once!"

"You stick two tampons up there?"

"It isn't rocket science for Christ sake. If you can stick a cock in there why not two measly tampons!"

"That's genius … I never thought of doing that. I wish you'd mentioned that before I was going into menopause!"

"It's the only way I make it through the night without wrecking my mattress."

"Well I don't use tampons unless I have to."

"And you'll keep bleeding all over your bed and your car and your clothes … it's not like there are studies that show they cause any major health risks. I don't know why you're so stubborn about them."

"It's just the way I am. And mom always says to avoid them just in case. There's that Toxic Shock Syndrome thing."

"Well you should all stop having your period soon. I haven't had one for nine months."

"I can't wait for that day!"

"Terri, what's Toby doing?"

"He'll stay still the house sells and he's undecided after that. He went to university here. His whole life is here, where the other two are Torontonian's through and through. They love it there. Naturally I'm hoping he decides to join us. I'll have my family living in the same city for the first time in six years ... happy days."

"I still can't wrap my head around the fact that you're moving. You're pretty old to start over girlfriend."

"I'm not starting over since I'll do the same job I did here only I'll work for the corporate office ... and they're paying more than the boys ever could."

"They better! You'll need more in that crazy city."

"They're also paying Andrew well to run the market, but he says it's going to be a big climb up out of the mess that he showed up to. He's been there since March staying with his sister."

"How's that going for him?"

"He can't wait for the weekend ... he'll just be happy to be reunited. We have never spent this much time away from one another!"

"I really hope it all works out for you. I wish you all the best."

"We've been gamblers most of our lives together and things just take care of themselves, even when it all appears to be impossible."

"Things don't just take care of themselves darling! You and Andrew have this way of staying positive and on course and you make it happen. Don't be thinking it's just luck."

"Yes, Mast'r Splinter I'll take ownership of my life!"

"Good, you've had a topsy-turvy one."

"Certainly no more than you lady. How's life at the hospice these days?"

"People die and then new people move in. Just like it always is. The key is to not get attached to them while they're with us."

Colleen has worked at an AIDS hospice for a very long time. She manages it and does all the cooking. They eat well during their time there because she can cook. She will make 'healthy' taste like 'heaven'.

Most of us have remained in our jobs for a very long time. Leslie always ends up back working for her usual lawyer. He and Leslie just seem to have this connection that keeps reattaching. Izzy is still at the girl's school. It was a lucky break for her to be there because then Hannah could be enrolled and got all the extra help she needed to succeed. Ruth has been at the same place since she finished high school. Sharon had a very long time not working and now she is back doing accounting for various offices. I worked for the boys running the office for nine years. They sold their business in February and have parted ways. Fortunately they have remained friends and I have no doubt that life will be better for both of them. They just needed a push off the cliff and they will find their wings. They have been standing on the edge for too long.

Mathew organized an amazing going-away party at a bar. He brought all the band equipment and Andrew got to play again. Mathew practically built our old office. One of the requirements while they were looking for office space was that there be room to set up a band. Mathew is a drummer and Andrew plays rhythm guitar. He also writes and will sing even though he has a very limited range … like a Neil Young range! The rest of the band just came together through friends and even clients. As soon as we walked in we knew that we had found our office. The upper loft became a kitchen with an island, beer on tap and a recording studio of sorts. We had many a party there and the boys jammed on Thursdays when we did Hen Night. A few times we surprised them with a groupie night and we would have a ball. Who doesn't love playing to an audience! Andrew got into playing guitar when his brother passed and he received all the music equipment. He will miss everything more than I will. He is more social and full of energy. For him nothing is an effort. We have more friends than anyone else I know. Andrew is a joy to be around and has a great sense of humour. I know most of our friends will be for life. We will pick up from where we left off with each visit. We will entertain them in Toronto and we will make frequent trips to Ottawa. I am planning on this change being the best thing that has ever happened to us. It has to be.

"Girls let's try to list all the different things we've done on Hen Night?"

"Does that include our girls' weekends?"

"Whatever you want to include … we've had a lot of fun together!"

"My personal favourite has always been our craft nights … I still have my Christmas snowman!"

"Funny! Do you remember all those times we went to Drew's bar when he was running it at Mooney's Bay. That should have been a destination … but those portable city bathrooms were gross."

"They were the same ones they used for the canal in the winter … they didn't smell so bad in -20C."

"What about Greek Fest, Blues Fest, Italian Fest?"

"I remember at Blues Fest that young boy hitting on Sharon and trying to find out her age and then she looks at him square in the eye and says, 'buddy I'm 37… 45 with the wind chill … beat it!' a classic."

"One of Colleen's trailer weekends where Leslie couldn't find a rolling paper and she was getting all cranky and then managed to use a tampon wrapper to get it done."

"Clothes swap nights … always rewarding."

"The evening we rented canoes at Dow's Lake then had cocktails on the patio."

"On one of our Chalet Renoir weekends it was freezing rain all the way there. It took us five hours to drive because they closed the road, so Leslie cracked open a beer at the two hour mark. Thank goodness we had that van and driver. We were all on the drunk side when we arrived."

"Except me cos I was pregnant for the third time. I wasn't missing another one of those trips because of that!"

"And the van couldn't get up the driveway so we schlepped everything up in the snow."

"And after our driver left, Lynn puts on her skates and goes down that crazy hill with them. You were so lucky you didn't kill yourself."

"The next night I went down with my skies. I wasn't going to Tremblant and not putting on my skies!"

"Going to see bands … so much music."

"Yeah….like Giant Tiger…"

"Enough, can you not get over that one?!"

"I don't think so…it's in the brain just like that night when this guy was really bothering you. I could see you might need some rescuing and then all of the sudden he made this face and disappeared. I went over and asked you what finally got him to move on…"

"Yeah that was just a moment of brilliance … I told him to lick my lightday."

"His face was priceless!"

"We went tobogganing a few times in the early days."

"Yes, and skating with flasks in hand."

We reminisce, but then we get bored and go back for a round of dancing. Hen Night isn't always about sex and drugs and rock n'roll. We do some meaningful girl stuff and get our exercise sometimes. We are a very versatile bunch.

"I knew it was going to happen one day but I didn't think I was going to start looking old yet. I see it in my skin now … the age spots and jowls I never had. I was screwing Andrew, and I looked down at my belly and shit it has changed. Gravity is not our friend. I don't think I'm going on top ever again!"

"All your bodies are starting to finally look like mine. Embrace and accept it girls, it's called aging and it happens to everyone."

"My teeth are a mess from years of smoking!"

"You should've quit with me Sharon."

"I don't think I ever could. What happens to me will happen, but I'll go out smoking a butt."

"Just like your mom."

"I hate you for being able to smoke only when you drink … who does that?"

"Me, and mom only smoked three a day when she did. Imagine she quit at 72! She says she has always missed it, but dad finally wore her down. She got tired of listening to him. At dad's funeral Leslie goes up to her and says, 'Mrs. Vetnor, I will find you a cigarette if you want one. He won't bother you about it anymore!'"

"Only Leslie!"

Some of the girls have left already and we all shared a moment. Obviously I am closer with the original Hens and that is who is left. I have to meet the real estate agent at 9:00 am to sign the papers and a wave of sad washes over me, and then it flips me and smashes me to the bottom of the sea. It is time to leave. I do not want to turn into a sniveling mess. I want to leave with a smile on my face and happy in my heart. I am excited for this change. I have been going through some crazy mid-life nonsense for years now. I have been as restless as a caged cougar! But, no, I can't just go shopping like normal woman! Instead I sell everything and have to start over.

"Girls I'm going to call it a night. Leslie, thank you so much for giving us your home every week, and thank you for calling all the girls."

"Don't be silly! Of course they all wanted to see you off. But why the fuck are your leaving so early?

"Because I'm going to start crying if I stay."

"I think I'll be able to handle myself till moving day and I'm coming to visit soon. It's not like I have much else going on! Like a boyfriend!"

"You know I'll live for that!"

"Right! You will be busy with work and your family. It's Sophie's last year and you'll be able to see all the plays and then just drive home!"

"C'mon everyone group hug." Izzy and Sharon both give a look … "I'll go between you two, relax … no touching required. I'm not even going to say goodbye because I'll be back lots. I want all of you to take good care of yourselves and your kids and your grandkid. Love you all."

"Love you back … safe travels sista."

I leave quickly with a lump in my throat and watering eyes. Leslie follows me out to the car and we hug for a long while, each of us crying quietly. I am first to pull away and I get in the car. I roll the window down and blow her a kiss and say, 'See you soon.' I turn the corner. Once I am out of sight I pull over because it isn't safe to drive while in that kind of crying despair. I can leave the other girls without too much trouble. Leslie has always been our link to one another. I could honestly say that I have had maybe twenty phone conversations with all the other girls combined in all these years of getting together. I call Leslie frequently and so do all the Hens. Yet we do not call one another. I suppose there is no need when you know that you will see each other. Leslie and I will always be BFFL's no matter where I live. I know this. We are so different yet so the same it is an interesting connection. She is Hen Night. She is who we all come to see. She is who we all love. She is the one who loves us all. I pull myself together and drive my shagg'n-wagon back to my perfect house, where I will see my not so perfect son and I will crawl into bed missing my nearly perfect husband. I can't wait for Saturday. I am 51 and starting a new life.

"Someday I'll fly; someday day I'll soar … cause I'm bigger than my body gives me credit for."

John Mayer

Hen Night Epilogue

I have lived in Toronto for just over a year. On my 52nd birthday I went for a jog along the lake for 52 minutes. I did 52 sit-ups and 52 push-ups. I did them in three different reps, but I did them. Sophie joined me on the jog. I love being close to my children and sharing life with them. I do still love this city, although it is much busier than I remember from 27 years ago. Driving around is challenging so I will bike, use public transit or walk whenever possible. The city planners are stupid and some drivers are crazy. They actually race around like they think they are going to beat me somewhere. I just wave at them at the next red light. If you can plan not to be in a hurry, life is better. Just double the time that Google tells you it will take, and you should be on time. Traffic is the one thing in life that Andrew hates. It is actually the only thing he hates in the whole world and I have dragged him here. I know him. I know he is not happy. He is content because he is with his family, but he is not happy. How could he be? So much change in one year … its madness.

We have been tested time and time again, yet I maintain that this is where our destiny lies. I feel it in my gut, or heart, or more poetically, in my soul. I am a spiritual person. After years of reading and pondering so many theories I believe that the sum of all human souls would create 'God'. What if our 'sixth sense' is in fact an infinitesimal piece of God? I think that without the unified belief in ourselves as a piece of God there can be no God; only fragments of Him showing up here and there. What if Jesus was just so revered and adored that between him and his followers' unfettered belief he was able to make miracles happen, and they happened solely because of their unity. I love to think that we all need each other and we can make our own miracles. With this ideal, morality is automatic and we are infinitely more powerful than we ever dreamed possible. My faith has served me well through the years. It has also disappointed me, but I have come to understand that there are reasons, and eventually the purpose becomes evident. I feel like I have finally made sense of what has never made sense.

It is Thursday and soon I will be Skyping into Leslie's kitchen. Cyber Hen Night is alive and well! I have some news I need to share. I only do this about once a month because watching it all on a computer is too overwhelming. Leslie has come to visit twice. The first time alone ... well sort of alone. She met a guy on the train and then invited him to Sophie's place for a drink. He was very nice and we had a great time. So she invited him to join us for dinner on Saturday. I have no idea how they fit in that single bed, but she said she slept great! The second time, she and Sharon came. I was so surprised to hear that Sharon wanted to come. It was then that I was finally able to talk with her about her estrangement. I couldn't understand why she would have believed Stan that we didn't want her in our lives anymore. You don't have to agree with everything your girlfriends are doing, but they are still your girlfriends. I never reached out to her and it was a big mistake. Sharon was in a bad place and she could have used the support. They came on Halloween weekend so I told them to bring some costumes because we may go to a party. We all got too drunk to go, but put our costumes on anyway and spun vinyl and danced all night.

Andrew and I live in a neighbourhood called The Beach and we love it. Our house in Ottawa sold eight months after it was listed and for $100,000 less than we had hoped for, therefore we are renting. Nothing has happened the way it was supposed to. It has been a case of careful what you wish for. Without a very large down payment, owning a property in Toronto is out of reach right now, where an average home is a million dollars. Just living here is also very expensive so we are trying to figure out how to save up the very large down payment required. Andrew's entrepreneurial spirit is alive and well and he has some pokers in the fire and we just need one of them to ignite. Andrew was a very well respected business owner in Ottawa. Here he knows nobody. I didn't realize exactly what I was doing when I pushed for this move. I didn't realize just how difficult it was going to be for him, for us. I thought we would arrive and we would conquer this town in no time. It is taking longer than planned, but we will conquer! It is time to call the girls.

"Terri can you see us?"

"Yes, you're there. I can only see you and Izzy?"

"That's all you get. It's just us tonight. Guess what, I have big exciting news!!!"

"Ok…"

"I'm getting hot flashes baby … I'm finally in the club!!!"

"Jesus Leslie, you say that like we did when we first got our periods and we were so elated. If only we knew what was ahead of us!"

"I know what's ahead of us and there should be noooo celebration for that sista," Izzy says.

"It's just I feel like I'm finally normal … I'm 52 and didn't have a single symptom of menopause."

"So where are all the others that they dare not show up?"

"Colleen is babysitting, Francine and Meagan are both on dates."

"Anyone I know?"

"Francine yes … do you remember the guy who was singing with Andrew's band for a bit?"

"Not Yves?!"

"No the other guy who only did a couple of gigs," Izzy takes a long pause … "Frank! That's it! I hate fucking menopause! See Leslie, this is what you have to look forward to."

"No way … that's great! He's a sweetie. I guess he broke up with his girlfriend."

"I hope so. We better get her to confirm that!"

"Now that I'm only Skyping into Hen Night does it still count as my 34th year of being a Hen?"

"Is that a rhetorical question dumbass? Once a Hen … always a Hen. How are you surviving without us?"

"I've been surprisingly OK on Thursday's. I guess it's because I talk to you more now than I ever did in Ottawa."

"Sometimes not quite enough, but I know you're busy."

"So I wanted to Skype you in person because I have more crazy change in my life!"

"Jesus, what now? You look happy it must be good."

"So Andrew and Corporate put the merger together with the two direct mail companies because he just couldn't make it work, but that's another story. It was more about all the contracts they had in place than anything else…"

"OK get on with it!"

"So we've been commuting to that office in Burlington for three months now. It takes anywhere from one and a half to two hours to get there."

"Shit that sucks … it's like working in LA, but without the fantastic weather!"

"I know right … so yesterday I got pulled into the boss's office."

"You look so excited he must have given you a big raise or something!"

"Not even close … I got laid off! They told me that now they've worked out all the administration duties with the merger and they feel they don't need me."

"Fuck! Well why do you look so happy?"

"I didn't really know why at first. When he told me I had to stop myself from smiling and look real disappointed … something just overcame me."

"So what'll you do?"

"I went straight to the UI office … I mean EI office. They even have to make being out of work seem positive somehow … I mean let's be realistic, it's Unemployment Insurance, it's not Employment Insurance! I wouldn't need fucking insurance if I was employed!"

"You must qualify? I know it's much harder to get these days."

"And so it should be … but yes, I do qualify."

"That's a relief. Wow! Could anything else go wrong since you left?"

"Yes, it could always be worse. It may be hard to get another job because for the last 10 years my office duties have had very specific software. I may have to do some upgrading and there's a place dedicated to that nearby. But, you can't spend the entire day looking for work. You do it all on line now. It really sucks because my strength is my personality and employers will just think I'm too old. They won't ever meet me! So, when I was walking home I was contemplating what else I could do with an eight month sabbatical of sorts ahead of me."

"It must be good because you're grinning ear to ear! And I wish like hell you would get on with it!"

"So I'm walking back from the UI office, and I get that feeling again that I had in the office when I was laid off. I feel fucking electrified and then I get zapped ... I know exactly what I'm going to do ..."

"Are you trying to drive us crazy because you haven't been able to very much lately?"

"Of course I am ... whenever there's an opportunity ... and this little project of mine may require some help from you."

"Really, how?"

"I Terry Vetnor am going to do something I've never done before in my life and always wanted to ... I'm going to leap from the cliff and find out if I fly or crash. I..."

"Jesus, if you were here I'd push you off the fucking cliff ... what's the big epiphany?"

"Girls, I'm going to write Hen Night!"

CPSIA information can be obtained at www.ICGtesting.com
Printed in the USA
LVOW10s0007300416

485956LV00034B/1135/P